ELIJAH
OF BUXTON

ELIJAH OF BUXTON

CHRISTOPHER PAUL CURTIS

SCHOLASTIC INC.
New York   Toronto   London   Auckland   Sydney
Mexico City   New Delhi   Hong Kong   Buenos Aires

This book was originally published in hardcover by Scholastic Press in 2007.

ISBN-13: 978-0-439-02345-0
ISBN-10: 0-439-02345-9

16 15 14 13   13 14/0

Printed in the United States of America   40
This edition first printing, February 2009

The author has used certain Canadian spellings to establish the setting of this novel. The text was set in Historical, Felltype Roman.

To the original twenty-one former-slave settlers of the Elgin Settlement and Buxton Mission of Raleigh: Eliza, Amelia, Mollie, Sarah, Isaiah Phares, Harriet, Solomon, Jacob King, Talbert King, Peter King, Fanny, Ben Phares, Robin Phares, Stephen Phares, Emeline Phares, and Isaac and Catherine Riley and their four children.

And to the Reverend William King and his love of justice.

❖ Acknowledgments ❖

Special thanks to Andrea Davis Pinkney and everyone at
Scholastic who helped make this so easy. Extra special thanks
to my editor Anamika Bhatnagar, who read this four million
times and still laughed in all of the right places.
I am very fortunate to have a group of wonderful readers
who help polish my writings. Continued thanks to Joan and
George (Mr. Congressional Gold Medal Award winner!)
Taylor, Mickial Wilson, Kaysandra Curtis,
Harrison Chumley Patrick, Kay Benjamin, Lynn Guest,
Eugene Miller, Teri Lesesne, Terry Fisher,
Janet Brown, Lauren Pankin, Debbie Stratton,
and particularly to my first three,
Pauletta Bracy, Richie Partington, and Steven Curtis.
Thanks to the Buxton National Historic Site
and Museum and Spencer Alexander
for their help with research.
And, as always, eternal thanks
to my parents, Herman and Leslie Curtis.

Chapter I

Snakes and Ma

It was Sunday after church and all my chores were done. I was sitting on the stoop of our home trying to think what to do. It was that time of day when the birds were getting ready to be quiet and the toady-frogs were starting to get louder with that chirpity sound they make most the night. I wondered if it would be worth it to go fishing for a hour afore it got dark. I got that question answered when Cooter came walking up the road waving at me.

"Evening, Eli."

"Evening, Cooter."

"What you doing, Eli?"

"I was thinking 'bout getting Old Flapjack and going fishing. You wanna come?"

"Uh-uh. I got something that's more interesting than watching you fish, I got a mystery."

This might not be so good. I ain't trying to be disrespectful 'bout my best friend, but there're lots of things that Cooter sees as being mysterious that most folks understand real easy. I asked him anyway, "What's the mystery?"

"I was cutting through M'deah's truck patch and seen some tracks that I ain't never seen afore."

"What kind of tracks? Were they big?"

"Uh-uh, they's long and wiggly. I followed 'em but they disappeared in the grass."

Cooter's pretty good at tracking so maybe this *was* a mystery after all.

"Let's go."

We got to Cooter's home, opened the gate, and went 'round back to his mother's truck patch. Cooter was right!

There 'mongst the rows of his ma's beets and corn and green peas were some of the strangest markings I'd ever seen.

I studied 'em real close. They were long and skinny and in six wiggling lines. Two of 'em were a good bit thicker than the rest. They started on one side of Cooter's ma's truck patch, went clean through her vegetables, then disappeared in the grass.

I got on my hands and knees to really give 'em the eye then told Cooter, "You got me. I ain't never seen such tracks nowhere. Let's ask my pa once he comes out the field."

But afore we had the chance to ask Pa, the Preacher

came walking down the road in front of Cooter's. He ain't atall like a common preacher that's got a church or nothing, but he tells anyone that will listen that he's the Right Reverend Deacon Doctor Zephariah Connerly the Third, and that he's the most educated, smartest man anywhere 'round. 'Stead of saying all those names, me and Cooter just call him the Preacher.

He leaned on Cooter's fence and called, "Evening, boys."

"Evening, sir."

"Hot one today, why aren't you two off swimming?"

Cooter said, "We trying to solve us a mystery, sir."

"Really? And what would that be?"

I told him, "It's some kind of animal tracks we ain't never seen afore, sir."

"Where are they?"

The Preacher opened the gate, walked into the truck patch, squatted down, and peered at the tracks just as sharp as I'd done. He took a jackknife out of his pocket and dug a little scoop of dirt out of one of the tracks. He looked at it so close that his eyes started to go crossed.

I quit breathing and my blood ran cold when all the sudden he shouted, "Lord, have mercy!"

The Preacher quick stood up and looked all 'round him the way you would if someone screamed out, "Wolf!"

Me and Cooter looked too. Who wouldn't've?

The Preacher said, like he's talking to hisself, "No! No! No! I knew this was going to happen, I just prayed it wouldn't be this soon."

Me and Cooter called out together, "What? What was gonna happen?"

The Preacher looked like his best friend just got killed. "I warned them they had to check out those new-free folks better, and now somebody's accidentally toted some of those horrible creatures up here."

I noticed that 'stead of folding up his knife, the Preacher kept it open. Then worst, he held on to it like he was fixing to stab something.

I said, "What somebody tote up here, sir?"

"Hoop snakes!" He said it in a low hissing way that told you whatever kind of snake this was, you didn't want to run up on one!

Cooter's eyes scanned right and left. "What? What's a hoop snake, sir?"

Being any kind of snake was enough for me to start getting nervous, but the Preacher made matters a whole lot worst when he said, "I suppose I have to tell you, but I don't want this to get any further than the three of us."

He used his boot to rub most of the tracks out of the dirt.

I said, "Please, sir, tell us what you mean!"

The Preacher started talking but never looked at me

4

di-rect, he was too busy eyeing the road and the woods. "Down home there's a vile breed of snake called a hoop snake. Not only can it outrun a racehorse, it's been known to kill a fully grown bear with one bite!"

I looked at Cooter and hoped that I waren't looking scared as him.

The Preacher went on, "They look like near any other snake, except for one thing."

"What?"

"They have the habit of sticking their tails in their mouths then biting themselves."

That don't make no sense, that don't make no sense atall! If what the Preacher was saying was true, these snakes sure ain't too sharp-minded.

I said, "How're they gonna bite you if they're clamping down on their own tails, sir?"

"Good question, Elijah. But they don't hold their tails when they're ready to bite, they hold them when they're ready to chase after you!"

Cooter said, "But . . ."

The Preacher held up his left hand. "Listen! And, my young brothers, you better listen good! This may save your lives. Once they've bitten their tails, they form the shape of a circle then stand up like a wheel or a barrel hoop and commence rolling after whatever they've decided to kill!"

The hairs on the back of my neck started jumping like a skeeter'd brushed up 'gainst 'em.

The Preacher said, "After they catch you and bite you . . ." He snapped his left hand shut like it was the mouth of one of these hoop snakes. ". . . the true horror begins. You're doomed."

Cooter said, "How come?"

"Because, Cooter, their poison gets into your blood too quick. Within hours you commence swelling till your skin looks soft and rotten as a ripe peach left in the noonday sun!"

Cooter said, "*What?* You swells up?"

The Preacher said, "You swell so much that after exactly seven and a half days the pressure in your body becomes too great and you *explode* like an overheated steam boiler! In seconds your stomach and your lungs and your other entrails are flung around you for miles and miles!"

I couldn't believe folks who'd got free would do this to us! Even if it was a accident!

But the Preacher waren't through. "Worse, the swelling affects everything but your head, so you're forced to watch the whole tragedy unwinding right in front of your eyes!"

Cooter edged close to me and choked out, "Well, sir, at least you dies quick and ain't left to do much suffering."

"No such luck, Cooter." The Preacher held up two fingers. "Two weeks! It's fourteen endless days after your explosion before you pass on. And it's no pleasant death either, you finally die from starvation."

Cooter said, "Starvation? How come you don't eat nothing, sir?"

"Because, Cooter, no matter how much food you swallow, it simply falls through the hole where your internal organs used to be and drops to the ground right in front of you!"

The Preacher stared hard in the direction the tracks were headed and said, "Those tracks were fresh, looks like a momma and poppa and a slew of babies! Which, God bless us all, means we're too late, they've already started breeding! And from the way those tracks were going, I'd say they're hungry and have started up a hoop snake hunting party!"

The Preacher threw his knife into the ground where the tracks use to be and put his hand on the fancy holster and mystery pistol he always totes. "Boys," he whispered, "I need you to solemnly promise me something. I want you both to swear on your mothers' lives that if I'm ever bitten by one of these beasts, you'll take this pistol and put a bullet in my brain! I'd rather be shot *dead* than face such a horrible, prolonged death! Raise your hands, I need

7

each of you to promise that you'll blow my head right off my shoulders!"

I near jumped to the moon when a loud bang came from behind me! I looked back and Cooter'd already run into his house and slammed and locked the door. He waren't 'bout to promise nothing!

Afore I knowed what was happening I was through Cooter's gate and right in the middle of a good long hard run home. I had sense enough not to take no shortcuts and stuck to the road so's I could at least see the hoop snake hunting party if I ran up on it. Ma must've heard me screaming from a ways off 'cause she was running out our front gate by the time I got there.

She said, "'Lijah? What on God's earth is wrong now?"

I busted through the gate, pulled Ma into the house, and slammed the door behind her. I was too worned out and shooked up to talk so she started looking me up and down and spinning me 'round to try and figure what was wrong. After a second she said, "'Lijah, sweetheart, you's scaring me to death! What's wrong, baby?"

Once my breathing caught up with me I let her know 'bout how the runaways from America had accidentally brung hoop snakes up to Buxton and how they were out in the woods rolling 'round looking for something to kill.

Ma looked at me like I was daft. She shooked her head and said, "'Lijah, 'Lijah, 'Lijah. What'm I gunn do 'bout you? How many times I got to tell you, a coward die a thousand deaths, a brave boy don't die but once?"

I didn't say nothing but I couldn't help wondering how that's supposed to be comforting. Seems to me after you die the first time, the ones that follow ain't gonna really matter too much.

I said, "But, Ma, I ain't looking to die even one time, 'specially not from no hoop snake bite! It's better to get your head blowed off!"

Ma kneelt down next to me, grabbed both my shoulders, and looked hard in my eyes. "'Lijah Freeman, you listen and you listen good. Ain't *nothing* in the world worth being that afeared of, son. Nothing."

I said, "What 'bout toady-frogs? How come you're so afeared of them? How's that any different?"

Ma couldn't hardly tolerate even hearing the word *toady-frog,* she'd near die if she ran up on one.

But just like that, the conversating was over. Ma stood up, smacked the back of my head, opened the door then said, "They *is* different. Them things is knowed to pass on warts and all other sorts of nasty dis-eases. And don't be back-talking me neither, 'Lijah Freeman. I ain't so scared of toady-frogs that I'm-a be running down the road in the middle of the day screaming my head off like you just done."

She kneelt back next to me. "Acting that way don't look

good on no child old as you is, 'Lijah. You got to learn to get control of you'self and quit being so fra-gile, sweetheart."

Ma started acting like she couldn't decide if she was gonna be nice to me or give me a good swatting. She ran her hand along my cheek and said in a kind way, "I don't know what I'm gunn do 'bout that Zephariah! I done axed you over and over not to have no dealings with him, Elijah. He need be 'shamed of hisself, scaring young folk with them nonsense stories."

She was still acting friendly and peaceable when she said, "And you, you poor thing, you got to start thinking things through, you got to try hard to understand if what folks are telling you make any kind of sense."

Then, just like that, she's back at being mad at me, she pinched my cheek hard and said, "But that ain't no excuse for you to be acting all fra-gile like you done, none atall."

She squozed on my shoulders 'cause being fra-gile's the biggest bone Ma's got to pick with me. There ain't nothing in the world she wants more than for me to quit being so doggone fra-gile. It's something I'm aiming to do myself, but the trouble is me and her have two different ways of doing it. And her way always seems to be the exact back side of mine. Whilst I try not to be fra-gile by sucking down the looseness and sloppiness in my nose when they come and by not screaming and running off at the littlest nonsense,

Ma sets 'bout it different. Most times she tries to encourage it by talking the subject near to death. And, doggone-it-all, learning a lesson that way just don't stick in your head.

But what's worst is when Ma quits talking and starts doing something to make a lesson permanent. The first time she tried to make me quit being fra-gile I didn't even know she was doing it, but that's one lesson that's stuck with me so good that it seems like it happened yesterday and not a long time ago.

Ma had been walking me 'round the yard near our truck patch, and I must've been mighty young 'cause I had my arm stretched way over my head to hold on to her hand.

I remember stopping to get a good look at a pile of dirt that was being scampered on by a bunch of bugs. I couldn't understand how things that small could be moving all by theirselves! I dug my toes down into the dirt to make Ma quit walking so's I could get a better look. It turned out to be one of the biggest mistakes I ever made.

I can recall squinting my eyes to look up at Ma and seeing her pull off her sunbonnet and wipe her forehead afore she squatted down next to me and said, "'Lijah, that ain't nothing but a anthill, sweetheart."

I reached out to pick one of the ants up. This was afore I'd learnt that bugs have ways of discouraging you from touching 'em. But afore I could get hold of one, Ma grabbed my hand. "Uh-uh, 'Lijah, they's some of God's hardest workers and just 'cause you's bigger don't make it right to mess with 'em."

Then she said, "Ooh, 'Lijah, lookit there! Ain't that the prettiest thing?"

She turned my hand a-loose and reached over in the grass and pulled out the most terrorfying creature that ever lived! It was twisting and whipping in a way that waren't one bit normal. And it didn't have a arm nor leg nowhere on it! It looked like it came straight out your worst nightmare. But the fearfullest thing about it was that it was right in Ma's hand, which up to then had been the best place to run if there was any kind of trouble.

Ma always counts that as the first time I ran off screaming, but who wouldn't've?

Near everything I learnt about snakes on that day and every day since shows that screaming and running from 'em ain't one bit atall fra-gile, it's sensical.

It waren't but a week or two later that me and Cooter were down at the river and he yelled, "Oh, ho . . . !" then snatched out a toady-frog big as a pie pan!

I was still smarting 'bout the way Ma'd made me feel fra-gile, so the first thing that came to mind was how fra-gile *she'd* get if she saw a toady-frog as big and round as this one.

Like most real good ideas, this one didn't come to us right off. One thing led to the 'nother, and after 'while me and Cooter came up with this plan that's got toady-frogs and Ma and her sewing basket all meeting up together. In Sabbath school Mr. Travis is always telling us that the Lord loves laughter, and what could be funnier than watching Ma reaching down into her basket and getting a little surprise?

After supper I wrapped the toady-frog in the sweater Ma had been working on and put it in her knitting basket and ran 'cross the road to hide in the drainage ditch with Cooter.

Then, just like they always do, Ma and Pa came and sat in their rockers on the stoop, getting ready to do some relaxing. They're laughing and carrying on and Ma put her sewing basket in her lap.

She took her knitting spectacles out of the basket then quick closed it to make a point 'bout something with Pa. She acted like she was set to reach in and pull her knitting out but stopped at the last instance to slap at Pa's arm. She even set the basket back on the floor and, doggone-it-all, it seemed her and Pa waren't gonna get nothing done but talking and laughing! I was *this* close to losing my mind!

Finally Ma put the basket back in her lap and reached in. She knowed right off something was wrong 'cause with that toady-frog added to it, her sweater weighed 'bout five pounds more than the last time she touched it.

She twisted her head to the side to look at Pa, unwrapped the toady-frog, and it dropped smack-down in her lap. She frozed up for 'bout one second, then jumped straight out the rocker. Yarn and needles and buttons and the toady-frog and the half-knit sweater flewed all over the stoop like your guts do after you been hoop snake bit! Ma's knitting spectacles jumped partway up her forehead and she started hopping up and down and slapping at her skirt like it's afire! The whole time she didn't scream nor say a word.

It was the funniest thing I'd ever seen in my life!

Me and Cooter near 'bout died peeking out of the ditch. It caint be good for you to try to keep a laugh inside, I was *this* close to busting clean apart!

Ma heard us trying to smother our laughs down and stared 'cross the road. She looked like she was fixing to say something but her mouth just opened and shut over and over. Didn't no words come out so she walked all a-shakeity into the house.

Pa called over to me and Cooter, "Don't y'all move."

He set Ma's rocker back up then collected all her knitting tools and put 'em back in the basket. He picked up the toady-frog and brung him 'cross the road right at me and Cooter.

He set the toady-frog down, shooked his head, and said, "Now, Elijah. You, me, and Cooter all thought that was funny. Your ma and that there toady-frog ain't likely to see the whole adventure quite the same way."

Me and Cooter tried to keep our faces serious whilst Pa was talking, but tears were rolling down both our cheeks.

Pa said, "Past a wart or two, I don't think the toady-frog's gunn cause you no grieving. But your ma . . ." He whistled low and long. ". . . she's a whole 'nother story. So whilst you's out here rolling 'bout in that ditch enjoying the tormentation you caused your ma and that toady-frog, why don't you save us all some trouble and go in them woods and break off whichever switch it is you wants her to beat you with. 'Cause you know the next time you and her is in the same room together, that's what's gunn happen.

"Cooter," Pa said, "today your lucky day, son. You's 'bout to get two shows for the price of one. If you thought that there was funny, you just wait till you see the way 'Lijah starts a-hopping and screaming once his ma lays that switch on his behind."

Pa smiled then walked away.

Me and Cooter had to run near a mile afore we figured we were far 'nough away to really let our laughs rip out. And rip out they did. I ain't *never* laughed so hard! We fell all over ourselves and couldn't barely stand up. We rolled and rolled whilst talking 'bout the way Ma looked when she opened that sweater!

We couldn't neither one of us get a whole sentence out.

I said, "Did you see the way —" then I commenced choking.

Cooter said, "And . . . and . . . and then she —" and started pulling at the grass and slapping at the ground.

Then I said, "I never knowed Ma could jump so —" and the laughing closed my throat right up.

Once me and Cooter were all laughed out and commenced walking home, things changed. A gloom started creeping over me the same way clouds'll all the sudden start sliding up to cover a full moon. Cooter was whistling and still laughing every once in the while and, doggone-it-all, I saw how unfair this whole commotion was turning out to be. He'd got just as much fun from everything that happened as I did, but it looked like *I* was gonna be the only one that had to do any kind of paying for the enjoying. I started working up a good apology fulled up with lots of sincereness for when I saw Ma.

When I got home, Ma didn't say a word! She must've thought the whole thing was too embarrassing and couldn't see no way of 'buking me without bringing up the subject of toady-frogs again, so she let it go.

I gotta say I was real proud of Ma 'cause of the good way she took the toady-frog joke. It's funny, just when you think you caint admire your folks no more than you already do, something like that happens and lets you know you're wrong.

Two days later I got back from helping Mr. Leroy down on Mrs. Holton's land. Ma and Pa were sitting on the stoop. Ma was back to working on that sweater and Pa was whittling away. She must've baked, the cookie jar was sitting twixt 'em.

She said, "How Mr. Leroy doing, son?"

"He's good, ma'am."

"You stop in and give my regards to Mrs. Holton?"

"Yes, ma'am, she told me to ask 'bout you."

"Mrs. Brown come by, axed if you's gunn go fishing tomorrow."

"Yes, ma'am, right after my stable chores."

"She done some baking too, say she hoping to trade for two of them big perch."

It waren't Ma that baked, it was Mrs. Brown! This made the baking in the cookie jar a lot more interesting!

"What she bake, Ma?"

Ma reached down and picked up the cookie jar.

She said, "You know how Mrs. Brown is, 'Lijah, always

trying something new. She baked some sugar cookies and some other kind of cookie she call . . ." Ma quit knitting and looked over her spectacles at Pa. "Ooh, Spencer, I must be getting old. I caint for the life of me recall what she said they was, can you?"

Pa held up on his whittling, looked at her, and said, "Naw, darling, I caint recall neither."

Ma slapped the arm of her rocker. "Oh yes! Now I 'member, she baked them walnut and sugar cookies and something she say she gunn call rope cookies. You's lucky they's some left. Was all I could do to keep your daddy out of 'em."

She tipped the cookie jar toward Pa and he reached in and pulled out a cookie that had walnuts stuck to the top of it and sugar dusted all over it!

Pa bit on the cookie and said, "Almost as good as your'n, Sarah!" He winked at me.

Ma leaned the jar at me but just as I was 'bout to reach in, she pulled it back and said, "Now, 'Lijah, you know better than that. You been working hard with Mr. Leroy. Go wash up first, son."

"Yes, ma'am."

I ran 'round to the back stoop to wash my hands quick as I could. When I came out front, Ma tipped the cookie jar at me again and I dug my hand right in.

Ma was right, it felt like Pa'd et near all of 'em. But as

I moved my hand 'round in the bottom of the jar, I felt one n'em rope cookies . . . and Mrs. Brown must've *just* brung these cookies over, 'cause the last one left was still warm!

I pulled the cookie outta the jar.

My heart quit beating, my blood ran cold, and time stood still!

My fingers were wrapped 'round the neck of the worst-looking snake in Canada West!

I screamed, "Snake!" and afore I knowed it, I was tearing off 'cross the road into the woods. By the time I worned myself out I must've run two miles. I stopped and leaned 'gainst a tree, waiting for my breathing to catch up to me. Something made me look down in my hand.

I screamed, "Snake!" for the second time.

But this time I remembered to turn the snake's neck a-loose and throwed it down.

I wouldn't've thought I had enough strength left in me to run, but being afeared and being tired look like two things you caint feel at the same time.

When I ran back up on our stoop, Ma's and Pa's faces were wet with tears. Pa was leaning over the side of his rocker like he's having a fit.

I'd been so afeared and trusted my folks so much that it didn't come to me till right then that that snake hadn't crawled into the cookie jar on his own, he must've had some help. It was a true shock when I figured out Ma was setting this whole thing up as a lesson!

When my voice finally came back I said, "Ma! How could you do that?"

They rolled!

Pa fought to catch his breathing. "Well, Elijah, seem to me what's sauce for the goose is sauce for the gander."

It's a horrible feeling when the people who're supposed to raise you go out of their way to scare you for no good reason, and making it worst was that they were getting so much enjoying outta it. 'Sides, fair's fair, and scaring your ma with something as harmless as a toady-frog calls for getting switched, not getting terrorfied.

"Why would you do that?" I was crying so hard that the words were getting choked down in my throat. "Ma, you're always telling me I can dish it out but I caint take it, so if you know that, how could you do this to me? And 'sides that, you know how much I hate snakes!"

"Mmm-hmm, 'bout the same 'mount that I hate toady-frogs."

"But, Ma! Toady-frogs ain't nothing! Snakes are dangerous! 'Twaren't no toady-frog that gave Adam and Eve a apple, 'twas a snake! And you ain't never heard of nothing called a hoop *toady-frog*, have you? No! That's 'cause they're harmless! It's snakes what'll kill you!"

Pa was slapping his sides so hard it's a wonder he didn't

bust no ribs. You couldn't do nothing but expect that kind of rudeness from him, but the way Ma was carrying on was terrible shocking!

"Ma! I thought we were trying to make it so's I wouldn't be so fra-gile! Look at me, I caint quit shaking!"

I could see I was wasting my breath. If people could die from laughing too hard, I'd be a orphan.

I know it probably ain't right to feel this way 'bout your own ma and pa, but I was sore disappointed in the way they were acting. Afore I got in bed that night, I even used a stick to flip my pillow over. I was so shooked up that I wanted to make sure Ma waren't gonna carry on this lesson no further.

→ CHAPTER 2 ←

Me and Mr. Frederick Douglass

'Bout the only good thing that came from Ma's snake-in-the-cookie-jar lesson was there waren't no one else 'round to see it, not even Cooter. It wouldn't've been no time atall afore everyone in the Settlement knowed 'bout what happened. And even if Cooter and me *are* best friends, and he wouldn't do nothing to on-purpose make me look low, I knowed that me running off from that snake like I'd done was such a good story that even a best friend couldn't've been blamed for letting it accidentally slip out. 'Specially a best friend like Cooter.

The whole adventure would just turn into another one n'em things that would be stuck onto my name forever. And, doggone-it-all, seems like what people enjoy sticking to your name permanent ain't never good things, they're always tragical. I ain't the kind of person that complains for no reason, but I gotta say, I already got one tragedy tied up with my name that is so horrible that it wouldn't be one bit fair that I'd get another.

The tragedy that's so horrible put a scar on me that I'm-a be carrying till the day I die. You'd think growned folks would cry when they saw me, but that don't happen atall. Even Ma and Pa try to act like it ain't all that noticeable and that they ain't 'shamed to have folks see they're raising me, but I know better.

It happened when I waren't nothing but a baby and I caint see why I'm to blame, but that's when the famousest, smartest man who ever escaped from slavery stood on a tall stage that had got built in the schoolhouse and raised me way up over his head in front of a crowd of people. From the way Pa tells it, the man must've had me twenty feet up in the air. He was giving a speech when the accident happened 'cause every time he made a point he'd give me a little shake way up there over top of his head.

I waren't even a year old back when Mr. Frederick Douglass and Mr. John Brown visited Buxton. Pa said all the Settlement people had got excited and worked up something terrible 'bout them coming and were dashing 'round trying to polish Buxton up, sort of like the way you'd rub the dirt off your Sunday shoes if you knowed Mr. Travis was gonna give 'em a hard look.

They rushed to get the new schoolhouse finished so's there'd be a place big enough for the meeting. They made sure the picket fences in front of everyone's home had got a good slap of whitewash on 'em. They made all kinds of food and such and they even had a special blanket made out of sewed-together flowers to go 'cross Flapjack the mule's back so's he could lead a parade.

All this fussing was going on 'cause folks in Buxton were gonna celebrate *three* special people at this big meeting. Special person number one was Mr. Frederick Douglass 'cause he use to be a slave, just like most the folks here in Buxton, and now they say he can talk the bees outta flying to the flowers. Special person number two was Mr. John Brown 'cause folks say, other than maybe Reverend King, the man who started Buxton, there waren't no white man ever made that was better'n him. And special person number three was me 'cause, it ain't something I ever boast on, but I was the very first child to be born free in the Elgin Settlement at Raleigh in Canada West, what we call Buxton.

Mrs. Guest, who's the best sewer and knitter in the Settlement, had even gone and knitted some fancy clothes for me that Ma still keeps in a peculiar-smelling box made out of cedarwood. Me and Ma have a pretty good disagreement 'bout them clothes 'cause to me they look a powerful lot like a girl's dress and bonnet. When I got growned enough to understand what it was they'd paraded me 'round in, I was just as much 'shamed 'bout the clothes they forced me to wear as I was 'bout the accident twixt me and special person number one.

Pa said everything was all right with the celebrating until the parade got to the schoolhouse and most of the speechifying was over. That's when Mr. Douglass came and took me from Ma, walked high up on the stage with me, and held me up in the air over his head.

Ma said she was worrying right off 'cause Mr. Douglass is a excitable man when he gets talking, and he started bouncing me up and down and swinging me 'round with joy, saying I was a "shining bacon of light and hope for the future."

I asked Ma what that meant and she couldn't say. Don't seem to me that getting called a piece of meat off of a pig is anything that you should get excited 'bout, but Mr. Douglass thought it was great and folks kept cheering and he kept tossing me up and down till the accident happened.

Ma says even back then I was a fra-gile child, and the more he tossed me, the more she was fretting. She said I was having a whole lot of fun then I smiled real big and, without no kind of warning atall, the accident happened. I throwed up everything I'd et all over Mr. Douglass's beard and jacket.

I learnt from Ma that people who use to be slaves love prettying up *any* kind of story. She says talking is near the only thing they use to get to do without no white person telling 'em how or when, so they make the most out of it once they get the chance. She says they love making a summer day a lot hotter than it really was, or making rain or drought last a whole lot longer than they really did, and they 'specially love telling you how their great-great-grampa or gramma use to be the king or queen of Africa.

Bad as my luck is, the people that live in Buxton ain't choosed to pretty up the fact I'm most proud of myself for, my rock chunking, they've prettified what happened twixt me and Mr. Frederick Douglass.

They'll tell you I throwed up on Mr. Douglass for a whole half a hour afore Ma came and snatched me away and pointed me out the schoolhouse window. They say I near drownded the man. Some folks swear I throwed up so hard that desks and chairs rose up and floated out of the schoolhouse. Mr. Polite said I throwed up so plentiful that didn't no deers nor rabbits die in the woods for five years after. He said the bears and the wolfs et my vomit for that long since it was considerable easier for them to do that than to try to run down some animal that waren't looking to get et.

And that don't make no sense. That don't make no sense atall.

First off, 'cause they're always telling us how smart Mr. Frederick Douglass is. They tell us he can talk Greek like a

Greek and Latin like a Latin, and anyone who's that smart ain't gonna sit and hold no baby over his head that's throwing up on him for no whole half a hour. I could understand it if he was surprised at first, ain't no one gonna expect to get throwed up on by a baby boy in a girl's dress and bonnet. But if Mr. Douglass is near smart as folks say, seems to me he'd've had the sense to aim me out the window hisself. Seems to me if I really did throw up for a whole half a hour, only the first five minutes would've been on Mr. Douglass, the last twenty minutes would've had to be out that window.

It also don't make no sense 'bout the bears and wolfs neither, 'cause if they were coming into the Settlement three times a day to eat what I'd throwed up, this would've been a mighty unsafe place, but didn't none of the growned folks act worried 'bout sending their children off to do no chores.

Back when I was 'bout five or six Ma told me to fetch a bucket and go into the woods behind our home and pick her some blueberries.

This is probably one of the reasons Ma thinks I'm a fra-gile boy. I remember soon's she told me to go I got all afeared and shake-ity.

I said, "By myself?"

She said, "It ain't that far, 'Lijah. I'm-a keep watch over you."

"But, Ma! What 'bout all those bears and wolfs? What if I'm out there when they come for their supper?"

She smiled and said, "'Lijah, don't be silly. Ain't no wild creatures like that been seen 'round these parts since afore you was borned."

I said, "But, Ma, how come everybody keeps telling me 'bout what I done to Mr. Douglass that got all the bears and wolfs coming to the Settlement looking for something to eat?"

She laughed and told me some of that growned-folks talk, some of that talk that makes it so's you ain't never sure 'bout much of nothing. She said, "Son, you got one n'em sets of mind what's gunn have you fretting 'bout the littlest things. Life's gunn be a tough row to hoe for you if you don't learn you caint be believing everything folks tell you, not even growned folks."

One minute Ma, who's got a good head for thinking, tells me I got to respect everything what growned folks say and the next minute she's wanting me not to believe some of the things the same growned folks tell me! If that don't leave you scratching your head you got a better brain than me!

→ CHAPTER 3 ←

Fish Head Chunking

It was Friday evening and I finished my lessons at school and started walking to the stable to do my chores. I was gonna have to work faster than I do most days 'cause a bunch of people were counting on me to bring 'em some fish.

Mr. Segee was next to the barn raking through his truck patch.

"Good afternoon, Mr. Segee."

"Why, 'lo there, 'Lijah. I always can tell when you on your way, Old Flapjack get worked up 'bout fifteen minutes 'fore you gets here."

"I don't know why people say horses and mules are dull, Mr. Segee, 'specially Old Flapjack. He's gotta be the smartest mule ever."

Mr. Segee snorted like he thought I'd lost my mind.

"Well, it's good you here, boy. Now go on in, them animals is waiting on you."

I separate my chores at the stable into two parts, the working part and the enjoying part. The working part is doing the things you wouldn't do 'less you were forced to. I get them done first. Things like cleaning the stalls and shoveling manure and taking it to the fertilizer pile, and feeding and watering the animals. This takes a considerable good 'mount of time.

The second part of my chores, the enjoying part, is divided into brushing the animals, tending to their hoofs, and my favourite part, helping make 'em comforted by keeping the horseflies off of 'em.

It waren't just for their good that this was my favouritest job, I was getting something out of it too. I was getting flies to use for bait. I figured out that this chore fit right in with the Buxton Settlement Creed: "One helping one to uplift all." It's the way all us in the Settlement look out for one the 'nother. We don't expect nothing in return, but if we see someone that needs a hand, we rush to give it. Good things always come from that.

I got my fly swah, pulled a milking stool next to Old Flapjack, and waited. It waren't long afore a good-size fly lit just above his rear hoof.

Crack!

"Blang it all!"

I ain't the type to make the mistake of cursing out loud like that, but sometimes swear words'll jump out of you afore you have a chance to remember they ain't proper. Those words came out of me from being frustrated. I waren't swatting flies just for the sake of killing 'em, and sometimes I got a little too strong.

I'd been swatting horseflies for so many years that I could tell by the sound the fly swah made once it hit if I was gonna be able to use the fly for fishing or not. And *crack* was a sound that most times waren't too good.

I looked under Old Flapjack and I was right. The fly was in the dust and nothing was moving on him 'cept for the green guts that were leaking out of his bust-up back end.

I picked him up by his wings, blew him off, and dropped him in the "dead" pouch.

Two more horseflies landed on Old Flapjack's flank and it was a chance to make up for the mistake I'd just made. I mean the hitting-the-fly-too-hard mistake, not the swearing mistake. Mr. Travis tells us that swearing's the kind of mistake that once you do it, there ain't no way to make up for it.

I studied the two horseflies that had landed on Old Flap real careful. When a couple of 'em land close together like this, it ain't long afore they take notice of one the 'nother and quit seeing anything else. It's kind of like they put a spell or a conjure on each other and, truth told, once they do, it's easier to hit two at once than it is to hit one.

The two flies saw each other at near the same time and frozed their moving, trying to see which one was toughest.

This waren't the right thing to do, 'cause waren't

neither one of 'em tough as my fly swah and it was 'bout to do a whole lot more bad to 'em than any other horsefly ever could!

Pah-dop!

Now that was a good sound! That meant I hadn't hit 'em hard enough to break no fly bones or nothing, but I had hit 'em so's they were gonna be a little dumbstruck. Most likely they wouldn't be doing no more flying but they should still be alive and kicking.

I looked under the mule again and there they were, wings still a-buzzing and each one of 'em spinning in circles on the ground, raising up two little clouds of dust.

I quick snatched 'em up and put 'em in the "live" pouch with the other ones that I was gonna use for big-fish bait.

The Preacher'll tell anyone that listens that the biggest, most ornery horseflies in the world live right here in Buxton. Mostly he tells the new-free slaves that come here 'cause he don't love nothing more than letting 'em know how amazing him and the rest of us folks in Buxton are. But, truth told, it's mostly how amazing he is.

One time, seven free slaves came into the Settlement all at once and the Preacher took it on hisself to welcome 'em. This was afore the Elders found out what he was doing and quick made sure it didn't happen again.

He told those seven new-free people 'bout what difficult days were ahead.

"Winters!" he shouted at 'em. "In your worst night mares you can't imagine how bad the winters up here are!

"Got so cold during the winter of 'fifty-three that flames on candles froze solid! Even the sun was frozen in place halfway across the sky! It didn't thaw out and commence moving again till the summer of 'fifty-four! Seven months of nothing but sunlight. Which explains why the horseflies up here are unnaturally large and ornery, since they had two growing seasons instead of the usual one."

The Preacher liked waving his arms 'round whilst he was talking, and he was really going at it to try to impress these new folks. "I was out in the field plowing with my mule that summer . . ." he said, which should've let on that this was gonna be a powerful stretching of the truth, 'cause don't no one 'round here ever recall seeing the reins of a mule nor any other kind of working tool in the Preacher's hands, ". . . when suddenly these two horseflies start buzzing overhead and one asks the other, 'What do you think, should we eat that mule here or drag him into the woods and polish him off?' The second fly says, 'Let's eat him here. If we take him to the woods the full-grown horseflies will snatch him away from us.'"

I ain't seen no signs of horseflies that big 'round here but it could be true, the Preacher's a mighty smart man. I only know that the fish at Old Flapjack's lake sure do think these horseflies are the best eating they've ever done.

Once I'd got enough flies and checked 'round the stable to make sure I'd done everything, I went back out to Mr. Segee.

"Everything's done, Mr. Segee."

"'Lijah, when you says everything's done, ain't no need for me to check. Ain't none the other children look after that stable the way you do. When's your next day?"

"Monday, sir."

"Well, then, see you on Monday."

"Yes, sir. Sir, is it gonna be all right if I take Old Flapjack out for a spell?"

It was the same thing every Friday, and he never said no, but Ma and Pa always say it's polite and proper to ask and not to make no assumptions.

"Why, let me think a second, boy, is it all right for you to take that old mule out?"

Mr. Segee leaned on the rake he was using and kind of stared up into the clouds. Then he said, "I think they done called off the horse racing for this evening, Elijah. Seem like all them horses, even Jingle Boy and Conqueror, done pulled out once they got wind Ol' Flapjack was running again, figure they ain't got no chance at whupping that mule. So it don't seem like you taking him is gunn be a problem."

Mr. Segee came up from Mississippi only a year ago, and Ma says we got to give him some allowance for the kind of things he thinks is funny, so I give him a little laugh every time he makes one n'em bad jokes.

I could tell Flapjack was raring to go, but 'less you knowed what to look for, you might not see it. His raring-to-go look's a powerful lot like his not-wanting-to-move look.

Soon's I led him out of the stable he started off on the road that runs through the main part of the Settlement. I knowed there waren't no rush to catch him, I knowed exactly where he was going. Once he got out of the stable he'd head straight down the road afore he cut off into the woods heading for the lake he first took me to 'bout a year ago.

I had plenty of time to put away the tools and the wheelbarrow and gather up my fly pouches and my chunking stones and my net-basket and the strings that I use for holding the fish I catch.

When I got done, I cut through some fields and caught Old Flapjack just as he passed Miss Carolina's house. I jumped up on his back and let him carry me to our secret lake.

Most folks say it's wrong, but if I had my druthers, I'd ride a mule over a horse any day. Horses do too much shaking of your insides when you ride 'em and they're a long way up if you lose your grip and fall.

Mules don't jar nothing when they walk, they like slow

and easy travel. They have a way of rocking you gentle like a baby in a crib. If you don't fall asleep first, you get a chance to think 'bout things when you ride a mule. With a horse, you don't get to think 'bout nothing but hoping you don't fall off and get coldcocked by their hoofs. If you fall off a mule, you're already close to the ground and got plenty of time to roll outta the way of their feet. Slow as Old Flapjack is, if you fell off him you'd have time enough to take a nap afore you had to worry 'bout him stomping on you.

Flapjack left the road and turned off into the woods just after we crossed out of the Settlement and passed the Preacher's house. It didn't look like the Preacher was home. Not that I'd've stopped and called on him, it's just that lately, since he's seen Jesus has been giving me gifts, he lets me come with him and watch when he practices shooting off his mystery pistol.

It just was last month that the Preacher snucked up on me whilst I was out in the Atlas Clearing chunking rocks. He came out from behind a tree and said, "Did I see what I think I saw or are my eyes deceiving me?"

He sounded so surprised that I looked 'round the clearing expecting something peculiar to be going on.

"What did you see, sir?"

The Preacher said, "I saw *you*, Elijah. I saw what

you were doing, and I'm afraid it has the look of conjuring to it."

I couldn't understand what he was talking 'bout. I was sure I hadn't done nothing that no one could claim was conjuring.

I said, "No, sir, I wouldn't never do nothing like conjuring. I waren't doing nothing but chunking stones."

He said, "That's what I'm talking about. I've never seen a soul throw a rock like you do and, Elijah, I have to tell you, I'm quite concerned. I have to do some serious pondering on this to see if it's the work of the Devil. You do know that being left-handed is one of the sure signs of being in Satan's clutches, don't you?"

I said, "No, sir!"

He said, "Keep that in mind. Come on with me, I'm going a little deeper in the woods to practice-shoot. And bring some of those rocks you have there."

I'd told Ma I waren't gonna go no farther than the Atlas Clearing, but since I was gonna be with the Preacher I figured it'd be all right if I followed him. 'Sides, if it meant I'd get to see him shooting off his mystery pistol, waren't nothing gonna stop me!

I'd spent lots of time sneaking through the woods, mostly at night, but I didn't recognize the way the Preacher started leading me. All I knowed for sure was that it was where me and Cooter'd been warned not to go, off toward the way where some of the white people that didn't like us lived. Pa'd told us it was a way full up with black bears and bats and, worst of all, millions of rattling-snakes!

I sure was glad the Preacher had his gun 'cause, truth told, whilst I knowed I wouldn't have no trouble chunking a rattling-snake with my rocks, I caint say for sure if I could stop one of those black bears.

Me and the Preacher must've walked for half a hour, but I couldn't be sure, when you don't know where you're heading, time don't seem to run by like it normal do. But with every step we took I was getting more and more disappointed in this new area.

From the way Pa had warned me, I'd always pictured these woods as having so many bears hanging out of the trees that the sunlight would've been blocked off from hitting the ground! I'd always pictured that there'd be so many rattling-snakes hissing and shaking in these parts that you'd near 'bout go deaf from the racket they made. But we'd been walking a good long time and there was still plenty of sunlight and I hadn't heard rattle the first. We hadn't even seen one bat.

Finally we got to another clearing and the Preacher said, "I'm going to give you some tests, Elijah, and I'm hoping that they prove you haven't been conjuring, because if you have, it's my responsibility to let the word be spread."

I waren't sure what he meant by that, but I knowed it waren't good.

He said, "I'm going to set these pieces of wood up at about twenty paces and I want to see how many of them you can hit."

I started thinking this over. Hitting something from twenty paces waren't nothing, but I wondered if I should miss one or two of 'em on purpose so's the Preacher wouldn't see no signs of conjuring.

But this was the Preacher, and he was so smart it'd be hard to fool him. He was always telling me he'd forgot more than I ever knowed, which don't make a lot of sense, but it was probably gonna be best on me if I chunked for real and didn't hold back.

The Preacher walked off twenty steps and set up five hunks of wood 'bout three feet apart one from the 'nother.

He came back and told me, "Let me see how many of them you can hit before I count five."

I put two stones in my right hand and three in my left.

The Preacher raised a eyebrow like he hadn't never seen nothing like this and said, "Set! Go! One . . ."

I throwed left, right, left, right, left.

The Preacher'd only counted to three afore I had all five of those wood hunks flying through the air.

He looked at me in a way that told me he thought for sure I was a-conjuring.

He didn't say nothing but he walked back the twenty paces and this time set up ten pieces of wood.

He came back and drawed his mystery pistol out of its fancy holster and said, "When I say 'go,' you hit the five on the right and I'm going to hit the five on the left."

I got my rocks ready.

"Go!"

The loud way the pistol exploded right next to me throwed me off and I missed the first piece of wood but quick knocked down the others. By the time I'd finished, the Preacher had only shot three of the wood hunks and was sighting in on number four.

He stopped and looked at me like he's puzzling, then said, "I'm going to have to do some more contemplating over this. On the one hand this might be an act of conjuration." He put his right hand out like he's expecting something to drop in it. "On the other hand . . ." His left hand came up. ". . . we might be witnessing a gift from Jesus Himself!"

He brung his hands together like he was fixing to pray. "I'm not ready to come right out and say whether this is conjuring or the Lord, but whatever it is, it sure is unnatural for a boy to be tossing stones like that."

A few days later, the Preacher let me and other folks know it had been showed to him that my rock chunking was gave to me as a gift from Jesus!

He told folks my arm and my eye were so true that I could knock the spots off a ladybug without harming her atall if I took the notion to do so.

He said what happened to a stone after I chunked it was like a ball shot out one n'em old muzzle-loader rifles. It waren't the quickest thing getting to where it was aimed, but once it got there, all sorts of who-struck-John busted loose.

I believed the Preacher when he told me what I got was a gift from the Lord, but that didn't mean I didn't have no doubts 'bout it from time to time. I'd been meaning to ask our Sabbath school teacher, Mr. Travis, if it was blaspheming to say this, but seemed to me if this rock chunking really was a gift from Jesus, it would be the sort of thing that would be there forever, and for me it waren't atall. This was a gift that needed lots of practicing else it went away.

Ma and Pa waren't too impressed by the Preacher saying these things neither. When I told Pa what got showed to the Preacher, he asked, "How come Jesus only choose certain folk to talk di-rect to? And how come they's always the ones what ain't got nothing atall in common with the Bible?"

Maybe I'd started dozing, I was surprised when Old Flapjack slowed down and I felt sticker bushes snatching at my brogans. He'd started picking his way through some blackberries and I knowed we'd just 'bout reached our secret lake.

It was these bushes that Old Flap spent all his time in whilst I fished.

I hopped off his back and walked down to the water. I went clean over to the other side of the lake and laid down my two pouches and my tote sack and net-basket and pulled off my brogans and all my clothes.

I divide this lake into two parts. First there's the fishing part, which was on the side where I came in at, by all the cattails and lily pads. Then there was the swimming part, which was where I'd walked to now.

I jumped in and let all the sweat from choring and riding Flapjack float off of me. I don't know how long I spent bathing, but after 'while I saw splashes and waves coming from the other side of the lake and I knowed the fish had started feeding.

I pulled my clothes back on, 'cepting for my brogans and stockings, picked up my sack and two pouches and net-basket, and walked back over to the fishing side of the lake, right near where Old Flapjack was still eating blackberries. I could hear him snorting and chawing and going at 'em pretty good.

There was a perfect spot for rock fishing just afore where the cattails got thick.

I opened the "dead" fly pouch and picked out 'bout four

of 'em that had a good amount of juices leaked out and I tossed 'em right into the spot near the cattails. This would get the little fish riled up, they'd bump at the flies and try to pull 'em under and would raise a ruckus that'd make the big fish wonder what the commotion was for.

I moved till the light was just so that I could see the flashing of the little fishes' scales. I went into my tote sack and picked out two good stones, one for my right hand and one for my left.

Next I reached into the "live" fly pouch and plucked out two that had a good bit of fight left in 'em. I tossed these flies at the fishing spot and one of 'em still had enough life in him to fly 'bout a little, but that didn't last long and he soon plopped into the water. Both of these flies waren't accustom to being wet and started whirring and splashing and skimming 'cross the top of the lake.

There's something 'bout the way those half-wit horse-flies move on the water that scares the small fish away and drives the big fish berserk! If I'd done everything right the big ones wouldn't have no choice but to come barreling out of the cattails and snatch at the flies.

I saw the little fish part 'round one of the flies and all the sudden there was a goldy-silverish flash shooting out of the lily pads. It's hard to explain, but I felt it more than I saw it.

I throwed left.

The rock and the fish and the fly all met up at the same spot at the same time.

It ain't boasting when I say it was a perfect throw. I can say that 'cause for a throw to be perfect, two things've got to happen. One, you got to chunk the fish so's he's knocked senseless right off and stays at the top of the water, and, two, the rock has got to bounce off him and land far enough away that it don't make no kind of splash that'll scare the other big fish.

After this rock got done chunking the fish in the head, it skipped four times 'cross the water and slipped down in the lake quiet as a duck going after minnows.

I throwed my net-basket out and hauled the fish in.

It was a good-size bass. I strunged it up and put it back in the water.

I don't know why it is, but something 'bout that basket don't worry the fish too much and I can toss it in over and over and not scare 'em atall. Maybe it's 'cause fish ain't real smart.

I knowed if I was a fish I'd've looked at it different. If I saw one of my fish friends go after a fly and all the sudden he was floating on the water not moving and had a big knot on his head, I think my appetite would leave me. And even if it didn't, I sure wouldn't have no enthusiasm for the next horsefly that showed up in the water. I'd've been smart enough to put one and one together and would have choosed something off the bottom of the lake for supper.

But I suppose if you're partial to swallowing horseflies whole, it's a pretty good sign that smartness ain't one of the things you been 'specially blessed with.

I chunked four more big fish and missed on two when Old Flapjack quit eating berries and gave a strange snort. I stopped moving and looked in his direction. From knowing this old mule, I knowed he'd seen something. Some folks have watch dogs, I got a watch mule.

He started right back up with his blackberry eating sounds, but I knowed something waren't right. I could tell he'd seen someone and that it was someone he knowed.

I looked real careful all along the blackberry bushes and the trees but didn't see nothing.

I waited and waited, then went back at the rock fishing. I missed three out of the next five, and I knowed it's 'cause my mind was still wondering why Old Flap made that sound. It seemed like if you waren't paying all your attention to rock fishing you waren't gonna be too good at it.

I tried to quit fretting but still missed on two of the next five stones I chunked.

Then the fish quit biting. I had me seven good bass and three big perch. I summed 'em up in my head as four for me and Ma and Pa, two for Mr. Leroy, two for Mr. Segee, and two that I was hoping to swap with Mrs. Brown since I knowed she was baking today. That totaled up to ten.

I emptied what was left of the dead flies in the water and emptied the live flies on a rock. If those flies ever did come 'round and got their senses back, it only was fair that their lives waren't all-the-way wasted and they'd have a chance to fly away.

Then I thought 'bout how pesty they are and what they eat. I changed my mind and brushed 'em all in the water.

I gathered all my throwing stones in my pouch and started putting my brogans on when a man's voice boomed out from behind me, "Now that was the most amazing thing I've ever seen!"

I whirled 'round and at the same time picked up a stone ready to chunk whoever it was that had snucked up on me.

My left arm went back and the man raised his hands and said, "No! It's me!"

'Twas the Preacher.

My breathing came back to me and I said, "I'm terrible sorry, sir. I waren't expecting no one to be out here."

The Preacher came out of the bushes and said, "How many of those fish did you stone like that, Elijah?"

I pulled my string of fish out of the water and showed 'em to him.

He said, "Sweet baby Jesus! The boy's out here fishing without line nor hook! Knocking fish in the head with rocks! Well, that really does confirm it, Elijah. You've been given a rare gift from the Lord!

"I'm reminded of Mark, chapter six, verses thirty-three through forty-four, where Jesus fed five thousand people with five loaves of bread and two fish. But instead of turning two fish into food for thousands, Elijah, you've turned stones into fish! Maybe turning water to wine is more impressive and practical, but what you've done is no mean feat either."

The Preacher put his hand on my forehead and said, "I've been thinking about how we can best use this gift, Elijah, and I think that we can do something with it to help the whole Settlement. You do want to help the Settlement, don't you?"

This was strange talk for the Preacher. He didn't live di-rect in the Settlement, him and a few other escaped people lived just outside our land 'cause they didn't want to follow all the Settlement's rules.

I said, "Yes, sir, I want to help the Settlement, but how . . ."

The Preacher said, "Now don't you waste a moment thinking about it. All I needed to know was if you were willing to help and now that I see that you're the fine Christian boy I thought you were, we'll work this out together."

I said, "Yes, sir, but I was wondering . . ."

The Preacher raised his hand and said, "You know

what, Elijah? The Lord has revealed to me that since he has given you this gift I should treat you with a little more respect. I should quit treating you like a child and start treating you like the man you truly are."

Pa says when someone sweet-talks you like this, you got to be real careful with the next words that come out of their mouth. He says the sweet-talking is like a rattling-snake's rattles, it's like you're getting a warning that you're 'bout to get bit.

The Preacher said, "So I was wondering since you're near full grown, maybe you'd like to come with me yon and see if your eye is as good for shooting this pistol as it is for throwing stones? I haven't forgotten the promise I made to you a while back."

The Preacher pulled his jacket back and showed me his fancy pistol.

Every thought I had 'bout rattling-snake words and sweet-talking and bites flewed away!

Then I remembered what happened last time, and how when it came to my turn to shoot off the pistol the Preacher'd said he'd run out of bullets.

I said, "You ain't funning me, sir? I'm-a really get to shoot it this time?"

He looked like I'd hurt his feelings.

He said, "Elijah, I'm talking to you man to man and you have doubts?"

I said, "No, sir, I just didn't think . . ."

The Preacher said, "Good! Let's go on over to that clearing and do some target practicing."

I said, "Yes, sir!"

But soon's I said it, I started thinking 'bout things, things like what if Old Flapjack didn't want to go no farther, and what would Ma and Pa say if they knowed I was shooting off the Preacher's mystery pistol, and how was I gonna explain to Ma why I was getting back so late? And folks *were* depending on me to bring 'em some fish.

I told the Preacher, "Sir, I don't think I can do it now, I gotta get back. Ma's expecting me to bring some fish home for supper and it's starting to get late."

The Preacher said, "You're right, Elijah. You're right, and that goes to prove my point about you being more man than child. What you've just done is show responsibility. We can shoot this gun on another day. Now you just go right ahead and take those fish back to your ma."

The Preacher waited a second then said, "That seems like an awful lot of fish for three people. I was wondering, is your family going to eat all ten of those fish?"

"No, sir. Usually I give some to Mr. Segee and some to Mr. Leroy."

He said, "A fine Christian thing to do! Now I was also wondering, Elijah, if you know anything about a word called *tithing*?"

"Yes, sir, Mr. Travis taught us 'bout that in Sabbath classes. It's giving a tenth of your belongings and your works to the Lord."

He said, "Yes, to the Lord *through* his servant here on earth. What do you suppose a tenth of those fish is? Three? Four?"

The Preacher might've thought he was the most educatedest man 'round Buxton, but it seemed like he was powerful bad at doing fractions.

I told him, "No, sir, a tenth of these fish is one."

The Preacher said, "True, if you figure a tenth by numbers, but I was thinking of figuring a tenth by age. Let me hold on to both of those stringers for a minute."

I handed him all the fish.

He said, "You're good at doing sums, aren't you?"

I said, "I'm tolerable good long's it don't get stretched into geometry."

The Preacher commenced pointing at each fish and calling out numbers and telling me to keep track of the total.

"This one's about fourteen years old, this one's twelve, this one just turned eighteen, this one's . . ."

It was the most amazing thing! Some of 'em he had to look into their mouths to get the age, and some of 'em he could tell just by holding up. But the Preacher knowed the age of each and every one of the fishes! By the time he was done I'd totaled up a hundred and twenty-two years!

"So what's ten percent of a hundred and twenty-two, Elijah?"

I moved the decimal point without using pencil nor paper and said, "One tenth of a hundred and twenty-two years comes to twelve full years and two-tenths of a year, sir."

The Preacher pulled the biggest two bass and the biggest perch off the stringers and said, "This perch is ten years old, and these bass are one year old each. How many years is that?"

"Ten plus one plus one equals twelve years, sir."

"So what's left?"

"Two-tenths of a year, sir."

"And how much time does that equal?"

I guessed. "That's 'bout two months and a little, sir."

He pulled the next biggest bass off the string and said, "I was thinking we should throw this one back since he's only a month and a half old, but that's close enough to two months that he balances things out nicely. I'll just keep him."

I didn't mean to show no disrespect but I couldn't help frowning. I'd started with ten fish and now I was down to six, and even though I ain't particular worthy at my schooling, it still seemed it'd take a whole lot of doggone humbug algebra and some trickaration geometry to make ten percent of ten come out to four.

The Preacher put the four fish on one of the strings and said, "I think I'll call on Sister Carolina and see if she's had fish lately. Maybe she can fry 'em up."

Then he was gone.

And so were four of my fish, and, hard as I try, I caint see that as one tenth of ten!

→ CHAPTER 4 ←

Kidnappers and Slavers!

I loaded all my fishing tools up, threw the stringer of fish over Old Flap's rump, and started riding back to the stable.

'Twaren't long afore the steady rocking of the mule had me wondering if I should sleep or think. Thinking won out 'cause I was still mighty sore 'bout having only six fish. I couldn't figure out exactly how the Preacher'd done it, but something with this tithing business stanked real bad. And that got me thinking that lots of what the Preacher did waren't right.

I'd heard Pa call the Preacher a jackleg man of the Lord once when he didn't know I was listening. I couldn't ask Pa what that meant without him knowing I'd been eavesdropping on growned folks' conversations, but I was catching on that it waren't a good thing to be.

And then lots of other things the Preacher did came rushing into my mind. Like him promising again to let me shoot that mystery pistol. We'd gone out two times afore and I still hadn't even touched that gun. The first time he'd ran out of bullets when it came time for me to shoot it, and the second time 'stead of shooting that silver-plate pistol, he gave me a old rusty one to fire. It got so hot after I shot it twice that it burnt my hand and I throwed it down.

All that did was make me want to shoot that mystery pistol off even more.

Folks did lots of speculating on where that gun came from, but that was 'bout the *only* thing the Preacher didn't do a whole lot of talking 'bout. I got real disappointed when he finally did tell Mr. Polite, 'cause 'stead of telling one of his usual interesting truth stretchers, he came up with the same story near 'bout any dull child would have. He said he found it in the woods. That disappointed me 'cause if the Preacher'd put his mind to it, I knowed he'd have come up with something a lot more exciting than that.

The gun first showed up in his hands 'bout three years ago when I was 'round eight. I got a real clear memory of it 'cause it was tied up with the last time we had slave catchers come to Buxton from America.

We'd been in the middle of Latin lessons when Mr. Brown came and knocked on the door of the schoolhouse and called Mrs. Guest outside. When she came back in I started fretting 'cause whilst she tried to keep her voice calm so's not to rile no one, I watched her eyes and saw the way she wrunged her hands whilst she talked and I knowed something was terrible wrong.

She said, "Children, we are going to postpone the rest of classes today. I want all of you to make certain your homework assignment is written down and your books are gathered. Then I want Rodney Wills, Emma, Buster, and Zachary to line up quietly at the door. Kicknosway, James, Alice, Alistair, and Bonita, you are to leave immediately and go directly home."

Near everybody but me was giggling and clowning and thinking this was something good, but I knowed growned folks waren't going to call off school 'less something powerful bad was 'bout to happen or had happened already. And why was Mrs. Guest sending all the white children and the Indian children home right off like that?

I quick looked out the window to the west and saw the sky was blue and sunshiny. That meant waren't no bad weather coming. That meant it was something worst, something dealing with people.

Another knock came on the door and Mr. Brown stuck his head in and said, "Ready?"

Mrs. Guest told him, "Yes," and said to us, "You will be taken home in groups of four. Those who live farthest from the school will go first. Your parents have been called in from the fields and will be waiting for you at home. They will explain what is happening. I will entertain no questions and I will tolerate no noise. Sit along the walls in the boys' cloakroom and keep away from the windows. Wait until I tell you to move. You have nothing to worry about."

Now even the children that waren't particular sharp-minded got nervous. Ain't too much that'll get you worrying more than a teacher telling you that you shouldn't, and we all knowed just about *nothing* could make growned folks cut out their work in the fields early.

Mrs. Guest opened the door and Little Rodney, Emma, Buster, and Zachary went out behind her and Mr. Brown. Mrs. Guest stuck her head back in the cloakroom and said, "I will be right outside. I want no talking and no moving about."

Soon's the door shut after her, Sidney Prince whispered, "I wonder what's wrong. This here's real peculiar."

Cooter whispered back, "Whatever it is, you's lucky Emma Collins left, 'cause she sure would've told Mrs. Guest you's in here talking."

Sidney said, "Well, you're talking too, Cooter."

Cooter said, "It don't count, I'm just trying to . . ."

Philip Wise said, "Y'all both need to hesh. I know what it is."

Everyone but me asked him, "What?"

Philip pointed at me and said, "It's him."

I felt myself getting warm. Me and Philip Wise didn't agree on near nothing.

He said, "Frederick Douglass is up in Chatham and told the growned folks he ain't coming down to visit in Buxton 'less they locks Elijah and all the other babies up. The man say he caint stand the thought of getting throwed up on again."

Most of 'em laughed but Cooter said, "Philip Wise, you ain't nothing but a fool. Everyone know you's just jealous 'cause Eli was the first child borned free in Buxton and you waren't nothing but third. Even Emma Collins beat you!"

Philip started to answer but the door came back open.

Mrs. Guest rounded up Philip, Cooter, Sidney, and Big Rodney, and they left. I was in the last group to go. Soon's we were outside I knowed I'd got afeared for a good reason. Mr. Brown and Mr. Leroy were standing on both ends of the schoolhouse holding on to double-barrel shotguns and looking 'round like they were ready for trouble!

If seeing the guns waren't scary enough, the sounds I was hearing were worst. The Settlement was quiet like it was for only a few minutes every day afore dark. You couldn't hear no trees being chopped nor no mules nor horses being pushed on to pull harder, nor no sounds from the road. You couldn't hear that big fifteen-horsepower engine that runs the gristmill and the sawmill thumping away. You couldn't even hear Mr. Leroy's axe!

The only sound was birds, and you wouldn't never think that birds singing would be something to make you skittish, but hearing 'em singing all by theirselves like that, they might as well've been haints or ghosts singing.

Pa and our neighbor, Mr. Highgate, both were carrying rifles and told us to walk in line.

I knowed right off what it had to be. I knowed there was only one reason they'd let the white children and the Indian children leave without no one watching 'em. I said, "Pa, there's slave catchers here, ain't there? Is that why everyone's toting guns?"

Pa said, "Don't fret, son. We's just being cautious. Ain't no one seen nothing for sure yet."

Pa told me that one of the Settlement's white friends from Chatham had come busting in on horseback and warned that there were two American scallywags with pistols and shackles and chains asking questions 'bout the best way to get to Buxton.

We all looked 'cross the fields and watched the edge of the woods, fearing that the American kidnappers were gonna come out firing, trying to snatch someone into slavery.

A little ways from home the Preacher came running at us holding on to a long sharp blade from off a scythe. He said to Pa, "I heard there are two of them. I'm going to check south."

Pa said, "Hold up, Zeph, they was supposed to be up in

Chatham, that means they gunn come from the north. 'Sides, you shouldn't be out there without no gun, someone with a firearm should go with you."

The Preacher said, "If it was me, I'd circle around and come from the south. You all go look north. I'm not expecting any trouble. These are my woods, I know what's what out here."

Then he ran off south.

Didn't nothing come from all the excitement we had. The worst thing that happened was we had twice as many Latin verbs to study at school when we went back.

The Preacher waren't seen for the next couple of days and that did cause some folks to worry, but everybody knowed he disappeared all the time so didn't no one pay it too much mind.

Two nights later I tiptoed out of my bedroom and peeked 'round the corner of the parlour to see if Ma and Pa were up. Waren't no candles nor lamps burning so I looked up the stairs to check their bedroom next. It was dark there too. I went up a few steps and heard Pa snoring, they were sleeping for sure.

I slipped out of my nightshirt, put some clothes on, then crawled out my window and dropped on the ground. I waited a second to make sure waren't nothing disturbed, then started running through the truck patch toward the trees.

I hadn't got ten yards into the woods when all the sudden my heart quit beating and my blood ran cold! Something tall and white and ghostish, like a giant haint, came walking slow out from 'mongst the trees.

My mind acted like it was gonna get all fra-gile but it didn't take much time afore I knowed it waren't nothing but a horse, a stranger horse. It didn't even take *that* much time for me to scat back home and jump into my bedroom window.

I slipped back into my nightshirt and ran up the stairs to Ma and Pa's room. I called out, "Pa?"

Everybody was still a little jumpy what with them paddy-rollers 'round somewhere and the Preacher not being seen for a while so Ma and Pa were up in a flash!

I told 'em, "I couldn't sleep and was looking out my window and saw a horse come from out of the woods!"

Pa said, "White folks?"

"No, sir, the horse didn't have no rider."

Pa said, "Were it one a our'n? You think someone left the barn door ajar?"

I told him, "No, sir. 'Twas a big white stallion with a saddle, nothing like none of ours."

Pa snatched on some trousers, ran downstairs, grabbed a torch and his rifle, then ran outside barefoot.

He hadn't said not to, so I followed close behind him.

Pa lit the torch and we started searching for signs of the

60

horse. Pa picked up his tracks and we found him just down the road.

The horse had camped hisself in front of the Highgates' home. His head was leaned down over their picket fence and he was chawing on bunches of flowers, uprooting most of Mrs. Highgate's black-eye Susies.

Pa handed me the rifle and torch and walked up on the horse slow. He patted the horse on the neck and said, "There, boy. There now."

The horse's eyes had a wild roll to 'em but he didn't seem to mind, so Pa picked up his reins and pulled the horse out of the flower garden.

I pointed at the horse's haunch. "Pa! Look! He's hurt!"

A big patch of dry blood was all over the horse's right-hand flank.

Pa checked the horse over good. He even pulled the saddle off and said, "Ain't him, but something's done bled bad here."

Pa gave me the horse's reins then went to Mr. Highgate's door and knocked loud.

Mr. Highgate's window rose up and his shotgun poked out.

"Who there?"

"It's me, Theo. Come on out, there's a hoss what ain't got no rider in your yard. Maybe someone's afoot somewhere."

61

Pa and Mr. Highgate stirred everyone and they lit torches and searched high and low but didn't come up with nothing or no one.

The next morning, since his hand got hurt at the sawmill and he caint work, Mr. Highgate took the horse and saddle to the sheriff in Chatham so's no one would say we stoled 'em. Some of the white people 'round here are always trying to blame everything that goes bad on Settlement folks and we waren't looking for no trouble.

Three days after that, the Preacher showed back up with the fancy holster and the mystery pistol. After 'while he told Mr. Polite he'd found them whilst he was out in the woods near the river. He said he went into Chatham to see if the gun belonged to anyone there but it didn't, so he was laying claim that it was his own.

People had a hard time believing the Preacher's story. They said someone *might* find a white man's pistol that had bounced out of his saddle or his jacket or his holster, but it waren't likely they'd find a pistol *and* a holster all together. They said 'bout the only way to get a white man away from his gun and holster was to take it off of him whilst he was at rest in his coffin.

Ma was right when she said people that use to be slaves love to talk, 'cause soon after that folks started prettying up some of the wildest stories you could think of 'bout why that horse came to Buxton. Stories started getting told that the Preacher had stoled up on those two white men with the blade from that scythe and slit their throats and cut 'em into hunks then throwed their earthy remainders in Lake Erie.

They said there'd been two white twins from America riding 'round Chatham on two white stallions whilst toting two of the fanciest pearl-handle, silver-plate pistols just like the one the Preacher said he found. They said whilst the Preacher was killing those men, one of the horses spooked and bolted and that was the one that wandered into the Settlement. Then, they said, the Preacher rode the other white stallion to Toronto and sold it and the second pistol in the market there.

I thought this waren't nothing but gossiping and story pretty-upping.

The way I figure, if the Preacher *had* took those guns from those men, how come he only said he found *one* pistol?

That don't make no sense, that don't make no sense atall. It's mathematics and I ain't real partial to that, but seems to me that as much as he enjoyed showing off the *one* gun he'd found, he'd've enjoyed showing off *two* of 'em *twice* as much! And everybody knowed it would be near impossible for the Preacher to keep a story as rousing as that all to hisself.

→ CHAPTER 5 ←

Sharing the Fish

By the time me and Old Flap got back to the barn, Mr. Segee had already shut everything up and went home. That was good for me. I'd been counting on giving him two of the fish I'd chunked to say "thank you, kindly" for letting me take Flapjack out, but since the Preacher had took near 'bout half of what I caught, I waren't gonna have no extras for Mr. Segee.

I got Old Flap back in his stall, shut the stable door, and started walking home.

Folks that had finished working and had cleaned up and already et waved or started calling to me from their stoops.

Mr. Waller yelled, "Evening, Eli. Them fish looks too heavy for a boy your size to be toting. You's 'bout to end up busting something on you that you gunn need one day. Why don't you ease your burden some, son, and set two or three of 'em over here?"

I told him, "Evening, Mr. Waller, but they ain't heavy to me. You must have forgot how strong I am.

'Member how I helped you move those stones and you told me you ain't never seen no boy young as me with so much strength?"

He said, "'Deed I do, Eli, 'deed I do. But ain't no harm in me trying for a little Friday night fish-fry now, is there?"

I said, "No harm atall, sir, but I already told Mr. Leroy I was gonna give two of 'em to him and I already got someone that I'm-a try to swap this here big perch with."

He said, "You keep me in mind next time, then, son."

"Yes, sir, I'll do that."

A ways on, Miss Duncan-the-first and Miss Duncan-the-second both said, "Evening, Elijah, looks like you done good!"

"Yes, ma'ams!"

A little farther toward home, Mrs. Brown stood up out of her rocker, waved a handkerchief at me, and called, "Yoo-hoo! 'Lijah Freeman! Yoo-hoo! Just the boy I been waiting on!"

I said, "Evening, Mrs. Brown."

"I just finish baking three cherry pies, 'Lijah, and Mr. Brown tells me he been having a powerful yearning for some perch. You suppose a pie be worth a perch?"

I said, "Yes, ma'am! I'd've had you two of 'em, but I had to do some tithing and got jacklegged."

She said, "One's fine, you know I don't like nothing but catfish no way."

I waren't never gonna catch a catfish rock fishing. Catfish must be the smartest fish there is, it's like them and carps were the only fish that added rocks and horseflies together and came up with something bad. They didn't come off the bottom of the water for nothing.

I walked up on Mrs. Brown's stoop. She always wore black and some of the times waren't in such a happy mind as she was today. Her only baby, a two-year-old boy, died hard of the fever two years pass and ever since that happened, Mrs. Brown was being bothered by spells.

If you were out sneaking 'round in the woods at night when you were supposed to be sleeping, you might get a terrible fright when you came through the forest and saw her leaning up 'gainst a tree, humming and rocking to and fro with her arms wrapped 'round herself.

But ain't *nothing* more terrorific than walking through the trees in the moonlight and coming up on her squatting down, brushing dirt from a spot on the ground that didn't look no different from any other spot in the woods. But there was *something* 'bout that one particular spot that was calling Mrs. Brown and telling her to brush at it with her bare hand. And she'd brush it till it waren't nothing but hard earth.

Other times, times like this, you wouldn't've knowed there was nothing plaguing her. 'Cepting for wearing nothing but black clothes she was just as right in her mind as me. She told Ma she waren't gonna start wearing colours again till the Lord blessed her with another child, but the midwife here in Buxton and the doctor from up in Chatham both said that waren't never gonna happen.

Some folks say Mrs. Brown's touched in the head, but 'cept for scaring me in the woods at night she treats me real kind. And everyone knows caint no one in the Settlement bake the way she does!

I ain't trying to be disrespectful of Ma's cooking when I say that neither. Ma can fry some tolerable good fish and make vegetables that ain't *exactly* horrible, but she caint bake for nothing. Pa would get pretty excited if I showed up with one of Mrs. Brown's pies. He never let on to Ma how happy those pies made him, but if he thought she waren't listening and couldn't see him, he'd give me some big hugs and spin me 'round the room and kick up his heels!

Mrs. Brown held her front door open and said, "Come on in and pick which one n'em pies you's partial to, 'Lijah."

I said, "Thank you, ma'am," and pulled off my brogans and left 'em on the stoop next to all my fishing tools.

The inside of her house had trapped the smell of the pies and soon's you crossed through the door you couldn't help but open your nose wide as it'd go, lean your head back, close your eyes, and breathe in as much of that air as you could!

I stood still and took me two more deep breaths. I learnt a long time ago that when you're smelling something real good, you only get two or three first-place smells of it afore your nose won't take no more notice. I didn't want to move or nothing so I could enjoy the smell afore my nose started recalling I was toting six dead fish.

After I took my fourth breath, I was smelling as much fish as I was smelling pies, so I opened my eyes and commenced breathing regular.

Mrs. Brown was smiling at me.

I smiled back. "They sure do smell good, Mrs. Brown."

"I ain't meaning to be unhumble, but you know they tastes better'n they smells, 'Lijah. Come on in the kitchen and pick you one."

We walked through her parlour. It was one of the Settlement's rules that all our houses had to look just 'bout the same on the outside. All of 'em had to have a stoop and a picket fence and a flower garden out front and had to be exactly ten paces off the road. It waren't till you went into the houses that you saw the different ways that folks set 'em up.

Mr. and Mrs. Brown didn't have much of nothing in their parlour. Where we had a table with a cloth and a vase for flowers and some chairs, they only kept a empty blue baby crib with a tired old white sheet over one corner. Where we had a big fireplace and mantel made out of bricks from the Settlement's brickyard, they still had a fireplace made out of clay and rocks. Where Pa had paid Mr. Leroy to lay some maplewood floorboards, they still had floors made from rough pine. Their home only had one floor whilst ours had two. They'd only come up from America a couple of years ago and were still struggling.

The Browns et in the kitchen so they kept their eating table in there. Ma told me that lots of folks that use to be slaves couldn't bust the habit of eating only in the room where they cooked, so heaps of people in the Settlement used their parlour for things 'sides eating food.

Mrs. Brown had the pies resting on a table near the back window.

Since I only had one perch for her, I picked the smallest pie and dropped the fish off the stringer into a big basin.

She said, "Thank you kindly, 'Lijah. Mr. Brown is sure enough gunn be surprised when he come home and have some perch!"

I took the pie. The tin was still warm! I said, "Thank *you*, Mrs. Brown. My pa's gonna be surprised too!"

I stepped out on Mrs. Brown's back stoop and scaled and cleaned the perch. I left the guts in the basin for her garden.

I went back into her kitchen. "I'll bring you your tin back tomorrow, Mrs. Brown."

"No rush, I ain't gunn be baking no more till middle of next week nohow, so take your time. Tell your ma I ax 'bout her."

"Yes, ma'am."

I took my five fish, my fishing tools, and my pie and started home again.

As I walked, I started calculating how I was gonna divvy up these last five fish. Three of 'em were enough for me and Ma and Pa if I didn't eat too much, so Mr. Leroy was still gonna get the two I'd promised him.

Once I got home, I cleaned all five of the fish and Ma fried 'em up. After we et, I'd go take Mr. Leroy his share. He was always doing extra so he was the last one to lay off working. He never et till it was late.

It was easy to find Mr. Leroy. All you had to do was pay attention to the sound his axe made.

'Round this time of day, when it's starting to getting duskish, the sound of Mr. Leroy's axe is so regular and natural that Pa says it turns into a part of the scenery and you wouldn't notice it unless you were trying to, or unless it stopped all the sudden.

It's like the way you don't notice the sounds toady-frogs make down by the river till they shut up. *Then* you say to yourself, "Them toady-frogs sure were putting up a awful racket, how come I didn't notice it afore?"

After I washed up I went out on the stoop to tell Ma and Pa I was gonna take Mr. Leroy his fish.

Ma's hands never quit knitting. She looked over her spectacles and said, "Don't you stay out too long, 'Lijah. If working with Mr. Leroy's gunn mess with you getting up early and doing your chores, you knows which one of 'em you's gunn give up, don't you?"

"Yes, ma'am."

Pa ain't like Ma, he holds up on his whittling to talk. He don't try to do whittling and nothing else together since he near whittled his little finger off that time whilst telling 'bout how hard he use to work in Kentucky. That finger still don't do everything he wants it to do, but at least it's still there. Mr. Leroy's got him a finger that ain't nothing but a nub.

Pa said, "You gunn work with him tomorrow?"

"Yes, sir."

"Good boy. On Sunday I'm-a help Mrs. Holton with some them stumps she got left. I'm-a need you and Cooter to come 'long."

"Yes, sir."

Ma'd put a rag on the plate of fish she'd fried up for Mr. Leroy, and I took it and headed down the road. Once I'd walked a spell I could hear him chopping in the south. He was down at Mrs. Holton's place. She's what Ma calls a unfortunate soul. Her husband got sick then got caught whilst they were getting free, but her and their two little girls got through.

She'd come to Buxton with lots of pieces of gold sewed up in her dress and bought fifty acres of land in the south of the Settlement. Everyone knowed 'bout her and talked 'bout her 'cause word was that out of the three hundred families here, she was the only one that never had to borrow no money to get her land. She paid for the whole thing cash on the barrelhead!

Folks are speculating all the time 'bout how much money Mrs. Holton has. She don't flash it 'round or nothing, but folks say anyone that can buy fifty acres without no loan must be rich as a slave owner!

If you buy land here in the Settlement, there's some rules you gotta go 'long with no matter how much gold you have, and one of 'em is that it ain't no one's job but your own to make sure you clear your whole fifty acres and dig a drainage ditch all 'long your property and the road.

Mrs. Holton's girls were way too young to do serious woodcutting, and it was the time of year that folks were so busy working from sunup to sundown that no one had the time nor the fight left in 'em to get a chopping bee going, so she paid Mr. Leroy to clear her land and dig her drainage ditch. He was always looking to do extra work 'cause he was saving up enough money to buy his wife and daughter and son out of America. That made him and Mrs. Holton a first-prize team.

Mr. Leroy was happy 'cause since Mrs. Holton and her children came to Buxton he didn't have to hire hisself out to none of the white farmers up 'round Chatham, and she was happy 'cause till her husband could escape again, she needed someone to do the heavy work 'round her home.

Mr. Leroy near 'bout built her house all by hisself, and since he was the best carpenter in the Settlement, she'd paid him to put all kinds of fancy pillars and posts and gewgaws and curlycues everywhere on the outside of her house. She'd draw him up a picture of something she remembered or thought up, and he'd make it outta wood in no time atall.

All Mr. Leroy's work had folks saying that Mrs. Holton was gonna win the Most Beautiful Home in Buxton Contest this year. That was something that didn't sit too good with our next-door neighbor, Mrs. Highgate, 'cause she'd won it for the pass five years one after the 'nother and waren't particular pleased 'bout someone else aiming at her prize.

I got to Mrs. Holton's house and knocked on the door to pay my respects.

"Evening, Eli."

"Evening, Mrs. Holton."

"Follow your ears. He way out back."

"Thank you, Mrs. Holton. Ma said to tell you she asked 'bout you."

"Tell your ma and pa I axed 'bout 'em too."

"Yes, ma'am."

There was a kind of music to him when Mr. Leroy was felling trees. From 'bout a mile off it sounded like one person playing and all you could hear was a steady, regular *crack!* sound that rolled toward you like it was being carried on the wind. That was the axe biting into the tree.

Once you got a bit closer, it started sounding like there were two folks playing music and you could hear something that sounded like *CHUH!* coming from Mr. Leroy. That was his breath getting squozed outta him once he hit the tree.

If you got close enough that you could see the sweat flying off of him, it sounded like someone else was joining in and you could hear a sound like *hoong!* That waren't nothing but him sucking air back in till he got set to swing again.

If you finally got close enough that you started getting nervous that the axe or them wood chips he sent flying were gonna hit you, you'd hear a sound that went *ka!* which was the sound of the axe getting pulled back out of the tree.

The harder and longer Mr. Leroy worked the more regular and music-ish the sound he made got. So when he first started, it would sound like *crack! CHUH, hoong, ka, crack! CHUH, hoong, ka, crack! CHUH, hoong, ka.*

But once he'd been going at it for a while, he got swinging faster and faster till he sounded like *crack!CHUH-hoongkacrack!CHUHhoongkacrack!CHUHhoongka . . .* so's he went from being music-ish to being machine-ish, which is what the Preacher said Mr. Leroy was. He said he'd heard Mr. Leroy's heart beating in his chest and that 'stead of sounding like it was made out of flesh and blood, it banged and pounded like it was made out of pure iron!

Mr. Leroy saw me and took one more *crack!CHUH-hoong* and left the axe stuck in the tree where it last bit.

He took a second to let his breathing catch up to him and said, "Evening, Elijah."

"Evening, sir."

"That time already, is it?"

"Yes, sir."

"Hadn't even noticed the sun was setting."

Mr. Leroy took a rag out of one of his overall pockets and wiped the sweat off his head. This waren't nothing but a waste of time, though, 'cause soon's the rag left his face, sweat rolled right back all over it. He rubbed his left elbow and arm and said, "You had you some luck fishing?"

"Yes, sir."

"Thank you kindly for remembering me, son."

Mr. Leroy sat on a stump and I sat on one next to him. He took a drink outta the jug of water he always keeps in the field and pulled the rag off the plate of fish Ma had fried for him. Ma had put some okree and potatoes and dandelion greens and a big piece of Mrs. Brown's cherry pie on the plate.

Mr. Leroy said, "You make sure you thanks your ma, Elijah. This is mighty kind of both of y'all."

Walking all this way to give Mr. Leroy a plate of food was worth it 'cause waren't nothing scarier nor funner than watching him eat fish. He didn't believe in wasting nothing, so he chawed every single piece! Fins and bones waren't nothing to him. Why, I bet if I'd left the scales and the guts on those fish he'd've chawed clean through those too.

The fish bones crackled and snapped in his mouth like dry corn in a mill.

I asked him, "Mr. Leroy, sir, ain't you never choked on one n'em fish bones?"

He said, "How you gunn choke if you's mashed 'em up good?"

"I don't know, sir. I try real hard to pick all the bones out of my fish, and when one of 'em does get through, it seems like it don't want to do nothing but stick in my throat sideways. It's enough to make you want to quit eating fish."

Mr. Leroy kept chomping and said, "Fish eating's like anything else in life, Elijah. If you go at it 'specting something bad to happen, all you gunn do is draw that bad thing to you. You caint be timid 'bout nothing you do, you got to go at it like you 'specting good things to come out of it. If I's to worry 'bout bones choking me, it'd happen every time I et fish. Ain't nothing further from my mind."

Fish bones snapped in his mouth like dry twigs.

Mr. Leroy finished off the vegetables and pie Ma'd gave him and handed me back the plate.

"Be sure you thank your ma and pa, Elijah. Tell your ma I 'preciate her thinking 'bout me.

"Now come on, we got us a lot of work to do."

CHAPTER 6

Mr. Travis Cheats Us Out of a Great Lesson

It don't seem fair, but since the start of this year Mr. Travis has been teaching us both our everyday school and our Sabbath school classes. And that means the man is on you like a tick, you caint get away from him no matter where you go. The biggest problem is if he pegs you as being not particular bright in everyday school, you ain't got prayer the first of having a clean slate when Sunday comes 'round and you got to go to Sabbath school.

When Mrs. Guest was our schoolteacher and Mrs. Needham taught us Sabbath school, you had a better chance of fooling at least one of 'em into thinking you were sensical, but with Mr. Travis running both schools, you ain't nothing but a dead duck.

What's even unfairer is that he mixes regular lessons up with Sabbath lessons, so they run one into the 'nother and you caint tell which one is which one. I know that ain't the way it's supposed to be 'cause if it was, they wouldn't have regular classes at the schoolhouse and Sabbath classes at the church.

I ain't trying to be disrespectful of teaching or teachers, but I've had enough classes with Mr. Travis to know that getting taught in a classroom just don't work. That ain't to say that he caint force you to study something till it sticks in your mind for a while, 'cause he can. But I don't care if you study on something all your life, it ain't gonna stick like if it happen to you personal.

Ain't nothing made this point better than the lesson Mr. Travis has been pounding on us lately, both in regular classes and Sabbath school. It started out 'cause Cooter Bixby went and sassed Mr. Travis when he didn't know he'd done it and when he didn't mean to do it.

I came to school on Monday and Cooter's waiting on me afore the bell runged. He's sitting on the front steps of the school so antsy and twitch-ity that he looked like he's sitting on a hot stove. Something had him awful riled up and happy.

I said, "Morning, Cooter."

"Morning, Eli!"

He jumped off the steps and pulled me over to the side of the schoolhouse so's no one else could hear us.

Cooter said, "Guess what! I seen Mr. Travis at the sawmill on Saturday!"

"So?"

"And he was acting more peculiar than he normal do!"

"So?"

79

"And we gets to talking and I seen he's mighty upset 'bout something."

"So?"

"So the more he talk to me, the more and more upsetter he's getting for no cause atall. So when he finally leave, I'm standing there scratching my head wondering what's plaguing him."

"What you figure it was?"

"I couldn't make heads nor tails of it till a minute ago when I seen him going at the blackboard like a demon had ahold of him! Then I finally knowed what it was!"

"Cooter, quit playing. What was it?"

"He was acting so peculiar 'cause of what he was planning on doing here at school today!"

"What's that?"

"Elijah, you ain't gonna believe what Mr. Travis is fixing to teach us 'bout this morning!"

I waren't gonna get myself worked up 'bout *none* of Mr. Travis's lessons. I ain't trying to say I'm smarter than Cooter, but I notice things a little better and carefuller than him, and Mr. Travis ain't showed no signs atall that he could come up with any lesson that was worth getting this excited over.

But if there was someone who waren't enthusiastic 'bout his studies more than me it was Cooter Bixby, so for him to be this riled up maybe it was gonna be something after all!

I said, "What's he gonna teach us?"

Cooter looked over both our shoulders then whispered, "Take a peek in that window and look what he's writ on the blackboard. You ain't gonna believe it!"

I stood on my tiptoes and looked into our classroom. Mr. Travis didn't usually write nothing on the board till we'd been studying for a while and children had started getting drowsy and droopy, but today he'd writ 'cross the blackboard in letters big enough that you could've read 'em from Lake Erie in the fog: FAMILIARITY BREEDS CONTEMPT!

You could tell Mr. Travis was feeling real strong 'bout this lesson, the words were underlined three times and you could even see that he'd been mashing on the chalk so hard that it had busted clean in two in a couple of places and he had to commence his underlining all over again! It waren't nothing to imagine Mr. Travis standing at the blackboard after he'd finished doing this writing, huffing and puffing with his eyes spitting fire!

Doggone-it-all, maybe Cooter was right!

I waren't too confident that he was gonna know but I asked him anyway, "So what do those words mean?"

Cooter said, "You don't know? I was kind of hoping you could tell *me*. But I done some thinking the way Mr. Travis's been telling us to. I matched up the two of them words I don't know with two words that I do know."

"What you come up with?"

"Like I said, I ain't got too much a notion what the first word and last word mean, I figure they ain't nothing but some fancy mumbo jumbo. But we *both* know what that word in the middle means, right?"

I must've been looking puzzled.

Cooter said, "Eli! You work in the stable, you *gotta* know what . . ." He checked over our shoulders again, leaned in real close, and whispered in my ear, "You just gotta know what *BREEDING* is, right?"

You didn't need to work in no stable to know what breeding is!

I said, "Yeah!"

Cooter said, "And look at that first word, *famili-arity*. That look a powerful lot like it got something to do with *family*, don't it?"

"It does."

Cooter said, "And the last word, *con-tempt*, it looks just 'bout the same as *contest*, right?

"I guess so."

"So what's that all sum up to?"

I shooked my head.

Cooter whispered, "Come on, Eli, put it all together and it come up to *family breeding contest*! He's gonna learn us 'bout having a blanged family breeding contest!"

"No!"

"What else could it mean?"

Cooter saw I waren't real convinced, he said, "My pa said that Mr. Travis is from New York City and growned up free. And that's two reasons what folks should be suspicious 'bout him for. Pa says him and n'em other growned folks was gonna have to keep a sharp eye on what Mr. Travis tried to learn us."

I said, "So?"

"Don't you see, Eli? Ain't no growned folks been checking up on Mr. Travis lately so he thinks the coast is clear and it's safe for him to give us some of that stuff what Pa calls 'up-north, big-city learning mess'!"

It sounded peculiar at first, but if you started thinking like you didn't have no common sense atall it seemed like Cooter'd put it all together real good!

Cooter saw I was starting to believe and said, "And if family breeding contests don't count as some up-north, big-city learning mess, I don't know what do."

I couldn't help myself from saying, "I'll be blanged!"

I know that's swearing, but compared to what our lesson was gonna be 'bout, swearing didn't seem like much of a sin no more.

Cooter said, "I just wish he hadn't gone and writ the lesson out on the board like that. What if that doggone Emma Collins or one n'em other persnickety girls run off and tell someone what we're 'bout to study? What if they stops this afore he gets to the real interesting, real nasty parts?"

By the time the school bell runged, Cooter had me so worked up that I was looking like *I* was sitting on a hot stove too!

We both knowed something big was 'bout to happen 'cause 'stead of saying his regular "Good morning, scholars, strivers, and questers for a better future! Are you ready to learn, are you ready to grow?" the way he does every other morning, Mr. Travis was sitting at his desk holding on to his pointing stick. His eyes were closed and he was so hopping mad that it was a miracle that smoke waren't pouring from his ears!

I knowed why too! He must've figured out that once he taught us 'bout family breeding contests, the growned folks were gonna hunt him down and give him a good tar-and-feathering!

I'd heard lots of talk 'bout such things, but hadn't never witnessed it myself. But I knowed if I ever ran into Mr. Travis again after this I was gonna have to apologize for spreading talk that he was a boring teacher. I was gonna have to eat my blanged words 'cause couldn't nothing in the world make you want to come to school more than learning 'bout a family breeding contest then watching the teacher that taught it to you get covered in hot tar and run out of the Settlement on a rail!

We all settled down at our desks and waited. Even the children who didn't know what today's lesson was 'bout sensed something waren't right and started looking at one the 'nother all nervous and worrisome.

Mr. Travis stood up and me and Cooter were 'bout to bust with excitedness!

Mr. Travis brung that pointing stick down on top of his desk so hard it was a miracle the desk didn't split clean in two!

All the other children were taking this in a very terrorific way. They were clenching on to the sides of their desks and looking as afeared as a horse that's seen a three-head snake. 'Cepting for Mr. Travis's heavy breathing, and the pointer sound echoing off the walls, the classroom was quiet as a dead squirrel!

Only me and Cooter were smiling 'cause we both knowed this was just the start of the best day of schooling we were ever gonna have!

I looked over at Cooter and he was looking just as happy as me.

Mr. Travis opened his eyes and saw Cooter smiling away, and if I live to be fifty years old, I hope I don't never witness another growned man go berserk like Mr. Travis did! It was a sight and a scar that'll be with me the rest of my life, right 'long with that trouble twixt me and Mr. Frederick Douglass.

The adventure got going so quick-like that I ain't sure of everything that happened, but all the sudden Mr. Travis was howling like a wolf and jumping clean 'cross the classroom and pouncing on Cooter Bixby like a owl on a rat! He moved so fast that Cooter didn't even have a chance to get the smile off his face afore Mr. Travis jerked him out of his chair by the ear and marched him to the front of the room!

I was shocked and couldn't've moved if I wanted to. Some of the other children waren't in as much shock as me and soon's Mr. Travis clamped down on Cooter's ear, they made a dash toward the doors. You caint blame 'em neither, ain't nothing in the world that can get you more frighted up than watching your Sabbath school teacher get took over by Satan and commence twisting the juices outta children's ears. Which is probably the first step the Devil takes when he's 'bout to wrestle your soul away from you!

Afore anyone could reach a door, Mr. Travis called out, "Return to your seats this instant!"

Everyone stopped where they were at and commenced heading back to their desks, all 'cept for Johnny Wells, who screamed like a haint had got ahold of him and jumped right out the window! The last I saw him, Johnny was tearing down the road toward the square, raising up little clouds of dust as he ripped along.

Once everyone got sitting again Mr. Travis kept ahold

of Cooter's ear and shouted louder than you'd've figured a proper man like him should, "Our people are still enslaved and treated like animals!"

Cooter couldn't tell that Mr. Travis had lost his mind! He was still smiling and nodding. And I knowed why too. Cooter ain't the sharpest tooth on the saw and he must've figured that if we were gonna get a family breeding contest lesson, then getting your ear pulled on a little bit waren't too much a price to pay!

Like I said, I ain't trying to say I'm smarter than Cooter, but I do study on things a little better and carefuller than he does, and I could see there waren't gonna be no kind of lessons on nothing till Mr. Travis was done dusting off Cooter Bixby and dusting him off good!

It ain't no real sign that I'm a fra-gile boy, but now I was sitting like all the other children. My hands were gripping on tight to the side of my desk, my breathing was coming raggedy, and my eyes were locked on Mr. Travis wondering how long 'twas gonna be afore he got back in his right mind. And if his mind didn't come back to him, I was wondering whose soul he was gonna grab next!

Mr. Travis said, "They are treated like animals! And though a very few fortunate ones of us know the sweetness of freedom, unfortunately, another very, very . . ."

Each time Mr. Travis said "very" he gave Cooter's ear a good little twist!

"... very ..."

Cooter's ear was getting wound up so tight that he started dancing on one leg trying to get some of the pressure off it. But he was still smiling!

"... very ..."

I couldn't stand it no more. Why, if Mr. Travis kept on twisting Cooter's ear like that, when he did turn it a-loose it'd be spinning and unwinding itself on the side of Cooter's head for a whole week!

I didn't care if it drawed attention to me or not, Cooter's my best friend and I knowed he'd do the same for me. I took in a deep breath to buck up my courage and finally raised my hand and yelled out, "Mr. Travis, sir, please forgive me for talking out in class, but I just gotta let Cooter know if he don't quit smiling, sir, he's gonna end up getting that ear ripped right off from the side of his head!"

Cooter heard me through his other ear and catched on to what a bad spot he was in. Finally he stopped smiling and started in howling. But Mr. Travis gave him a couple of more *verys* anyway.

"... very, very few of us don't have an appreciation of whence we have come."

Cooter yelled, "I 'preciate it! I 'preciate it!"

Mr. Travis said, "Oh, you do?"

Cooter screamed, "Oh, sir, you caint know how much I do!"

Mr. Travis said, "And where, may I ask, was your appreciation of that fact this Saturday past at the sawmill?"

You could tell Cooter didn't have no kind of answer, but something 'bout getting your ear twisted must make your mind work real clear. Cooter said, "I'm sorry! I don't know what I done, but I'm powerful sorry, sir!"

Mr. Travis eased back a notch on Cooter's ear and tells him, "Read what's on the blackboard, Mr. Bixby."

Cooter didn't even look, he called out, "It say, 'family breeding contest,' sir."

He couldn't help but notice the surprised look on Mr. Travis's face so he decided he'd best add some more. He said, "And I don't care what happens, sir, I ain't gonna breathe a word to no one if you teaches us 'bout that. But look at them there girls, you know Emma Collins is gonna snitch!"

Mr. Travis commenced twisting on Cooter's ear some more. He told Emma, "Miss Collins, read what I've written on that blackboard!"

Emma jumped up like she sat on a tack and said, "Sir, it says, 'Familiarity breeds contempt,' sir." Then Emma started in with her bawling.

Me and Cooter both were surprised at this. Not 'bout Emma bawling, that girl'll cry if you ask her what's two and two. We were surprised that Emma Collins, being as smart and fra-gile as she is, would be brave enough to call them words out right in front of everyone!

"Miss Collins, you may be seated. Mr. Bixby, do you understand what that means?"

Cooter thought on it for a second then said, "Well, sir, I thought I did. But now I'm thinking that maybe Elijah give me some bad information!"

I couldn't believe it! Here I'd helped save Cooter's ear, and the first chance he got to throw me to the wolfs he did it!

Mr. Travis said, "It's quite obvious you have no idea. It means once a person, let's say a person like you . . ." Mr. Travis went back at the ear twisting. "Once a person feels too comfortable around someone who is his elder, or his superior, or his teacher . . ."

Cooter went back to howling.

". . . that person has a tendency to not treat his better with the respect that's due!"

Cooter got it now. "What did I do, sir? I didn't do nothing!"

Mr. Travis said, "That's exactly it, Mr. Bixby! You did nothing! When you met me at the sawmill, you did not remove your hat when you walked up to me and spoke, you did not wait until I was finished talking to Mr. Polite, you did not address me in the proper manner. . . ."

Cooter said, "But, sir, I was surprised and happy to see you! I didn't say nothing but 'Hey, Mr. Travis!'"

Mr. Travis's mind left him again and he started winding Cooter's ear back up.

"That's it! Hey? Hey? *Hey!*"

Now *hey* was the word Mr. Travis used every time he gave Cooter's ear a crank.

"*Hey?* Last time I checked, Mr. Bixby, hay was for horses, not for one's instructor! I've grown angrier and angrier. You are so fortunate to be freed from the yoke of slavery, you have this wonderful opportunity to improve who you are, and instead you choose to behave toward me in a manner one would expect of a poor ignorant soul who has lived his entire life in bondage!"

It was 'bout this time that the door flewed open and Mr. Chase came busting in toting a broadaxe and dragging a screaming, kicking Johnny Wells behind him.

Johnny was yelling, "Please, sir, don't make me go back in there! He already killed Cooter Bixby!"

Mr. Chase looked 'round the classroom, saw Mr. Travis, brung his axe down, then said to Johnny Wells, "If you ever drag me out the fields over some nonsense like this again, boy, I'm gunn hide you, then give you to your pa so he can do the same! Do you see any haints in here? Do you see anyone what's dead in here?"

Mr. Chase pulled off his cap and looked back at Mr. Travis twisting and Cooter dancing and said, "I give you my regrets for coming in here like this, sir. You can carry on with your lesson."

Things got pretty bad after that. We didn't learn nothing 'bout no family breeding contests, and Mr. Travis commenced handing out lines as punishment and licks as reminders. I got three swats and had to write *Familiarity Breeds Contempt* twenty-five times for speaking out in class and for providing Cooter with bad information on what it meant. Johnny Wells got five swats and had to write it fifty times for running off and snitching on the teacher. Cooter got ten licks and had to write it one hundred and twenty-five times for being what Mr. Travis called "riddled with disrespect for his superiors."

Unfairest of all, since Cooter was my best friend I knowed I was gonna have to help him out, so I'd probably end up writing fifty of his doggone lines myself.

I knowed the reason why Mr. Travis went and made us write all them lines and passed out all them swats, it was 'cause he was trying to make the "familiarity breeds contempt" lesson stick. But classroom learning just don't work the same as when something happens to you personal.

That ain't to say that the lesson ain't gonna be with me for the rest of my life. But it don't have a thing to do with Mr. Travis, 'cause it waren't but a few days later that the lesson got taught to me in a way that caint help but last forever.

→ Chapter 7 ←

Mr. Leroy Shows How to *Really* Make a Lesson Stick

The on-again-and-off-again clouds got to be always on and they ended up blacking out the moon two nights later. Since it's dangerous to work with a axe when there ain't no light atall, Mr. Leroy figured he had to lay off his work early. It ain't our usual custom. Most nights he kept on working till long after I was home and sleeping, but this night we started walking together out of Mrs. Holton's field.

I don't work nowhere near as hard as Mr. Leroy, but that don't matter, I was good and tuckered out. Betwixt schooling and studying and choring 'round the Settlement and working till past dark with him for most of the last couple weeks, I'll own up that I was lagging that night and my mind might not've been quite right. That ain't to make no excuses 'bout what happened, it's just telling the truth.

Most times me and Mr. Leroy don't say much whilst we work, not only 'cause it's hard to talk to someone that's knocking away at trees and swinging a heavy axe, but also 'cause Mr. Leroy don't seem partial to running his mouth nohow. To my way of thinking, that meant us walking home together was a good time to get a whole lot of the conversating done that we'd been missing out on.

Most every other night I gotta walk home by myself, and I ain't complaining, but sometimes it does seem like the walking would be a lot easier if I had someone to do it with.

It ain't no sign of being a fra-gile boy, but if you have to walk home on a night where the moon's got blacked out, you just might get surprised and find yourself jumping at noises coming from the side of the road or from out the woods and then running all the way home screaming.

Anybody that has some sense would be a little afeared that one of those bears or snakes or wolfs might've wandered out of their regular area and come over here, so maybe twixt the being real tired from all my work, and the being real happy 'bout having some company, my mind didn't have no chance at being right that night when the moon was covered and Mr. Leroy and me walked home together.

Since he waren't much of a talker, I figured he had plenty of practice on being a listener, and I was jawing at him pretty regular and fast. Even though it happened two whole days ago, I was still mighty worked up 'bout Mr. Travis near snatching Cooter's ear off and not teaching us 'bout family breeding contests. So after I talked for a while 'bout fishing and animals in the woods and Ma's scratchy sweaters and how many first-place ribbons Champion and Jingle Boy got at the fair, I started in on what happened when I got all those lines forced at me.

Whilst we were walking for the first mile or so, Mr. Leroy would grunt and nod his head every once in the while, like he was paying some mind to what I was saying. But by the time I started in on talking 'bout Mr. Travis, we'd covered us two miles easy and Mr. Leroy waren't showing no kind of interest in nothing I was having to say. He just tromped on ahead looking like he was wishing I'd be quiet. But like I already owned up to, lots of things were coming together to make me want to talk and not pay too much mind to who it was I was talking to.

I said, "And Mr. Travis went berserk and afore you can blink he jumps clean 'cross the room and I caint say how he did it but he must've been flying 'cause to get at Cooter Bixby he had to go over three rows of children and didn't one n'em desks get knocked aside nor toppled over nor didn't one n'em children have no footprints on 'em nor bruises from where he must've stepped . . ."

I could tell Mr. Leroy didn't particular want to hear all this. He didn't tell me to be still, but he did pick up the pace of his walking like he was rushing to get home. I warent 'bout to miss the chance to get this off my chest so

I started halfway running and halfway walking to keep up with him.

I told him, "So Mr. Travis has got Cooter's ear wound up so tight that it's starting to look like somebody's finger 'stead of somebody's ear and it's 'bout the most awful thing you ever seen in all your days. . . ."

Then I said 'em, I said those words that made it so the lesson 'bout familiarity and contempt'll be fixed in my mind for's long as I live, even if that's to fifty. I said, "And me and all 'em other little nigg —"

I knowed better. Ma and Pa didn't tolerate no one saying that word 'round 'em. They say it's a sign of hatred when a white person says it and a sign of bad upbringing and ignorance when one our own calls it out, so there ain't no good excuses.

I knowed better.

I didn't think Mr. Leroy was paying me no mind. I didn't even get the chance to get the whole word out. I never even saw it coming.

It felt like whatever rope it was that was holding up the moon gave out all the sudden and the moon slipped free and busted through the clouds and came crashing down to earth afore it exploded square on top of me!

All I saw at first was a bright light. Which I figured was Mr. Leroy backhanding me 'cross my mouth. Then I felt my senses flying away. Which must've been me falling toward the ground. Then I felt like I'd been chunked by the moon. Which would've been me knocking my head 'gainst the ground.

I don't think I was out for more'n a second, but when I came to, I wished I'd been out for a whole lot longer 'cause Mr. Leroy was standing over top of me with his hand drawed back, fixing to crack me all over again.

He made up for all the not talking he'd been doing whilst we walked. Now he commenced jawing at me just as hard as I'd been jawing at him.

He shouted, "Is you out your mind?"

I was 'bout to say, "No, sir," but I figured this was one n'em questions people ask just for the sake of asking it, they don't really want no answer. I probably couldn't've said nothing no way, my tongue was too busy roaming 'round my mouth, checking to see if any of my teeth had got set a-loose by Mr. Leroy's slap.

He said, "What you think they call me whilst they was doing this?"

He opened the front of his shirt and showed me where a big square with a letter T in the middle of it was branded into him. The scar was raised up and shiny and was real plain to see even if there waren't no moonlight atall.

"What you think they call me?"

Mr. Leroy was screaming like it was *him* that lost his mind.

"What you think they call my girl when they sold her? What kind of baby they call her from up on the block?"

Mr. Leroy was spitting and looking mad as a hatter. I sure was glad he'd gone and dropped his axe when he'd first busted me 'cross the mouth.

I said, "Mr. Leroy, sir, I'm sorry . . ."

"What name you think they call my wife when they take her to another man for his own? What?"

"I'm sorry, sir, I'm sorry . . ."

"How you gunn call them children in that school and you'self that name them white folks down home calls us? Has you lost your natural mind? You wants to be like one n'em? You wants to be keeping they hate alive?"

I saw that Mr. Leroy really *was* out of his mind! He must've thought I was a white person that said that word.

I begged him, "Mr. Leroy, sir, please! I ain't white! Please don't hit me no more!"

He raised his left hand and I closed my eyes and tried to mash myself down into the dirt.

He said, "White person? You thinking this here's 'bout some white person? Look at this. Look!"

I opened my eyes and saw he waren't gonna slap me again. He was showing me where his littlest finger on his left hand use to be. He was pointing at all that was left there, a little stump.

He said, "Who you think it was cut my finger off? Who?"

I didn't know if I should answer him or just keep quiet and let him have his say. I shrugged my shoulders.

He said, "A slave, that's who. And the whole time he slashing and stabbing at me trying to cut my throat, what name he calling me? What name?"

I said, "I know, sir, but I ain't gonna say it no more."

He said, "You thinks just 'cause that word come out from twixt your black lips it mean anything different? You think it ain't choke up with the same kind of hate and disrespect it has when *they* say it? You caint see it be even worst when *you* call it out?"

I told him, "Sir, I only said it 'cause I hear lots of children say it."

"What difference it make who you hear say it? I can understand a little if one of y'all freeborn use it, y'all's ignorant in a whole slew of ways. Y'all ain't been told your whole life that's what you is. But someone what was a slave, or someone whose ma and pa was a slave and raised them good like your'n done, that just shows you believing that what we be. That just shows you done swallowed they poison. And swallowed it whole."

There waren't gonna be no more hitting, I could tell Mr. Leroy was calming down. He commenced rubbing on his left arm then reached his hand down to help me up.

Once I got up I quick wiped away the tears that were trying to get in my eyes. It ain't being fra-gile, but don't nothing in the world make you want to bawl more than getting a good backhand slap when you ain't expecting it.

Mr. Leroy said, "Now belting you like that probably waren't the right thing to do, 'Lijah, but I ain't sorry I done it. If my boy, 'Zekial, was to call someone out they name like that, I prays to God someone would bust him up too. Y'all young folks gotta understand that's a name what ain't never called with nothing but hate. That ain't nothing but a word them slavers done chained us with and if God's just, like I know he is, one day it gunn be buried right 'long with the last one of 'em. That ain't one the things we need to be carrying to Canada with us.

"Now if you and me's gunn do any more working together, you know what you gotta say."

I did. I told him, "I'm sorry, Mr. Leroy, I ain't never gonna use that word again."

He said, "You got to always keep in mind, Elijah, that I'm growned and you ain't. You got to always 'member that we gets 'long just fine but I ain't your friend. I cares 'bout you like you's my own boy, but you always got to give me my respect. You saying that word ain't showing no

100

respect for me, it ain't showing no respect for your folks, it ain't showing no respect for you'self, and it ain't showing no respect for no one what's had that word spit on 'em whilst they's getting beat on like a animal."

Mr. Leroy used his hat to brush the back of my shirt and pants off and reached his hand out for me to shake it, then said, "Elijah, it's my hope that there ain't no hard feelings twixt you and me. I likes the way you owned up to what you done."

I shooked his hand and said, "No, sir, ain't no hard feelings atall."

Some of the time when a growned person asks you a question, you're smart to tell 'em what it is they want to hear, but that waren't what I was doing.

I said there waren't no hard feelings 'cause I meant it.

Pa's always telling me that people that use to be slaves are toting things 'round with 'em that caint be seen with your regular eyes. He says once someone was a slave there's always gonna be a something in 'em that knows parts 'bout life that freeborn folks caint never know, mostly horrorific parts.

He tells me that's why I got to be sharp on my guard when I'm talking with anyone that got free. They've seen people acting in ways that caint help but leave scars and peculiarities. Things that I might not think mean nothing, but things that can cut 'em to the quick. So I waren't doing nothing but telling Mr. Leroy the truth when I told him I waren't holding no grudges and that I waren't gonna use that word again.

He said, "Good, son. 'Cause I really want you to know what I'm trying to say and sometimes I ain't too good with my words."

I said, "I know what you're trying to say, Mr. Leroy. It boils down to familiarity breeds contempt."

Mr. Leroy picked up his axe and swung it 'cross his left shoulder then put his right hand on my head. I'll always remember Mr. Leroy's hand on my head and the words he told me. I'll always remember that night when there waren't no moon and me and Mr. Leroy walked home together.

CHAPTER 8

The Most Exciting Night
of My Life So Far

The next day after school, I was in the stable shoveling manure when Old Flapjack gave a snort. I looked up and the Preacher was standing in the doorway.

"Evening, Elijah."

"Evening, sir."

"Do you remember when I asked if you'd be willing to do something to help the Settlement?"

"Yes, sir."

"Have you changed your mind?"

"'Bout what, sir?"

"Helping the Settlement."

"Why, no, sir, but what was it that . . ."

The Preacher unfolded a piece of paper and handed it to me.

COMING TO CHATHAM,
THREE NIGHTS ONLY
Sir Charles M. Vaughn and his world-renowned CARNIVAL OF ODDITIES

will be traversing through Canada West on their way from Chicago, Illinois, to Buffalo, New York, and points east. Sir Charles has graciously agreed to allow the citizens of Chatham, Buxton, and nearby environs to witness for themselves what they have only read about in the nation's finest newspapers. Hear the Calliope!!! Taste the Sugared Treats!!! See the Most Unusual Freaks of Nature You Can Imagine!!! Witness the World's Greatest Hypnotist!!! Rare Patent Medicines Available. Games of Chance!!! Members of All Races Welcome. Wednesday, Thursday, and Friday Only!!!!

Cooter'd already told me about this carnival, but he'd made the mistake of asking his ma if he could go. She'd asked him if he was daft then said she was gonna make sure he didn't sneak out by having him sleep at the foot of her bed on Wednesday, Thursday, and Friday.

I told the Preacher, "All the growned folks said we gotta stay away from this. They said there's gambling and all sorts of horrible things going on there."

He said, "So what do *you* think about it? I've thought of a way we can use your God-given gift to help get some money for the Settlement, but if you're having second thoughts . . ."

"But Ma and Pa wouldn't never let me go to something like this."

"Elijah, there are lots of things that you do that I'm sure your mother and father would be shocked about. I'm positive they have no idea how much time you and Cooter spend wandering about in the forest late at night, do they? This wouldn't be much different than that. It would simply be a matter of meeting me later tomorrow night and then the two of us going to the carnival. I'd be there to make certain nothing bad happened to you. But, if you've changed your mind about helping the Settlement, I understand. It's easy to talk about being helpful, but actually doing what one has promised can be a lot more difficult."

I saw what the Preacher was doing, I saw how he was using growned folks talk to paint me in a corner. But the way I look at things, there's accidentally getting painted in a corner and there's not minding getting painted in a corner. And, truth told, I didn't mind getting painted into this one. What could be more exciting than going to a carnival to see freaks of nature and watch someone get hypnotized? Plus, the Preacher had figured out a way for me to help the Settlement too, what could be better?

"But I ain't got no money to get in, sir."

"Elijah, your money is no good when I'm around. Besides, if you insist on paying me back you can always double up on your tithing when you go fishing."

It waren't for myself exactly, it was for the good of the Settlement, so I said, "When should I meet you, sir?"

"That's my boy! We'll meet tomorrow night. Bring a sack full of your stones."

As interesting as this was starting to sound, there waren't no way I was gonna miss going to this carnival!

On Friday night, me and the Preacher first came to a clearing that was a bit off from the main set of noise and excitement. In the middle of the clearing was a tent that had a big fresh-painted sign out front that said:

**See Madame Sabbar,
the Royal Huntress from Sweden!
She Has Slain 541 Swedish Moth Lions
with No Weapon Other Than
Her Slingshot!!!!**

A white man with a walking stick and a straw hat stood on a box shouting to people to pay a dime to come see this hunting woman. He yelled, "Marvel at the deadly accuracy of Madame Sabbar's slingshot! Come one, come all! You will be amazed at the things she can do with a simple stone. You will want to come back again and again. Your friends and neighbours won't believe you when you tell them about the power that Madame Sabbar's simple weapon possesses! Witness for yourself the astounding little lady who has killed five hundred and forty-one of the fiercest beasts in all of Europe, the dreaded Swedish moth lion!"

One of the white farmers called out, "That's a load of hogwash! There ain't no lions in Sweden!"

The white man pointed his walking stick at the farmer and said, "You're absolutely right, sir! Which is further proof of Madame Sabbar's skill; it shows she's wiped out the entire lot of them! Now, you'll have to hurry. Our next-to-last show begins in two minutes. Who's going to pay the ridiculously small sum of one thin dime to see this amazing woman?"

I couldn't believe it! The Preacher pulled me into the line and we waited to go in and see this woman! I started shaking right off. I hadn't never seen no one who'd killed a lion afore! I hadn't never seen no one that's ever *seen* a lion afore!

When we got to the front of the line the Preacher put down two American dimes and we went into the tent. We sat on a row of benches right up near the front of the stage. On one end of the stage there were five bull's-eye targets.

Next to the targets was a big board that had a thick, dark green forest painted on it.

You could tell it waren't no forest from 'round here 'cause these woods had monkeys hanging in the trees. There were also six holes the size of supper plates cut into the board so's it 'peared to be a big knothole in each one of the trees. Under each one of the holes was a fancy writ number going from one to six. 'Cross the top of the board, spaced the same distance one from the 'nother, were ten lit candles and under the candles it looked like someone had throwed a sheet over the very top of the board. The sheet said, THE JUNGLES OF SWEDEN!!!

We didn't wait but a minute afore the white man with the walking stick and straw hat came out on stage and told some jokes that didn't no one think were funny. After he saw he waren't gonna encourage nothing but hisses from the crowd, he introduced us to the slingshot lady, and fierce-looking as she was, it was easy to tell she really had killed five hundred lions!

The man said, "Please, ladies and gentlemen, boys and girls, help me welcome Madame Sabbar, and perhaps she will show us her dexterity with these deadly slingshots."

The man pointed at a table that had on top of it three fancy slingshots. Next to the slingshots were little piles of things I figured the woman was gonna shoot. There were some grapes and some peculiar-looking stones with holes in 'em and some real pretty marbles and some rocks that looked a little too light to be proper chunking stones.

A tiny amount of clapping came out the crowd and Madame Sabbar picked up one of the slingshots and one of the marbles. She aimed at the first bull's-eye target and shot off a marble. It hit dead centre and busted through some paper and runged a bell. She did the same thing with the next four targets, ringing a bell every time.

Folks didn't think this was such a big ruckus, 'specially not one worth paying no whole American dime for! Only one or two people clapped, but there was a lot more grumbling and hissing going on too.

The man said, "Astonishing! Astounding! But it doesn't end there, ladies and gentlemen. Once she has prepared herself, she moves on to a more challenging task. It is a well-known fact that the Swedish moth lion is drawn to candlelight, so once the roar of one of these fierce Scandinavian cats is heard, Madame Sabbar's first duty is to extinguish all of the candles as quickly as she possibly can!"

The man put his hand on his ear and said, "Hark! What was that?"

All the sudden it looked like we were gonna get our dime's worth after all!

Somewhere from behind the stage came a roar that sounded like Mr. Brown clearing flum outta his throat, but a lot louder, and Madame Sabbar sprunged to work! She picked up a different slingshot and all sorts of who-struck-John busted loose!

First thing she did was aim at the ten candles sitting atop of the board with the six holes. She was using the odd-looking stones with holes in 'em and when they flewed 'cross the tent they made a sound like one n'em fat lazy Buxton bumblebees. Once the buzzing stones got to the candles, they put the flame out quiet as a whisper. Waren't a *one* n'em candles disturbed neither! The only thing that moved on each one was the wick. Why, with the tent getting fulled up with the buzzing of ten stones and the flames getting snuffed out one after the 'nother, 'twas a sight I'd've paid one of my *own* dimes to see!

But what she did next topped even that. She turned the slingshot out at all of us in the crowd and commenced firing over our heads, putting out all the candles that runged 'round the tent!

Seems like thinking you're 'bout to get busted in the head with a buzzing stone and not having it happen makes you want to give a good old whoop. Folks that'd ducked down or throwed their arms atop their heads came right back up cheering and clapping!

Madame Sabbar gave one n'em lady curtsies.

The man said, "Did I mislead you? Did I not tell you you'd be amazed? But, oh, ye of little faith, the story is not even half told!"

The man pointed his walking stick at the board with the jungle and the six knotholes.

"For not only must Madame Sabbar be on the lookout for the dreaded Swedish moth lion, she must also keep a sharp watch for the lion's allies, the savage members of the Swedish Mobongo tribe, and especially the young chief of the tribe, MaWee!"

From behind the holey board came a set of screams and yelps and jibber-jabber, then a little white boy hanging on to a spear and sporting a big old soup bone on top of his head marched onto the stage. The only clothes he was wearing was the bottom half of a woman's dress that looked like it waren't nothing but a bunch of long leafs sewed together. On his cheeks were painted black stripes. He was hopping from one foot to the 'nother whilst someone banged on a drum. If he'd have done it any faster and with any kind of rhythm, it would have come pretty close to being dancing.

"Beware, Madame Sabbar," the man shouted. "Young MaWee is very angry because he knows of your reputation."

The boy shooked his spear at the slingshot lady, but 'stead of being angry, the look on his face made it seem he was afeared.

"But, what is this? Oh, no! MaWee has used some of his conjuring powers on Madame Sabbar and has rendered her blind!"

The little boy reached in a bag on his waist and throwed

something all sparkling and flashing at the woman. The white man with the walking stick tied a blindfold 'round Madame Sabbar's face then pulled a cloth sack over that so's we could tell she waren't seeing a thing.

"And now that he has blinded her, MaWee will hide behind one of the trees in the Swedish jungle and most foully lie in wait for an ambush!"

The man turned the slingshot lady so's she was facing the board with the holes in it di-rect. MaWee walked behind it. But afore he went I got a good look at him. This waren't no Swedish jungle chief atall! This was Jimmy Blassingame, one of the white children from Chatham that studied at our school!

The man said, "Madame Sabbar, what can you see?"

The woman raised the sack so her mouth waren't covered and said, "Alas, I see nothing. The heathen's magic has left me completely sightless."

The man said, "Oh, woe! And look at the cowardly savage! He's preparing to attack! What shall we do? How shall we save this innocent white woman? I can give her a weapon, but in her state how shall she use it?"

The man reached onto the table next to Madame Sabbar and put a different slingshot in her left hand. In her right hand, he put a bunch of the purple grapes. She plucked one of 'em and set it in the sling.

All the sudden Jimmy Blassingame's face popped out of the hole that had the fancy THREE writ underneath it, the last hole on the right in the top row.

The man screamed, "Madame Sabbar! The coward is attacking! Fire your weapon!"

Madame Sabbar lifted the slingshot and let one n'em fat purple grapes fly. It splashed on the side of the tent five feet above Jimmy's head.

"Oh, no! She *is* blinded! And look! The savage is moving to another spot from which to waylay this innocent white maiden!"

Jimmy's head came outta hole number five, which was on the bottom row in the middle of the board.

"I've got it!" the walking stick man yelled. "You good citizens of Chatham can help by calling out the number of the hole in which that black . . . uh . . . that black-*hearted* barbarian is hiding!"

Jimmy's face showed up in the last hole on the right in the bottom row and 'bout half the crowd shouted, "Six!"

Why, that hunting lady couldn't see a thing but she shot one n'em grapes so fast and true that it caught Jimmy square in the middle of his forehead! He'd ducked his head so that was all that was poking out of the hole.

Everybody laughed so hard that the tent shooked!

Jimmy went to hole number five, hole number four,

hole number one, and hole number three, and every time his forehead popped out, the crowd snitched on him and Madame Sabbar gave him the same treatment.

After 'while, all the grapes that got smashed on Jimmy's forehead started leaking down into his eyes so he bended over to wipe at 'em. But when he did this he was right in front of the fifth hole and the crowd shouted, "Five!"

Madame Sabbar raised the slingshot and fired the next grape so straight that it catched Jimmy, who hadn't had no chance atall to bend his face down, right twixt his eyes.

And waren't a person more shocked by this than Jimmy Blassingame! His mouth came wide open, he stood up, his face was now in front of the second hole and, doggone-it-all, some of the rotten folks in the crowd hollered out, "Two!"

Madame Sabbar quick shot another grape and it disappeared down Jimmy's throat, making a sound like a soap bubble getting busted!

Jimmy's hands came up to his neck and he staggered out from behind the board with the jungle and the holes and started flopping 'round on stage like a fish tossed out of water.

The man with the walking stick commenced cursing and saying words I ain't never heard afore. He picked Jimmy up and gave him a squeeze 'round the middle. The grape popped outta Jimmy's mouth and rolled out into the crowd.

You'd have thought 'twaren't a funnier thing in the world had ever happened.

Even the Preacher, who most times is a pretty serious man, took to throwing his head back and howling.

Jimmy Blassingame didn't even have sense enough to get off the stage. He sat plumb up there where the man had dropped him and cried so hard that purple and black streaks ran down his cheeks and splashed onto his chest.

It sure was a good thing for Jimmy that I was the only one from school who saw this. Sitting there with purple and black streaks running down his chest and bawling whilst wearing half a woman's leaf dress was the kind of thing that no one wouldn't let him forget about for years. It would have got tied up with his name same way mine's tied up with Mr. Frederick Douglass!

The man with the straw hat and walking stick pointed at Madame Sabbar and said, "Please, give yourselves a hand for saving the purity of this poor white damsel, and let us show our appreciation for the most accurate hunter to ever roam the jungles of Sweden!"

Everybody 'cept for me, the Preacher, and Jimmy Blassingame clapped and hollered and whistled hard as they could.

The Preacher leaned down and yelled, "There's one more person I have to talk to," and pulled me out of the tent.

→ CHAPTER 9 ←

The Mesmerist and Sammy

Me and the Preacher walked through a patch of woods toward the sounds that were cutting through the night air. When we stepped into the Atlas Clearing it was like we'd fell off a cliff right into a whole 'nother world. What I saw was so shocking that at first everything on me acted like it wanted to draw up and squeeze together, the same way your body does if you're walking 'cross some ice that gives way and dumps you into frozed-up winter water. It was like it was too much coming at you all at once, like it would steal your breathing away from you. But I think that's what the carnival folks were trying to do.

Everything in the Atlas Clearing was set up to get your head started whirling and keep it going that way, and there waren't no hiding from none of it! Every part of my body was trying to grab attention away from the next part. My ears were steady picking up sounds that I hadn't never heard nowhere else. There were hoops and hollers from children and growned folks both, screams that had you thinking someone was looking death right in the throat but that quick turned to laughs that were kind of 'shamed-sounding.

There was a powerful hissing music whistling from a wagon that was throwing fog and songs out of a row of pipes, sounding so hot and hard and pointy that you'd've thought you'd took a knife and were scratching at something deep inside your ear.

But soon's it felt like the *sounds* were gonna cause your head to bust open, your eyes started taking over and noticing separate things out of what at first didn't appear to be nothing but a blur of colour and torches.

There were more of the walking stick–holding, straw hat–wearing white men singing out for you to come see what they had hid up in their tents. They kept calling out the same words over and over, sounding like the choir on Sunday but without no real feeling of happiness in the words.

There were bright red and blue and green and yellow banners strung up 'longside dull brown, high-reaching tents. On the banners were pictures of things that you had to pay a whole nickel to go in and get a look at. Why, terrible as those pictures were, I'd have paid a nickel to *not* go in and see 'em!

There was a painting of a white man that appeared to be half a human and half a alligator, joined up so's you couldn't tell if what you were seeing was the rear half of a alligator swallowing up the top half of a man, or if it was a man that had been born without no legs who had sewed the back half of a lizard onto hisself to see if maybe he could do some walking that way!

There was a picture of a white woman that looked like she had some child's arms and legs poking out of the side of her neck! And another white man that was picking up a full-growned elephant and holding it over his head like he was 'bout to toss it into the next county! Another banner showed a white man that was wide as a barn holding hands with a white woman that waren't much more than a stick with a hank of yellow hair on top. They were standing under a big red heart that said, BIZARRE LOVE!!!!

But the drawing that I knowed would keep *me* awake nights and discourage me from wandering 'round in the woods for a good long time was the one of a white man who had to be a conjurer! He didn't have no animal parts stuck on him, nor no parts of other people growing out of him that would invite staring, he had something worst. Something that I tried hard to look away from but waren't no way I could do it.

He had sharp, yellow, jaggedy-looking bolts of lightning shooting di-rect out of his eyes! The bolts were making the normal-looking white man in the picture with him float off his feet and scramble and scratch at the air like he was 'bout to drift up to the clouds! It would cost you a whole quarter of a American dollar to go in the tent and see the conjurer do this! I'd've gave *two* quarters of a dollar not to!

But sure as shooting, this was the other person the Preacher said we were gonna have to go see. He pointed at the drawing of the man with the lightning-bolt eyes and said, "He's the owner of the carnival. I want to get a look at what kind of rigmarole he's got going before I talk to him."

Another straw hat–wearing, walking stick–waving white man was out front of the tent calling, "Last show of the evening, last show of the year, last time in Canada, last chance of your lifetime to see the fantastic Vaughn-O working his powers of mental prestidigitation!"

The Preacher slapped two whole American quarters on a table and told the white woman sitting there, "Me and my boy want to see the mesmerist."

I spoke right up and said, "No, sir! You go on in and see him. I'll wait over yon by that tree."

The Preacher grabbed hold of my collar and pulled me into the tent. This one didn't have no benches in it to sit down on, so we were standing shoulder to shoulder with a bunch of folks from Chatham. Soon's we were inside and worked our way up to the front, I clamped my hand 'cross my eyes.

The Preacher put his mouth near my ear and said,

"No-siree-bob. I paid a whole twenty-five cents for you to watch this and that's just what you're going to do." He jerked my hand away from covering my face.

The first thing I did was look straight up, partly so's I wouldn't have to see the stage, but mostly 'cause if the Preacher was gonna force me to watch and get floated off by lightning coming outta some white man's eyes, I wanted to see if there was something I could latch ahold on to afore I ended up in the clouds.

If I was gonna get lifted away, this was a good place to do it 'cause I couldn't've got no higher than the roof of the tent. There were torches high up on the walls that I'd have to be careful of whilst I was floating, but I figured if I kept a keen eye and kicked at 'em, I could get by without burning nothing 'sides my brogans and maybe the cuffs of my trousers.

I looked all 'cross the top of the tent and my heart started slowing down. It was a true relief to see that there weren't no one from the earlier shows still stuck up there. Maybe that meant the conjuring wore off after while and you'd come a-crashing back down.

If I'd've knowed this was gonna happen I'd have brung me a length of rope and tied it 'round my ankle. That way if I started floating, the Preacher could have pulled me 'long home like a kite. I'd have felt a lot better 'bout waiting for the conjuring to wear off back in Buxton than here 'mongst a bunch of strangers.

Afore I could do any more worrying, a curtain on the stage got whipped aside and a tall, round white man in a long black cape was standing right in front of us. His eyes looked a whole lot more like a dead person's eyes than a live person's. They were blank and blue and they 'peared to be looking square at you, but you could tell they waren't really seeing a thing.

A bevy of laughs and moans and screams came out of everyone that was jammed up in the tent. It ain't being fragile when I say that I was 'mongst the screamers.

I grabbed hold of the Preacher's shirtsleeve and mashed my face into it. He just as quick snatched it away and said, "I told you you were going to watch this. You can learn about how a flimflam works."

I noticed my own arm was being held on to tight and looked to see who'd grabbed me. A little white stranger boy, near 'bout as old as me, was laughing and carrying on something wild.

He swore, "Blang it all! This here's the fourth time I seen him and I still near 'bout jump out my skin when he first come on stage!" He talked like he was from America.

I said, "You saw him four times! Ain't you afeared of getting floated off?"

He laughed and said, "Pshaw! He just a old humbug! He can't float naught nowhere."

The boy had a head of thick curly red hair and a nose that looked a whole lot like a bird's beak. His eyes were a scary gray and blue colour, 'bout the same as the sky afore a storm. He waren't nothing but a child but the smell of cigar smoke came outta his mouth strong!

I said, "He really caint float nothing away?"

"Naw! Watch what happens. What's your name?"

"I'm Elijah."

The boy looked like I cursed at him. "*Elijah?* You sure?"

"Course I'm sure."

"You live down in Buxton?"

"Yes."

"Well, I'm-a tell you something, Elijah. You'd best not tell no one from Chatham that that's your name."

"Why not?"

"'Cause there's a rapscallion in Chatham what's already laid claim to that name, and he ain't the kind to be sharing nothing with no one! There was a boy up here whose name was Edward, and Elijah from Chatham didn't want no one else having their name even *start* with the same first letter as his, so he made the boy change his name to Odward! And Odward's own ma and pa calls him that now 'cause they didn't want no trouble with the real Elijah. If I's you I'd find me another name 'cause Elijah from Chatham ain't gonna be real happy 'bout meeting you, particular not with you being a slave boy from Buxton."

"I waren't never a slave. I was freeborn."

"Don't matter. Just you be mindful of who you say that name to. Elijah from Chatham ain't to be trifled with. He already killed a full-growed Indian man! And didn't kill him with no knife or gun or sword, killed him with one hand! His left one! And he ain't but twelve years old!"

Those words hadn't had no chance to sink in good when the conjurer on stage came to life. He flunged his arms to the sides and showed that under his black cape he was wearing a something blue that looked a powerful lot like a dress with all sorts of shiny, sparkling, silvered stars and crescent moons. Why, it was pasted with as many moons as stars! And that don't make no sense, that don't make no sense atall.

All the folks that were screaming and laughing a minute ago set up a mess of oohs and aahs that would have you believing they were seeing the real heavens 'stead of a dress with sham stars and way too many moons stuck all over it.

The little white boy dugged his elbow into my ribs and said, "Keep a watch on his eyes!"

The most amazing thing happened! The conjurer's eyes rolled back in his head and their place was took right away by *another* set of eyes! Only difference twixt 'em was that these two eyes were brown, and whilst the other ones seemed staring and empty, these eyes were looking dead at you! And worst, waren't no doubt that *they were seeing you!*

I felt my legs commence shaking and grabbed ahold of the white boy so's I wouldn't fall.

He said, "Them first eyes is painted on his lids, I was out back smoking a see-gar with him and seent it myself. He ain't real atall!"

The conjurer was slow as anything peering hard at everyone in the crowd. When his eyes hit 'em, some folks screamed, some folks laughed, some folks cried, and some folks 'peared to be dumbstruck. I ain't sure which group I was 'mongst 'cause the fearing in me was too strong.

The white boy said, "Watch this. I'm-a have me some fun here!"

When the man's eyes struck him the boy stood bolt upright and his face frozed stiff as a stone! I quick unloosed his arm so's the conjurization wouldn't have the chance to jump off of him and onto me.

The man pointed spot-on at the boy and called out, "You!"

The boy's eyes near bucked right out of his head!

The conjurer-man's finger commenced crooking and bending in a way that got more screams and confusion to rise up from the crowd.

The boy looked at me, his face unfrozen for a second, and one of his gray eyes winked. Then quick as anything his face frozed up again, looking all stupid-fied, and he started pushing his way through people and heading to the steps on the side of the stage. You'd've thought the conjurer's finger was a magnet and the boy was made outta iron filings! When folks saw the spell he was under they stepped aside like he was toting a bucket that was overflowing with the plague!

He got up on the stage and the conjurer waved his cape over the boy's head twice. He said, "Boy! Do you know me?"

The boy said, "No, sir, you's a perfect stranger."

"Then we've never spoken?"

"No, sir, and I ain't never smoked no see-gar with you behind the tent neither."

Some folks that didn't know how frightsome this was laughed and the conjurer screamed out, "Silence! Do you not see that this boy is already under a spell and talking nonsense? Why, if I were to misdirect my attention away from him for merely one moment he'd be in danger of remaining a babbling idiot like this for the rest of his life!" The conjurer-man talked like he came from England.

Most folks got quiet like they were in church.

The conjurer waved his cape over the boy's head again and said, "Look into my eyes! Look deeply into my eyes!"

The boy couldn't help hisself, he looked and the conjurer started blinking first one eye then the other so's on
one side of his face you were seeing a live brown eye, and on
the other side you were seeing a dead blue one. Then he
opened both dead eyes at once then both live ones till by
and by your head was back to whirling and you knowed this
boy had been wrong, this conjurer was real!

I snatched back ahold of the Preacher's coat sleeve.

The conjurer said, "Look even more deeply into my
eyes!"

The boy's head started going back and forth fast like a
pendulum in a clock that the weight's fell off. Then his chin
dropped down on his chest and it 'peared he was out cold,
'cepting he didn't fall in a heap!

The man said, "You are entering a realm of velvet sleep,
golden slumbers, and dappled dreams. Once I snap my
fingers, you will lose yourself in my voice. Upon the sound
of my fingers snapping, my simplest wish will become
your irresistible command!"

He slow raised his right hand over his head, waited for
what felt like was a hour, then snapped his fingers. At the
same exact time someone banged a drum one terrible
boom, and a flash of red and yellow powder exploded and
popped and hissed all 'long the front of the stage. Screams
and smoke from the powder rised up to the top of the tent,

and, truth told, my scream was 'mongst the loudest and longest lasting!

The conjurer said, "When I count to three you will open your eyes and hear no voice other than mine! One . . . two . . . three!"

He snapped his fingers again and the boy's eyes came open and were staring di-rect at the conjurer! I knowed the poor boy was under the man's spell 'cause one of his eyeballs started looking right whilst the other one was looking left, then they commenced going in circles and rolling back in his head! My blood ran cold thinking 'bout how this boy thought this was all a flimflam, and now he'd gone and let this horrible-looking man snatch ahold of his soul! I knowed it waren't gonna be long afore this poor white boy would be scratching and clawing at the roof of the tent!

The conjurer said, "What is your name, boy?"

The boy started talking slow, having a hard time getting the words out, "My . . . ma named . . . me Samuel . . . but most . . . folks . . . calls me . . . Sammy."

"Samuel, who is the only person in the entire world whom you can trust?"

"You, master."

"That's right! And do you believe everything I say?"

"Like your mouth's a prayer book, master."

"Then why are you speaking to me in English? You are

not a little boy, you are a chicken! And unless the chickens in Canada are very much brighter than American chickens, they do not speak English!"

'Twas the most amazing thing! The little boy started clucking and pecking 'round on the stage then he commenced scratching at the floor with his bare feet and you'd have swored he was digging up worms!

Near everybody in the tent acted like this was something funny! None of 'em thought to worry what Sammy's ma was gonna say when the son she sent to the carnival as a little boy came home as a giant bird! And even worst, a giant chicken!

The conjurer waved his cape again and called out, "You are no longer a chicken, you are a boy again! But wait, the weather has changed! It's positively freezing in here!"

Why, the boy took to shivering and teeth-chattering and knee-knocking so doggone much that I felt a chill of coldness run down *my* back! And this waren't no flimflam neither, 'cause Sammy started turning blue the way they say white people do when they're dead or just 'bout ready to die!

The mesmerist yelled, "Egads! This Canadian weather! One second it's freezing and the next it's like the fires of Hades! This heat is enough to kill!"

Sammy quit shivering and commenced wiping his brow and pulling at the collar of his shirt and saying "Whew!"

so's you'd have thought he'd just got done plowing fifty acres in the middle of July with a mouse for a mule harnessed to a knife for a plow!

Folks laughed and screamed so much that you could see why this cost a whole quarter of a American dollar to come in and see.

The mesmerist said, "And what's that I see right in front of you, young Samuel? It appears to be the waters of Lake Erie, cool and deep and inviting!"

Sammy started brushing at the stage like it was covered with sand and he was clearing a spot to spread a blanket. But afore he could set hisself down, the mesmerist said with a voice that was fulled up with disappointment, "Sam-u-well, Sam-u-well, Sam-u-well."

Sammy frozed up and the man told him, "How can you even think of relaxing at the seashore when you are just a very few feet away from bathing in this great lake's waters? You should jump right in!"

Sammy slapped his own forehead like he was thinking, "How come I didn't think of that?" and stuck one of his toes out to test the water. He let out a long "Ahhh!" and got ready to put his whole foot in this lake that couldn't no one but him and the conjurer-man see.

Afore even his ankles got wet the mesmerist said, "Sam-u-well, Sam-u-well, Sam-u-well."

Sammy didn't step no farther into the water and the

conjurer looked at all of us who were watching and said, "Have any of you here ever heard of a boy going to bathe fully clothed?"

The crowd shouted outta one throat, "No!"

I kept my eye on Sammy and for a second the dumbstruck look flew off his face and his brow wrinkled, but just as quick he went back to looking stupid-fied.

The mesmerist said, "Of course not, particularly not when you are wearing the finest silk shirt that the most talented tailor in Toronto has to offer! Samuel, your mother would be appalled if you were to get that beautiful, expensive, and rather stylish shirt wet!"

Sammy slapped his forehead again and started pulling the shirt over his head. Once he had it off he waren't wearing nothing but a raggedy undershirt and commenced tiptoeing back into the lake. But afore the water could cover even his knees the mesmerist said it again, "Sam-u-well, Sam-u-well, Sam-u-well."

Sammy stopped with one foot in the air and looked back at the conjurer.

"My word! Ladies and gentlemen, would you look at this young man! He is a stubborn and ungrateful lad! Not only has his dear, beloved mother seen fit to clothe him in a fine silken shirt, she's also given him a silk undershirt! Please, Samuel, off with it before it's ruined by the waters of Lake Erie."

This time Sammy cut a look at the mesmerist that waren't the least bit dumbstruck, it was kind of edging on being worried.

He pulled his undershirt over his head and a bale of laughs echoed 'round the tent. Laughing is a peculiar thing 'cause there're lots of different kinds. There's the laughing you do at the end of a good story, the laugh you give when you're scared then find out you didn't have no cause to be, and the laughing that was bouncing 'round in this tent. It waren't a happy kind of sound atall. It mostly reminded me of the cutting sounds that a pack of hounds makes once they commence to ripping a possum to shreds. It was more like the sound you'd think the Devil would make if he had a good sense of humour and you'd told him a joke.

I waren't doing none of the kinds of laughing. I could see that if this started out being fun for Sammy, it sure was turning into something else.

Ma and Pa must be right 'bout what smoking does to a child, 'cause once his undershirt was off, we could see Sammy was right skinny and sickly-looking, and though standing in front of all these people without no kind of shirt on atall would have shamed me near to death, the conjurization was on him so strong that Sammy kept on doing it. But it *did* seem like his enthusiasm for the whole show was getting littler and littler.

He hugged his arms 'round hisself and started back to

tiptoeing into Lake Erie. But Sammy gave a long pulled-out groan when the mesmerist and most the folks in the crowd moaned out, "Sam-u-well, Sam-u-well, Sam-u-well!"

A hoop and a holler came out of the crowd 'cause we were all pretty sure that even though Sammy's trousers looked like old and worned-out dungarees to us, to the mesmerist they were gonna be some more of that fine Toronto silk that caint stand getting wet.

"Egads, boy! I've never seen such a privileged yet undeserving child. Your mother's love for you knows no bounds! Silken trousers as well, can you believe it?"

This time the stupid-fied look left Sammy and afearedness and shaming took over. The red from his hair started leaking down onto the rest of his face. His ears started up glowing like hot pokers.

But he turned his back to the crowd and started unbuttoning those trousers!

He held up once they're all unbuttoned, but the mesmerist had no mercy in him atall. He waved his cape and said, "Off with the silken trousers!"

Sammy gave a gulp so loud everyone in the tent heard it, then he let loose of his pants and they dropped right 'round his ankles.

The crowd sucked in air then got real quiet 'cept for one man who hollered out, "Shucks, if his dern ma loved him so dern much, you'd think she'd have bought the boy *some* kind of underdrawers, silk or not!"

The laughs and howls and hoots must have raised the roof of the tent five feet, all 'cause Sammy was naked as the day he was born. And he turned red as any cardinal I'd ever seen. I'd druther have got floated into the ceiling for two hours than to stand there like that for two seconds.

The mesmerist's mouth flew open and he quick clopped Sammy in the head then pulled his cape 'round him and said, "The spell's over, pull your pants up, you little chowderhead. Have you lost your blasted mind?"

After they rough-handed Sammy and booted him out of the tent, the conjurer mesmerized two or three other folks but waren't a one of 'em nowhere near as interesting as Sammy.

It must've been getting near midnight when me and the Preacher left the tent and he said, "When we get to this next place just go along with everything I say, and fight that urge of yours to talk so much. Don't open your mouth unless you're spoken to."

"Yes, sir."

We walked a little ways into the woods and sat on a couple of stumps whilst folks cleared out of the carnival. Finally the Preacher said, "Let's go. And remember, the less you say the better."

CHAPTER 10

Meeting the *Real* MaWee!

Me and the Preacher wandered 'round the carnival for 'bout another hour. Then we walked back into the Atlas Clearing and headed for a tent where most of the carnival workers were sitting. A big, rough-looking white man with bright red hair stood up and put his hand on the Preacher's chest and said, "Show's over, boy. We's pulling up stakes tonight and don't need no more workers."

The Preacher slapped the man's hand off his chest and stood so his jacket was open and that mystery pistol was showing. He said, "I look like a boy to you? I'm not here about work. I'm looking for the owner. And if you put another hand on me you'll be pulling back a bloody stump."

The tall conjurer-man with the two sets of eyes jumped up and said, "Hold on a moment, Red. I own this carnival, sir. How may I help you?"

The Preacher pushed past the red-hair white man and said, "Sir, I just want to start by telling you what a wonderful carnival you have here."

The conjurer reached his hand to the Preacher and

said, "Why, thank you, sir. Whom do I have the honour of addressing?"

"I'm the Right Reverend Deacon Doctor Zephariah Connerly the Third. A pleasure to meet you, sir."

"Reverend Connerly, I am humbled to be in your presence. I am the lowly Charles Mondial Vaughn the *Fourth*, Knight Commander of the Most Honourable Order of the Bath. Knighted a mere fourteen years ago."

The Preacher said, "I'm the one who's humbled, sir. I've been to many such carnivals and have never seen anything that matches this one. You must be very proud."

"Indeed, indeed. I've worked years to assemble this family."

The Preacher said, "Which is why I wanted to speak with you."

The conjurer took a long pull on his cigar and blowed the smoke to the side, then said, "And what may I do for you, sir?"

"It's more what I can do for you."

"I'm intrigued. Do tell."

The Preacher pulled me from behind him and said, "Sir Charles, allow me to introduce the most amazing child ever to have lived in Buxton. Although he was born and reared in Africa, he has lived with me for these past four years. Maybe in your travels you've heard of the tribe he's from, the Chochotes?"

Sir Charles said, "Can't say that I have."

"There's a good reason you haven't. Sad to say, little Ahbo here is the last surviving member."

"Well, Reverend, that is indeed sad, but what does that have to do with my carnival?"

The Preacher commenced waving his arms, really warming into this tale he's 'bout to spin. "The Chochotes were fierce warriors who hunted and even fished with nothing but stones. Stone throwing was a skill passed from generation to generation, and little Ahbo's father, who was the king of the Chochotes, passed on the secrets of stone hunting and fishing to his son just before he was tragically murdered."

The Preacher sounded so heart-busted about this that even I was getting sad for little Ahbo, and I knowed that he was me and that there waren't probably gonna be a lick of truth in the whole story.

The conjurer said, "Pity that. But wait, do I understand you to be saying that this boy can catch a fish underwater? By throwing a stone?"

The Preacher said, "If only we were at a lake so he could show you."

The conjurer winked at the big, rough, red-hair white man and said, "If he can do that, he must have an unusually keen eye. Could he, mayhap, demonstrate his skill some other way?"

"Of course he can. I watched your Madame Sabbar earlier tonight, and while she was most impressive, I didn't see her doing anything little Ahbo couldn't match."

"No?"

"No. Perhaps we could go to her tent and show you."

"Well, sir, we were actually preparing to break things down, but I think little Ahbo might provide an interesting, but brief, diversion."

The Preacher, Sir Charles, and the other white man started walking toward the slingshot lady's tent with me trailing behind.

The conjurer looked back at me and said loud and slow, "Do . . . you . . . speak . . . any . . . English?"

It was kind of hard to look at him with his two sets of eyes, but I said, "Why, yes, sir, and some Latin, and I can understand a little Greek."

Oops! That must've been too much talking. The Preacher gave me a hard look then told the conjurer, "Plus, of course, he's fluent in Chochote."

One of the conjurer's eyebrows raised up and he said, "Indeed? To my ear it sounds as if the boy is very Canadian."

"That's because not only is he the best stone flinger since David, he's also uncommonly bright. He's lived with me for only four years and he's picked up the language and customs of Canada West so quickly it's truly astounding."

All the sudden a stranger boy came up 'longside of me and gave me some unpleasant looks. His hair was all matted up like a bird's nest and his clothes were so dirty that not even Cooter would've been caught dead in 'em.

He said, "Who you?"

I just 'bout said my name then remembered what Sammy had told me 'bout saying "Elijah" 'round here. I knowed the boy waren't from Buxton and I was pretty sure he waren't from Chatham but I couldn't be total for certain. I thought it'd be best if I didn't take no chances. He was littler than me so I said, "Why you want to know?"

He said, "Where y'all going?" He sounded American.

"Over to the slingshot lady's tent."

The boy spit, kicked his bare foot at the dirt, and said, "I knowed it!"

I could tell he was sizing me up to see if he could lick me. I puffed my chest up some whilst we walked.

The boy said quiet, "I's the *real* MaWee! But you's fixing to take my place, ain't you?"

"What?"

"That white boy waren't no good, I seent it, so now Massa Charles looking for *you* to take my place."

He tilted his head toward the conjurer and said, "He done tolt me it was just for whilst we's in Canada, but I knowed he was a-lying."

"Lying 'bout what?"

"You's trying to be the next MaWee, ain't you?"

"*What?*"

"But I'm-a tell you right now that you ain't gunn like it. You ain't gunn like roaming 'bout with 'em one bit. They ain't gunn say nothing at first but you gunn have to clean all them animal cages and fetch for 'em all times of the day or night, and the 'gator man gunn beat you every chance he get and you gunn be cleaning all they clothes, and they stingy with what they feed you, and it even ain't no fun after 'while getting hit in the face with them grapes neither."

I said, "I'm not taking no one's place. The Preacher's just bragging on me so's that man with all those eyes can see how good I chunk stones."

The boy gave me another rough look.

I said, "You travel 'round with these people?"

"Course I do, I tolt you, I'm the *real* MaWee."

"Your ma and pa travel with you too?"

"I ain't got no ma nor pa."

"You a orphan?"

"You best watch what you's calling me. What's a orphan?"

I said, "How old are you?"

"I ain't sure."

"You ain't had no schooling atall?"

"What I need schooling for? You ax too much questions."

"Who takes care of you?"

"Massa Charles do. He look after me good. He done paid more'n a hunnert dollars for me down in Loos-ee-anna."

"*Paid?* You're a *slave?*"

"Naw! I seent how slaves get treated. I ain't no slave."

"You ain't never tried to escape?"

"What you mean? If Massa cut me a-loose, what's I gunn eat? Where's I gunn sleep?"

"But this is Canada! You ain't but three miles from Buxton! You ain't never heard of *Buxton?*"

"Massa Charles say Buxton why he have to get a white boy to pretend he MaWee. He say y'all up here ain't gunn think it funny to see *me* get pelt with no grapes. Now he seent that white boy ain't no good and he gunn try you next."

I told him, "My ma and pa ain't 'bout to let me travel with no circus. Buxton's my home."

The inside of Madame Sabbar's tent looked a whole lot smaller without all the people piled up in it. Madame Sabbar herself was sitting on the stage smoking a cigar.

MaWee pointed at the white cloth atop the jungle board and whispered, "Can y'all read? What that say?"

I told him, "It says, 'The Jungles of Sweden.'"

"It don't say nothing 'bout MaWee?"

"No."

"That what I thought. He lie!"

The Preacher and the conjurer stopped talking and Sir Charles told MaWee, "Go light the candles as if it's a show."

"Yes, sir!"

MaWee struck a match and set all the candles on the board burning.

"Them other ones too, boss?"

"Yes, everything."

MaWee grabbed a lighting pole and went 'round the tent lighting the candles up high. When he was done he came back and said, "That all, boss?"

"Yes, MaWee, but don't leave. We're getting started in a moment."

"Yes, sir, boss."

"Now, Reverend Connerly, perhaps little Ahbo can demonstrate his skill."

The Preacher waved for me to come up on the stage.

He whispered to me, "First time through, just use your right hand."

This waren't gonna be nothing! It waren't even twenty paces twixt me and the candles that were sitting atop the Swedish jungle board. I reached in my tote sack and pulled out ten of the chunking stones and set them on the table next to me.

I looked at the Preacher and he ducked his head at me. I held on to my breathing and chunked with my right hand and passed stones into it with my left.

When I was done, all the candles had been put out just as smooth as the slingshot lady had done it.

The conjurer and the other white man looked at each other. Madame Sabbar blew a long cloud of smoke out of her nose holes. The Preacher winked his eye at me.

MaWee called out, "Woo-ooo-ooo-wee! He good, Massa Charles! Y'all caint use him for nothing but tossing stones, he that good!"

The conjurer said, "You're right, MaWee, that was most remarkable! Now how 'bout the others?" He pointed at the higher-up candles.

This waren't gonna be as easy. The farthest candles appeared to be 'bout thirty, thirty-five paces away, and it was dark up that high.

The Preacher saw I was fretting and came up on the stage.

"What's wrong?"

"I don't know if I can put out the flames on the two at the back, sir."

"Just aim to knock them down, then."

"Yes, sir. Just my right hand again?"

"Yes."

I held on to my breathing and threw at the twelve candles runged 'round the tent. When I was done, one of 'em at the back had got knocked over and I'd clean missed on the one over the doorway.

Sir Charles and the other white man brung their heads together and started talking.

MaWee said, "Massa Charles, Massa Charles! You got to have that boy take over from Missy Sabbar! He good 'nough to take her place!"

The Preacher said, "And that's not half the story, Sir Charles. No disrespect intended, madame, but while you are without doubt a deadly accurate slingshotist, little Ahbo's skills include something else."

The Preacher's hands started unfolding and waving right along with the story. He said, "One of the reasons the Chochote tribe is now nearly wiped from the face of the earth is that they shared their land with an insect so vile that it is called the horrible giant Bama bee. Bees so large that they've been known to carry away a full-grown man as easily as a hawk carries a mouse. And they attack in swarms of ten, which forced the Chochote to learn to throw not only with accuracy but with speed as well. Might I propose, if she is not too tired, that Madame Sabbar and little Ahbo have a side-by-side demonstration that includes speed?"

Sir Charles said, "A race? Why, that might prove to be quite interesting. Madame?"

The slingshot lady didn't look too happy 'bout doing this but she chomped her teeth on her cigar and stood next to me.

The Preacher said, "If the young boy could light the ten candles on the board again, we can get this started."

MaWee waited till Sir Charles nodded at him then lit up all the candles.

The Preacher said, "Why doesn't the madame pick one side of the board and put out candles toward the middle and little Ahbo will do the same with the other side. We'll see who puts out the most the quickest."

The woman chomped her cigar harder and said, "Left." She raised her slingshot.

The Preacher whispered to me, "Use both hands. Beat her good."

He told Sir Charles, "You start them."

The conjurer-man said, "Both of you start on the count of three. One . . . two . . ."

Folks from Sweden must not be real good at counting. The conjurer hadn't even finished saying "two" afore Madame Sabbar put out the first candle on the left.

". . . three!"

I throwed left, right, left, right, left, right.

I'd got six of 'em in the time she got four.

She spit her cigar out on the stage and said, "Light them candles up again, you little fool."

MaWee waited on the conjurer to nod then lit 'em all up.

This time I got seven and she got three. She knocked one of 'em over too.

She dropped her slingshot and walked out of the tent.

MaWee shouted, "Ooo-ooo-wee! He done run her off! He way better than her, you gunn let him take her place?"

The conjurer said, "My word, Reverend, you didn't exaggerate in the least. I think little Ahbo will fit very nicely into our family."

MaWee said, "He gunn take *her* place, boss? I ain't never seent no one what throwed so good! Lots of folks pay to see that boy throw! It be a waste of time having him get pelt with grapes."

The conjurer said, "Start breaking things down in here, boy. I want to leave by noon tomorrow. Red, go see if Madame Sabbar is all right. Reverend, we need to talk."

Him and the Preacher stood next to the stage.

Sir Charles said, "I assume you've had some expenses in raising little Ahbo. I'm willing to give you some consideration for that. You say the poor lad is an orphan?"

"Yes, I'm the only one he has."

"How much are you looking for, sir?"

The Preacher said, "Hold on here, you've misjudged me. I don't deal in human beings."

"Then what is it you're proposing?"

"The boy and I would be willing to travel with you for a while if you're willing to make certain guarantees."

"Such as?"

"Such as how much we would be paid. Such as what it is we would do in your family. Such as what it is we *wouldn't* do."

Sir Charles blowed out another long puff of cigar smoke at the roof of the tent and said, "Ahh, well, Reverend, what is it *you* propose doing? I can see that little Ahbo would be able to carry his weight and contribute to the family with his stone throwing, augmented, of course, by several other chores, but I really do not have a need for anyone else. I *would*, however, handsomely reward you for your transference of guardianship of the boy."

MaWee'd pulled all the candles off the top of the Sweden jungle board. He said, "Pardon me, boss, you wants me to take this sign 'bout that white boy off of here? We gunn put it back saying this here's the real MaWee's jungle, ain't we?"

The conjurer-man kept his eyes on the Preacher but nodded his head at MaWee.

MaWee pulled off the white sheet that said THE JUNGLES OF SWEDEN!!!

Writ out underneath the sheet in letters di-rect on the board was:

The Jungles of Darkest Africa!!!
Help Madame Sabbar Capture MaWee,
the Chief of the Pickaninnys!!!

All the sudden the Preacher was done talking. He grabbed hold of my collar and we marched out the front of the tent. Afore you could blink we're walking down the road back to Buxton.

Things happened so quick that I had to ask the Preacher, "Why'd we leave without saying good-bye to no one?"

He said, "It wasn't what I thought it was."

"What'd you think it was? Waren't it just a carnival?"

"Forget this happened. It was a bad idea from the start."

"What was?"

"Nothing, Elijah. I was simply looking for a way to help the Settlement."

I tried a couple more times but I waren't getting no more explaining from the Preacher. It 'peared he didn't want to talk no more, which I look at as he wanted to do some listening, so I told him all 'bout Sammy and how scared I was 'bout getting floated away and 'bout how Sir Charles paid a hundred American dollars for MaWee. I kept on talking all the way to Buxton but the only subject the Preacher seemed to take any kind of interest in atall was MaWee. He had me tell him 'bout it three times. I asked the Preacher if you were still a slave if you didn't mind working for someone and didn't have nowhere else to go.

Only thing he said was, "Yes, you're still a slave. But you're worse than a slave. You're an ignorant slave."

When we got home, the Preacher waited whilst I climbed in through my bedroom window. Once I got in I waved at him and he waved back and walked away. It waren't till I was in bed thinking 'bout the most exciting day I'd ever had in my life that it came to me that the Preacher'd headed back down the road to Chatham 'stead of toward his own home. That was just as peculiar as a whole lot of the things the Preacher did that night. I just chalked it up to some more of that growned-up behaviour that don't make no sense, it don't make no sense atall.

On Monday morning, me and Cooter joined up in front of the schoolhouse. I was 'bout to explode wanting to tell him some more 'bout the carnival, but afore I could open my mouth he said, "Don't it seem odd ain't no one else here? Doggone-it-all, Elijah, the same thing happened to me last month when I lost track of the days and sat out here for a half a hour on Sunday morning wondering where everyone was at. Today *is* Monday, ain't it?"

"Yes, don't you 'member sitting in church all day yesterday?"

"So where's every . . ."

We both heard someone say, "Oooh!" and walked 'round back of the school. All the other children were crowded up in a big circle way out in the field. Wouldn't no one dare fight this close to the school so me and Cooter ran over to see what the commotion was.

I said, "I bet they found another dead body!"

Cooter said, "Uh-uh, Emma Collins is standing there and she'd have run off and told someone first thing. I bet one n'em moth lions from that circus you was telling me 'bout busted loose and they's holding him down till someone come to get it."

I looked at Cooter and couldn't help hoping that thickheadedness ain't something you can catch like a cold.

When we busted into the circle it waren't neither a dead body nor a lion. 'Twas a little stranger boy standing there looking like he's 'bout to cry.

I knowed this boy, but I couldn't get ahold on from where.

Then it hit me. 'Twas MaWee! Somebody had cut all his wild hair off and put him in some proper clothes.

I said, "You escaped! You're free!"

'Twaren't odd for folks that just got freed to look and act confused, but I hadn't never saw no one that looked and acted like they were mad 'bout coming to live in Buxton afore. And MaWee was good and mad. Why, he was pouting and looking like he had rocks in his jaws and was grumbling so's everyone was wondering if he was crazy.

Emma Collins asked him, "What? You're wishing you hadn't escaped? You're wishing you were still a slave?"

MaWee rubbed his hand over the top of his head like he was still wondering where all his hair was at.

"I done tolt you I waren't no slave. And I didn't do no escaping neither. I gots snatched off by *his* friend!"

He pointed spot-on at me.

I said, *"What?"*

"After y'all left, your friend come back and stoled me from Massa Charles."

I couldn't help myself, I knowed I should've kept my mouth shut, but I said, "The Preacher?"

MaWee said, *"Preacher?* He sure don't act like no preacher I ever seen."

Cooter said, "What happened?"

"Soon's we got done breaking everything down, that friend of his bust in holding on to two guns and set to pistol-whipping Massa Red. Then he grab Massa Charles' hair like he 'bout to scalp him. He shoves one n'em guns right in Massa Charles' nose.

"We all thinking it gunn be another stickup and boss is sure afeared of this man and say, 'Ain't no need to hurt no one, just take the money.' But that there boy's friend . . ." MaWee pointed right at me. ". . . say he ain't looking to rob us and then he point the gun what ain't jammed up Massa Charles' nose dead at me! He tell the 'gator man he gots one minute to tie my hands up. All the time he got that pistol up in Massa Charles' nose so deep, blood running down his face."

Tears were pouring out of MaWee's eyes. "Once the 'gator man got me roped good, that preacher tell 'em this here's Canada and folks is free and he taking me to Buxton and he gunn kill anyone what try to stop him. Then he tell Massa Charles that once we gets to Buxton, y'all's army gunn make sure don't no one come and try to get me back. He say he got him the fastest horse in Canada tied out in the woods but it waren't gonna be no different if he had a old broke-down mule 'cause he ain't gunn gallop him nor trot him nor rush him atall. He say he ain't 'bout to run from no one, 'specially not in his own country. Then he tell Massa Charles the way to come if he want to find where y'all live. He tell 'em that the road to Buxton branch off to the right 'bout half a mile down and if they daft 'nough to follow him and wants to meet the Lord that bad, then that the way they gots to turn."

Everybody was looking shocked at MaWee's story.

He wiped his nose on his shirtsleeve and said, "Then he pull me outta the tent and tug me off into the woods and put me on top that pretty horse and tie me to the saddle and tie them reins 'round his waist and put one n'em pistols in each his hands and we starts walking right down the middle of the road.

"I just knowed Massa Charles and them gunn come rescue me and I'm hoping when they kill that man they aims good and they don't shoot me by mistake."

MaWee kicked at the ground and said, "Only thing I can figure is they took the wrong branch once they come to where the road split up at. But don't none y'all be surprise if they come busting in that there schoolhouse and take me back with 'em."

Emma Collins said, "Why're you wishing for that? You're free now."

MaWee said, "How's I free when they tolt me I ain't got no choice but to go to school? How's I free when they got that Johnny boy and his momma watching over me like a sheriff?"

The bell runged and it came to me that I was gonna have to be careful with MaWee. If Emma Collins or one n'em other girls got wind that I was wandering 'bout past midnight at the carnival they'd get me stewed up in a world of trouble.

As we walked up the steps into the schoolhouse, Mr. Travis said, "Good morning, scholars, strivers, and questers for a better future! Are you ready to learn, are you ready to grow?"

He saw MaWee and said, "Well! Congratulations! They told me you'd be joining us today. Welcome, young man."

I could tell being free was gonna be a hard row to hoe for MaWee. 'Stead of answering Mr. Travis in the proper way he, bold as anything, said to him, "How many people in y'all's army anyway?"

Children jumped to the side and cleared out of the way so's not to interfere with Mr. Travis getting a proper snatch at MaWee. But Mr. Travis surprised us. He didn't cane MaWee nor scold him nor 'buke him in the least. He gentle laid his hand on MaWee's head and, without no sting in his voice atall, said, "My name is Mr. Travis. When I call on you to speak you will address me as that or as 'sir.' I have a feeling you and I are going to be spending a great deal of time together. Once again, welcome and congratulations."

MaWee said, "Thank you, sir." Both me and him kept peeking out the window all through the day waiting for Sir Charles and the rough, red-hair white man to come. But they never did show.

→ Chapter 11 ←

Emma Collins and Birdy

It was early Saturday morning, a week after the carnival, and Pa and Old Flapjack and me and Cooter were down on Mrs. Holton's land uprooting stumps. Everything was going fine when all the sudden Old Flap gave one n'em snorts that let me know he'd seen something or smelt something that waren't regular. Deers and other four-leg animals ain't nothing to him so I knowed this sound was for a stranger. A person stranger.

I kept guiding Old Flap along, tugging his reins as he leaned into the chains that were snatching at the stump, but I cut my eyes 'cross the field to find what it was that got him snorting.

I spotted 'em in the tree line.

Folks that are trying to hide in the woods that ain't real comforted being there always make the same mistake. If you want to know exactly where they're at without doing a whole lot of searching, all you gotta do is find the biggest tree or rock around. They always think that behind it is the best place to hide. Whoever these folks were, they'd choosed the biggest maple standing on Mrs. Holton's land.

I saw two heads peeking out from 'mongst the green behind the maple 'bout fifty yards off. I kept working and whistling Old Flap on, pretending I hadn't seen nothing atall.

I said, "Pa, Old Flapjack just got wind of some folks in the trees off to the east."

Pa didn't quit working nor look 'round nor act like I'd talked to him, he just said, "Is they white?"

"No, sir."

"How many of 'em is they?"

"All I saw was two, sir. Looks like a man and a boy."

Pa said, "Cooter, head on back and find where Emma Collins is at. Tell her she needed. Don't be looking back, and once you're out of sight, run hard."

Cooter knowed why Pa wanted Emma so he said, "Yes, sir," and acted like he was strolling away.

It seems peculiar but we had to act like this so didn't no one get spooked.

Most times when new-free slaves come to Buxton they get helped here by a Underground Railroad conductor, but every once in the while they find us all on their own. When that happens someone usually spots 'em 'mongst the trees or bushes, stealing looks and studying us hard, not sure if it's safe to get noticed. Even if they ain't seeing no white people they still caint bring theirselves to show who they are.

We learnt a long time ago not to make no big commotion when we first see 'em. We learnt that all the running they'd been doing, all the looking over their shoulders and not knowing when they were gonna eat again or where they were gonna sleep or who they could trust made 'em skittish and even dangerous and not likely to take to no one running at 'em. Not even if you were smiling and waving and showing how happy you were that they got through. Afore you'd reach 'em they'd just melt back into the woods and you'd be standing there wondering if you'd really seen anything atall.

If a bunch of us went charging at 'em whooping and raising Cain they might disappear back into the forest for another two, three days. And that was two, three days that they were free but didn't know it, which Pa says is tragical 'cause you ain't never gonna know how much time you got here on earth and each day you're free is precious.

That's why after we'd tried a slew of other things, we found the best way to welcome new-free folks to the Settlement was to use that crying little brat, Emma Collins.

Cooter waren't gone for no time atall and came back towing Emma with him. Cradled up in her arm she was holding on to her doll. It waren't nothing but a old sock that someone had jammed stuffing up inside the toe part and then tied string tight 'round and 'round the neck to turn it into a head. It had two big brown buttons sewed on for eyes and six little white buttons sewed on for teeth. It even had a bunch of braided black yarn sewed on for hair that was supposed to look like plaits. Emma'd gone and put little ribbons on the end of each plait and had made the doll a blue dress and a red apron. Total all them things together and you end up with a frightsome mess that's likely to give you nightmares. But Emma toted it near everywhere but school.

She said, "Afternoon, Mr. Freeman. Afternoon, Old Flapjack. Afternoon, Elijah."

That's one of the main reasons don't no one like Emma, she thought it was funny to speak to a mule afore she spoke to me. Just like Philip Wise, she ain't never got over that I was the first child born free in Buxton. Ma and Emma's ma were in a race to see who was gonna be firstborn and Emma didn't come out till six days after me. Since me and Ma won the race, Emma's always let the sin of envy choke her heart.

Pa pulled his hat off and answered her. I pulled a face.

He wiped his forehead and said, "You still seeing 'em, son?"

I patted Old Flapjack's flank and kept my head pointed

157

at Pa but I turned my eyes back to that big maple. There was still one half of a head peeking at us 'bout three feet off the ground. It was the boy.

"Yes, sir, one of 'em's still there."

Pa said, "They's yon, Emma, by that biggest tree di-rect under the sun."

Emma looked out of the corner of her eye and said, "I see the tree, Mr. Freeman," and started off walking slow away from us.

When Mr. Frederick Douglass is speechifying he says that the second hardest step in making yourself free is the first one that you take. He says after you make up your mind and take the first step, most of the rest of 'em come pretty easy. But he says that the *most* hardest step to take is the very last one. He says that finally crossing over from slavery to freedom is the most horrifyingest, most bravest thing a slave will ever have to do. In my eyes it's odd that Emma Collins is the one who's best at carrying folks that last step into being free but, truth told, couldn't no one else do it near as good as her.

Ma says it's 'cause Emma's a lot like me, but she don't mean that in a good way, 'cause Emma caint chunk stones worth spit nor tend to animals so's they're happy like I can. And I ain't nowhere near as good as her in my studies and schoolwork. Ma means we're alike 'cause Emma's fragile too.

But she's a whole lot more fra-giler than I *ever* been, and whilst you'd have to study me real hard to see it, with Emma it's something that's plain and right out front. Fra-gile-ness is sitting on her bold as one n'em awful flowery church hats Ma and the other women wear on Sunday. But the fra-gile-ness does make it easy to tell that Emma don't mean no one no harm, and that makes the runaways more comforted once they see her.

Emma Collins didn't make no beeline for the big maple. She kind of zigged one way then zagged the 'nother, moving slow, but always ending up going in the direction of the tree.

It looked to be a whole lot of lollygagging and a walk that should've took 'bout a minute to make ended up taking a whole lot longer, but she knowed what she was doing. She bended over to pull up a yellow flower, acted like she was showing it to that terrorific doll, moved on a bit, squatted down to lift up a rock to see what was underneath, put the doll's face close to the ground so's it could get a good look too, moved on some more, twirled and spinned 'round a couple times, moved on a little more, brushed something off the doll's dress and, afore you could say how she did it, she'd wandered right up next to the big maple.

That was when she finally quit moving and looked dead at the tree. I knowed she was talking gentle to whoever it was that thought hadn't no one seen 'em.

She was too far off and talked too soft for me to hear but I knowed she was saying, "Hello, my name's Emma Collins. I'm the first girl who was born free in Buxton, and now you're free too. We're very pleased you are going to be our new neighbours. Come, everybody's waiting to meet you."

Emma finished her speechifying and reached her right hand out toward the tree.

Didn't nothing move for the longest time, then, slow as can be, a man came out from behind the maple holding on to his hat. He talked a bit, pulled his hat back on, then dropped on one knee and reached his hand out to Emma.

Emma took ahold of his hand, he stood up, and she commenced walking the man right to us.

I said, "She's got him!" and Pa finally looked over and waved.

The man didn't return Pa's wave or nothing. One of his hands was holding on to Emma and the other one was behind his back. He was looking side to side and all 'round, seeming like he was 'bout to bolt if someone said, "Boo."

When he was 'bout twenty paces from us the man turned Emma's hand a-loose, pulled off his hat, and called to Pa, "Pardon me, sir. The child right? This here really Buxton?"

"Morning. Yes, sir, it is, and y'all's really free!"

The man brung his hand from behind his back. He was clutching on to a long, shiny knife!

He looked at it then back at Pa and it seemed like he was fixing to cry.

He turned the knife so's he was hanging on to the blade and said, "I's terrible sorry 'bout this here dagger, sir, but . . ." He wiped at his eyes. ". . . but we's so tired of running, we's come so . . ." He couldn't talk no more.

Pa walked right up on him and wrapped his arms 'round the man and said, "Don't say nothing more, brother. I know. I know it ain't been easy but you found where you're supposed to be. You're home. You alone?"

The man said, "No, sir," turned back toward the maple and whistled, then waved both his arms over his head.

A woman, a boy, and a girl, hanging on to one the 'nother's hands, stepped out of the woods and started heading slow toward us. They were walking low and their heads were ducking and shooting from side to side just like the man's had been. 'Stead of taking the di-rect way to us they skirted 'long the woods and the part of Mrs. Holton's land that Mr. Leroy'd already cleared.

The woman was toting a bundle tied to her back. I knowed it was a baby 'cause it was tied the same way all the Settlement women do when they're working and want to keep their children with 'em.

'Bout halfway 'cross they broke 'way from the tree line and started moving faster and faster through the clearing toward us. Their mouths were pulled wide open like they were fixing to scream, but didn't no sounds come from 'em. After a second they started running all out, acting like the Devil hisself was on their tail. Then they commenced making a sound that made my skin all twitch-ity with gooseflesh. It waren't like no human sound atall, it was a kinda wail and a moan and a yell all stirred up together. It was something terrible to hear.

The man throwed the knife down and ran out at 'em. They crashed one into the 'nother so hard you'd think they'd've knocked each other over, but they didn't. They stood all knotted together keeping up those horrible noises and holding on like there waren't no tomorrow. They acted like they hadn't seen one the 'nother in a hundred years 'stead of just a minute or two.

The little boy, who 'peared to be 'bout five years old, was blubbering and churning his legs up and down like he was still on the run but he waren't moving nowhere. He was running in one spot clutching on to his mother's and father's legs. It must have shooked him up bad to see his ma and pa crying and looking wild and carrying on like this 'cause all the sudden the front of his britches started getting covered with a dark stain. I had to turn my head so's not to shame him.

162

I looked over at Emma and, doggone-it-all, she was squeezing that awful doll and starting to pull her lip down and cloud her eyes up, getting ready to bawl right along with the new-free folks.

I'll be blanged if bawling ain't something akin to the measles or the chicken pox or the plague, once it grabs ahold of one fra-gile person, seems like it snatches on to every other fra-gile person that's anywhere near. I'd been working hard to fight it, but I didn't have no choice but to commence crying right along with Emma and n'em.

Pa and Cooter didn't try to shame me or nothing. Cooter looked at his shoes and Pa looked at me. His shoulders dropped some, and he allowed a long slow breath to come out of him. It looked a lot like disappointment, but at least he didn't say nothing.

The woman broke away from the others and ran hard at Pa, unwrapping the baby off her back and holding it out front of her.

She said, "Sir, my baby! My baby girl sick!"

She showed the baby to Pa and he said, "We got some nurses what'll tend your child, ma'am. How long she been ailing?"

The woman said, "She ain't woke up since yesterday morn. Two nights ago they was some paddy-rollers right on top of us. She always been a quiet child but since we been running she been likely to bawl, so I had to give her some of this else they'd've caught us for sure. I ain't had no choice, but I's 'fraid I give her too much!"

She pulled a brown tonic bottle out of her dress pocket.

Pa said, "She drawing breath strong. We gets lotsa young uns what's had too much sleep medicine, and all 'em done good after 'while."

The man and the two children bunched up 'round the woman and the sleepy baby. Pa unharnessed the chains off of Old Flapjack and tied him to the stump we'd been pulling on.

Pa walked back over to the family and said the same thing we say to all the new-free folks when they first get to Buxton. It's the way we greet 'em into being free.

Pa pointed up and said, "Looky there! Look at that sky!"

I'd heard Pa and other growned folks say this plenty of times, but I couldn't help but follow where Pa's finger was pointing. Everybody did, we all looked up at the blue sky that didn't have cloud the first in it.

"Ain't that the grandest sky y'all ever seen?"

Pa smiled and pointed out 'cross the field. "Look at that land! Look at them trees! Has y'all ever seen anything that precious? It's the land of the free!"

The family kept following where Pa was pointing.

"Now look at you'selves! Look at 'em babies! Has y'all ever looked this beautiful? Today be the first day don't no one own y'all but y'all. Today be the first day that don't *no* one own them babies. Today be the first day you ain't got cause to blame no one for what gunn happen to you tomorrow. Today y'all's truly set you'selves free!"

Then he opened both his arms and said to the people, "And y'all choosed the most beautifullest, most perfectest day for doing it! Only thing I's got to ask is, what kept you?"

It was peculiar 'cause it didn't matter if it was raining or snowing or even if the sky was being ripped by lightning and thunder, we always would tell the new folks that it was the most beautifullest, most perfectest day to get free. Far as I can tell, the weather didn't have a whole lot to do with it.

Pa said, "Come on, we gunn go into the Settlement and let everyone know y'all made it. Cooter, Emma, Elijah, y'all come too. Leave the mule, we ain't gunn be long gone."

Pa and Cooter and the new people started out toward the road.

Fra-gile-ness is mighty embarrassing, even if you're a girl, so me and Emma both hanged back a little to get the sniffling out of us. Emma set her doll and the little yellow flower on the stump and pulled out a 'kerchief to wipe her eyes and nose.

I've had it explained to me plenty of times, but I ain't never gonna understand the purpose of having a piece of cloth made just for blowing your nose into. Seems real dirty and nasty to me. Makes a whole lot more sense to me to plug up one of your nose holes and just blow what you gotta blow out of the other one onto the ground. Least that way you ain't constantly toting no dried-up things from your nose 'round in your pockets. But Ma's always telling me not to do that, 'specially 'round respectable folks.

Far as I can tell, Emma ain't the least bit respectable, but for Ma's sake, 'stead of blowing my nose onto the ground, I blowed it into my shirtsleeve.

Emma gave me a dirty look and I gave her one right back.

I remembered the knife that the man dropped and left in the field. I picked it up and ran to catch up with Pa and n'em.

I said, "Sir, you forgot this."

I reached the knife at him. Him and the woman looked at one the 'nother and soured up their faces. He said, "Thank you, boy, but we's free now. I don't want to see that dagger never no more."

I couldn't help but be surprised.

The man said to Pa, "Sir, I swored wasn't no one gunn take us back 'less it be over my dead body. I swored it and I proofed it wasn't no bluff, but now ain't no more need for that dagger, ain't no more need to be thinking 'bout the dirt what all over it. It sullied, it ain't clean."

I looked at the knife. It looked like the blacksmith had just got done making it. I said, "But, sir, it looks like it's new, it ain't dirty atall, it looks like . . ."

Pa told me, "Elijah, put the knife in your tote sack, and be still."

He said to the man, "Don't worry, sir, I'm-a take care of the knife."

I hoped Pa was gonna tell me what this meant later, but I knowed by the way he'd done everything quick-like that I shouldn't say nothing more 'bout it for now. I took a rag out of my tote sack and wrapped the knife in it so's it wouldn't bang up 'gainst none of my chunking stones.

We started back up walking and Emma zigged and zagged her way up to the new-free girl. The little girl acted like Emma was a haint and hugged in closer to the boy with the wet trousers.

Emma smiled at the girl and tried to hand her the yellow flower she'd picked. The girl looked at the flower then at Emma but still held on to her brother. Then Emma stuck the flower down in that terrific doll's apron and reached the two of 'em out to the new-free girl.

The girl kept gripping her brother with one hand but raised the other one slow to take the doll. Once she got ahold of it she hugged it into herself hard, staring at Emma.

Emma said, "Her name's Birdy. I suppose you can call her anything you want to, but she's always liked the name Birdy best. She's kind of shy so she wants me to ask if you'd mind being her new ma."

The girl looked long and hard into the doll's brown eyes then smiled like she saw something there 'sides a couple of buttons and some thread. She shooked her head up and down and moved her mouth like she was saying, "Thank you, ma'am."

Emma smiled and said, "You're welcome."

I might've said something welcoming to the boy, but I'd learnt from it happening to me personal that if you wet your pants in front of a bunch of strangers, you don't really want no one talking to you. You don't want no one asking why you're walking stiff-legged or doing *nothing* that will draw no attention to yourself. My keeping quiet waren't from being ignorant and unwelcoming, it was done so's not to shame him. 'Sides, after he got done walking all the way to the Settlement with that pee chafing 'round in his pants rubbing him raw, he waren't gonna want to talk atall!

Cooter said to me, "They's the first new-free in four months, Eli! You done the last ones, so it's my go to ring these here folk in."

Cooter was right. I had runged in the last new-free people so it was his turn now.

I said, "Pa?"

He said, "Y'all run on ahead."

Me and Cooter both said, "Yes, sir!" and tored off toward the Settlement.

Near everyone in Buxton who could would come a-running once we started tolling the Liberty Bell!

→ CHAPTER 12 ←

The Secret Language of Being Growned

Me and Cooter ran all the way back to the schoolhouse using the best shortcuts so we'd get there long afore Pa and Emma and the new folks. Pa would walk 'em slow along the road, talking to 'em gentle and starting to get 'em use to the way we do things in Buxton.

Waren't no one in the schoolhouse on a Saturday so me and Cooter opened the door and headed to the steeple to ring the Liberty Bell.

The Liberty Bell ain't no regular schoolhouse bell. It's a five-hundred-pound bell that came all the way from America. Not nowhere as close as Michigan, America, neither. It's from a city called Pittsburgh, far, far down in the United States. And we didn't have to pay nothing for it, it was gave to us by other folks that use to be slaves.

It took 'em a whole bunch of years, but they saved up every penny they could and had the Liberty Bell made then sent all the way to Canada. And these were poor folks too, but they were so proud of us that they didn't mind

170

doing without some things so's we could have the bell. They wanted it to be something that we'd always hear and see to remind folks in Buxton that prayers from America were always riding 'longside us.

They even had words writ onto the bell so's we'd never forget who gave it to us. It said, PRESENTED TO REVEREND KING BY THE COLOURED INHABITANTS OF PITTSBURGH FOR THE ACADEMY AT RALEIGH CANADA WEST. LET FREEDOM RING!

"Raleigh" is what some people who don't live here call the Settlement.

Whenever new-free folks come to live in Buxton, we ring the bell twenty times for each one of 'em. Ten times to ring out their old lives and ten more to ring in their new ones, their free lives. Then, we ask the new-free folks to, one by one, climb the ladder of the steeple and rub the bell with their left hand. Most times when you're doing something important you're supposed to use your right hand, but we ask 'em to use their left hand 'cause it's closest to their hearts.

Mr. Frederick Douglass said he hopes so many people get freed and mash their hands onto the Liberty Bell that a shiny spot, bright as gold, gets worned into the brass. But so far that hasn't happened.

Anyone in the Settlement that hears the ringing quits

doing whatever they're doing and comes to the schoolhouse to welcome the new people. Then, if the new-free folks say they want to live in the Settlement, everyone decides where they'll stay till they get their own place and get comforted 'bout being 'mongst us.

There's always a box full of cotton in the school's steeple so's you can stuff your ears whilst you're ringing the bell. It's loud enough that you'd be hearing it and nothing else for the longest if you didn't shove something in your ears. Me and Cooter jammed our ears up tight.

Cooter said, "So how many times I gotta ring it?"

I said, "What?"

Cooter yelled, "How many times I gotta ring it?"

Multiplying something by twenty's easy, you just double it then add on a zero. I said, "Five doubled equals ten, then adding a zero to ten equals a hundred."

Cooter said, "Eh?"

I told him louder.

Cooter said, "You sure? Don't seem like it should be that much."

I said, "What?"

Cooter said, "A hundred sound like way too much rings."

I spread and closed my fingers ten times and said, "Nope. Look. Ten, twenty, thirty, forty, fifty, sixty, seventy, eighty, ninety, one hundred."

Cooter said, "I guess that's right, but it sure do seem like a lot."

"Eh?"

Cooter yelled, "You's better 'n me at sums so I'm-a listen to you."

He jumped up to pull the rope and get the bell ringing. Since he was the one who was doing the ringing, I had to do the counting so whoever was listening would know how many people got free.

Dong!

I yelled, "One!"

The first ring was always the weakest. It waren't till about five or six rings that the bell got tolling real good.

DONG!DONG!DONG!

"Two, three, four . . ."

It waren't long afore we got to ninety-six.

DONG!DONG!DONG!DONG!

". . . ninety-seven, ninety-eight, ninety-nine, one hundred!"

By the time me and Cooter were done, there were already some people standing outside the schoolhouse waiting to welcome the people that Pa was walking in.

Miss Carolina, Mr. Waller, Miss Duncan-the-first and her sister, Miss Duncan-the-second, and Mr. Polite all said, "Morning, Cooter. Morning Eli."

Cooter said, "Pardon me?"

Mr. Polite said, "I told you, 'Morning.'"

I said, "'Scuse me, sir?"

Mr. Polite yelled, "If you two cabbage-heads don't take that cotton out your ears, I don't know what I'm-a do to y'all!"

Me and Cooter pulled the cotton out.

Miss Carolina said, "How many folks was that, Elijah? Nine? Ten?"

"No, ma'am, there's just five of 'em, a man, a woman, a girl, a boy, and a sick baby."

Mr. Polite said, "Only five? You sure you done your counting right, boy? Much as y'all runged that bell, I's expecting to come down here and see that half of Tennessee done got away."

"No, sir, that was only a hundred times for five people."

Cooter said, "I told him that, I told him it seemed like a hundred was too much for just five people."

I said, "But it ain't! Five times twenty equals one hundred."

I started spreading my fingers to count it off again but afore I could even get to forty, Pa and the new-free folks turned up the road heading toward the schoolhouse. Emma Collins and the little girl were each holding on to one of the arms of that blanged Birdy doll swinging it twixt 'em to and fro.

Pa said, "Morning, y'all. This here's the Taylors, just come up from Arkansas. Been hearing 'bout us for the longest. The baby gunn need some tending."

It was okay to rush up on 'em now that Pa and Emma had settled 'em down some. Everybody quit fussing with me and went right up to where Pa and the new people were standing.

Folks that had been farther out whilst we runged the bell started showing up. Ma and Mrs. Guest came in too.

The new people were looking lost and confused and shy, so many of us came up on 'em and patted 'em on the back and shooked their hands and welcomed 'em to Buxton. Mrs. Guest took the woman and her baby to the infirmary. Ma looked at the boy and pulled him away. I knowed the next time I saw him he'd be smelling like powder and wearing a old pair of my britches. I knowed that even with that it was gonna be a while afore he waren't walking stiff-legged.

Then things got real confusing 'cause 'stead of greeting the people and making 'em feel comforted the way it happens most times, Miss Duncan-the-first started up asking questions.

She held Emma's new friend's face in her hand and said to her sister, Miss Duncan-the-second, "Dot, I know you waren't but eight and it been fifteen years, but who this child bring to mind?"

Miss Duncan-the-second studied the little girl then said, "She don't look like no one I know. Who you talking 'bout?"

Miss Duncan-the-first said, "How old is you, girl?"

The little girl pulled Birdy's arm away from Emma and hugged back up on her father. The man said, "Don't be shy, Lucille. She ain't but six, she little for her age. Who she favour?"

Miss Duncan-the-first said to the man, "What your woman name be?"

The man said, "Liza, Liza Taylor, ma'am."

Miss Duncan-the-first said, "Y'all married?"

"Yes, ma'am. Seven years."

"What her name afore she got married?"

"She was a Jones, ma'am."

"Where 'bouts she from?"

"Fort Smith, Arkansas, ma'am."

"She born there?"

"Yes, ma'am."

"Who her mama?"

"She never knowed her, ma'am."

"Who raise her?"

"Her aunty."

"Her aunty by birth?"

"Yes, ma'am."

"Her aunty ain't told her who her mama is?"

"No, ma'am."

Miss Duncan-the-second said, "How come she ain't told her?"

Mr. Taylor looked at the women and frowned. He looked like he was fixing to say something, but Miss Duncan-the-first jumped in and said, "What she know 'bout North Caroliney?"

"She don't know nothing 'bout it, least she ain't never said nothing."

Miss Duncan-the-second looked back at the little girl and all the sudden slapped both her hands over her ears, her mouth jumped open and she 'peared to be dumbstruck.

Miss Duncan-the-first said, "Sir, judging by the look of your daughter, I knows your wife, I swear I do. But her name be Alice, not Liza."

Miss Duncan-the-second looked stupid-fied. She pulled her hands off of her ears and whispered, "Naw, it caint be, that woman look too old. Alice ain't no more than twenty-six by now."

Mr. Taylor said, "Naw, ma'am, you's mistaken. We ain't 'xactly sure how old Liza be. She got five children elsewhere and the oldest one 'bout fourteen years old. Liza's somewhere twixt thirty-five and forty near as we can figure. But she ain't no young woman, she caint be no twenty-six."

Miss Duncan-the-first said to Mr. Taylor, "She *is* that

young! She done birth — Emma, how much do five and three come to?"

Emma said, "Five plus three equals eight, Miss Duncan-the-first."

Miss Duncan-the-first said, "She done birth eight children since she waren't nothing but a baby herself. That's why she be looking that old."

She said to Mr. Taylor, "She got a scar like a sliver of the moon on her left shoulder what run over and down on her chest." It waren't a question.

Mr. Taylor sucked in air and stared hard. He pulled his daughter to him and said, "What you know 'bout that?"

"She got burnt when she pull a frying pan down on herself when she waren't but four years old. Her real name be Alice Duncan, she born in Ajax County, North Carolina. Her and our brother, Caleb, got sold away fifteen years pass. Your wife's our baby sister. Do she know where Caleb at?"

"No, ma'am, far as we knowed, she ain't got no kin but her aunty. This gunn come as a mighty shock to her."

Then things got real, real confusing, 'cause 'stead of Miss Duncan-the-first screaming "Hallelujah!" or "Praise be!" or something else full of joyfulness that you'd think she'd scream, she said, "Please, sir, don't say nothing 'bout this to her till we's had some time to think on how we gunn let her know. She gone through enough without being burdened with this."

He said, "Thank you, ma'am, I's thinking the same thing. This just gunn be a disturbing that she don't need right now."

This was another one of those confusions that got me wondering if I'd ever have sense enough to be growned. 'Bout the only thing I could say for sure is that being growned *don't* make a whole lot of sense. Maybe that's why it takes so long for you to grow up, maybe enough time's gotta go by for all the sense to get worned right out of you.

If it was me that just got freed out of America and ran all those miles and ended up finding one of my sisters, I'd've been so happy I'd have busted, but not the growned folks. Whilst Miss Duncan-the-first had been asking Mr. Taylor all those questions, it seemed like every growned-up that was listening had their face getting longer and longer and their foreheads getting more and more wrinkled.

I could understand part of the reason. Pa's always telling me how being in America is unbelievable hard for slaves. He says it seems don't no one get out of America without paying some terrible cost, without having something bad done permanent to 'em, without having something cut off of 'em or burnt into 'em or et up inside of 'em.

Maybe that's why when growned folks see someone who's long-lost, they don't get riled 'bout it much as a young person would. Maybe it ain't nothing but being afeared they're gonna have to hear about all the bad things the person they loved had went through whilst knowing there waren't nothing they could do 'bout it. Maybe all the sad things 'neath the scars and burns and the pieces that were missing off of their kin were stories best not looked at too hard.

This thinking like a growned person was starting to be sensical.

Doggone-it-all.

→ CHAPTER 13 ←

Mail from America

One of my favouritest chores is going to Chatham to check on the mail. It's not something that happens regular 'cause we have our own post office here in Buxton, but every once in the while the mail won't come for two or three weeks and someone's got to go find out why. It's one of my favouritest chores, but that's only true if I'm allowed to take Old Flapjack 'stead of one of the saddle horses. Even when those horses are walking slow they're still too fast for my taste.

On Wednesday, right after school, Pa told me to go straight to Chatham for the mail. He didn't come right out and say to take a horse, so when I got to the stable I asked Mr. Segee for Old Flapjack. I knowed it waren't right, but it didn't seem like it was wrong neither, it was kind of middling twixt the two.

Me and Old Flapjack waren't but two miles out of Buxton going slow and easy toward Chatham when I started wishing I shied away from the wrong and gone more to the right. Old Flap gave one n'em snorts that let me know he sensed something dangerous. He even kicked his front heels off the ground 'stead of his rear ones, something I didn't know he could do!

I grabbed ahold of his mane and looked hard at the woods.

I couldn't see nothing at first. Maybe Old Flap had smelt something wrong. Then, for the second time, he did the trick he'd just learnt. The first time was practice, now he was better at it. He throwed his front heels up so high that I slid right off his haunches. Me and my tote sack and the empty mailbag spilt out onto the road!

I didn't hurt nothing, but soon's I jumped back up, Flapjack did another trick I hadn't never seen him do afore. He started running! It was real stiff-legged and clumsity-looking, but no other word but *running* would come to mind.

Ain't nothing in the world more disturbing than watching your mule, who you thought was one of your best friends, try to gallop away after dumping you in the road so's you could get et by whatever it was that got him so afeared.

I grabbed my tote sack and pulled three chunking stones out. I turned to the woods ready to throw. But waren't nothing there. Whatever scared Old Flapjack must've took off soon's I hit the dirt.

I looked a little farther down the road and saw Old Flapjack had decided he waren't too fond of running. He'd quit and gone over in a field to chew on something. I ran to him, gentled him down some, then climbed back on top. We started back toward Chatham.

But this was a trip that waren't meant to be. 'Twaren't but five minutes later that Mr. Polite came out of the woods holding on to the necks of three pheasants and a shotgun.

"Afternoon, Mr. Polite."

"Afternoon, Elijah. Where 'bouts you heading?"

"I'm going to Chatham."

"What for?"

"To check on the mail, sir."

"Not on that worthless mule, you ain't. You head right on back to that stable and tell Clarence Segee to give you Conqueror or Jingle Boy. I been 'specting a package from Toronto and I needs to have it afore the twentieth century gets here."

"Yes, sir."

I turned Old Flapjack back toward Buxton to trade him for one of those doggone horses.

When me and Jingle Boy got to Chatham we went right to their post office. I tied the horse out front, waited for my insides to quit shaking, then stepped onto the stoop. I pulled on the doorknob and near 'bout jerked my shoulder out. The door was locked, which was mighty peculiar 'cause it couldn't've been much past four o'clock. It waren't till then that I saw the sign someone stuck up in the window:

CLOSED UNTIL THE FIFTH. ANY ENQUIRERYS SEE GEORGE AT THE DRY GOODS STORE.

I went next door to MacMahon's Dry Goods.

The place had a great smell. It was fresh-cured leather and new material mixed up with fancy powder and soap. When you opened the screen door a bell runged to let people know you were there. It runged again when you left so's folks knowed you were gone.

The white man that was folding up sheets of cloth for women's dresses behind a counter looked up at me.

"Why, hello, Elijah. How're you?"

"Fine, thank you, Mr. MacMahon."

"And what can I do for you today, laddy?"

I'd learnt a long time ago that Mr. MacMahon didn't mean nothing bad when he called you laddy. It sure sounded like he was mispronouncing *lady* but we'd got told to ignore it.

"I'm here 'bout our mail, sir. The sign said come talk to you."

Leastways that's what I hoped it said. *Enquirerys* was one n'em words that I ain't got notion the first about.

"Oh. I was wondering when someone from Buxton would come. Then you haven't heard what happened?"

"No, sir."

"Well, laddy, we've had to find a new postman. Larry Butler had an absolutely terrible accident."

When Mr. MacMahon said words like *terrible* he made it sound like they had seven or eight Rs in 'em 'stead of just one.

"What happened, sir?"

"As near as we can figure, his horse threw him and trampled him. Hoof caught him right in the head."

This was more proof that a mule is way better than a horse. If Mr. Butler had been riding Old Flapjack, he'd still be delivering mail.

Mr. MacMahon said, "Give me one more minute, Elijah. I know there's a package in the post office and perhaps a letter or two. Not much."

"Yes, sir."

He finished folding the cloth and picked up his crutches to take me back to the post office.

A long time ago Mr. MacMahon had a bad run-in with a horse hisself. That's why his right leg ended at his knee 'stead of at his foot.

When he was on his crutches he moved real graceful and smooth. He'd been without that leg for so long that it looked like the crutches were a part of his body. It almost looked like he was dancing when he walked.

When we got inside the post office Mr. MacMahon hefted a box onto the shelf then looked in a mailbag that had BUXTON writ 'cross the front.

"Hmm, seems to be only one package and one letter, Elijah. I could have swore there was more."

He handed me the letter.

"Thank you, sir."

"Someone's going to have to come pick up the mail until the fifth. The new man should be up and running by then."

"Yes, sir. Tell Mr. Butler I'm sorry 'bout his accident."

"Thanks for the kind words, laddy. Wouldn't matter much what we told him, his mind isn't amongst us anymore."

Mr. MacMahon danced to the door then locked up behind us. He went over to Jingle Boy and patted him on the neck. "Most beautiful horse I've ever seen, Elijah. Hard to believe he's so fast."

"He is, sir."

I lifted the box onto the saddle then jumped up myself. What with seeing all the damage horses had done in

Chatham and being natural nervous 'bout being up this high, I didn't look to see who the letter was to until we were halfway back to Buxton.

My heart sunked when I saw what was writ 'cross the front in proper letters: MRS. EMELINE HOLTON, NEGRO SETTLEMENT AT RALEIGH, CANADA WEST.

On the back, above the red wax seal, it said: APPLEWOOD, FAIRFAX COUNTY, VIRGINIA, UNITED STATES.

This was trouble. Didn't nothing good ever come out of one of these letters from America. If the words on the envelope were writ in regular old plain letters that looked like someone had fought hard and long to get the writing down, most times it meant that some person who was a slave had snucked it out and it was full of rotten news. It was gonna tell 'bout a father getting sick or a brother getting whupped bad or a mother's children getting sold away. If the letter was writ fancy, like this one was, with swirlingness and curlycues and such nonsense it only meant one thing: A friendly white person was writing to let you know somebody was dead.

Since this letter was addressed to Mrs. Holton, it probably had some bad news 'bout her husband.

My ride back from Chatham weren't a good one. It weren't that the road had gone bad or the skeeters were heavier than they were afore or that Jingle Boy was bouncing more than regular, but the fancy writ envelope in the pouch made the ride home long and sad.

I left Mr. Polite's package on his stoop then took Jingle Boy back to Mr. Segee. 'Stead of taking the letter di-rect to Mrs. Holton, I walked back home with it to see what Ma was gonna say.

I pulled my brogans off and went in through the front door.

"Ma?"

She waren't in the parlour.

"Ma?"

Nor upstairs in her bedroom.

"Ma?"

Nor my bedroom.

"Ma?"

Nor the kitchen.

There was one of her peach pies on the kitchen table cooling and I thought for a second 'bout lifting a piece of the crust and digging a couple peaches out of it with my finger. Then I thought better of it.

I pulled my socks off and went out the back door. Ma was squatted down tending to her truck patch.

She saw me and smiled and was just 'bout to say hello.

Mas are some amazing and scary people. Seems like

they got ways of seeing things that ain't showing, and hearing things that ain't being said. I didn't even open my mouth but Ma knowed by some mystery way that something waren't right. She quick stood up and said, "'Lijah? What's wrong?"

The trowel she'd been using and a fistful of weeds fell out of her hand.

"What happened?"

She ran up to me and I showed her the letter from America.

She wiped her hands on her coveralls and said, "You see I ain't got my spectacles on. Who it to, who it from?"

All the growned folks that hadn't never learnt to read nor write whilst they were 'slaved in America had to take lessons at the schoolhouse at night. Between cooking and cleaning and gardening and sewing and knitting and working the fields at harvesttime and helping out at the chopping bees and the raising bees and tending to her sheep and shearing 'em and gathering wool and carding it and spinning it, Ma had been lazy and was slacking off on her school lessons and they waren't sticking particular good.

I told her what was writ on the envelope and she said, "Awww, no. No, no, no. Don't it never end?"

Ma didn't waste no time, she said, "Go get your Sunday clothes on, 'Lijah. We gunn go together to tell her."

I knowed I was gonna have to read the letter out loud

to Mrs. Holton too. She was taking lessons with Ma, and I don't mean no disrespect to Mr. Travis, but it 'peared he was having a powerful bad time in making his lessons stick with any of the growned folks.

I changed to my Sabbath school clothes and walked into the parlour. Ma had already put on her Sunday dress and was carrying that pie she'd baked.

She said, "Good thing I baked this here pie. I hate to go for something like this barehand."

She set the pie down and opened her arms.

I walked in and she kissed the top of my head and mashed her cheek there.

Her voice and the warmness from her face both spread 'cross the top of my head. "Now, 'Lijah, you knows you most likely gunn be breaking some bad news to Mrs. Holton so don't forget, I'm-a need you to be strong. I'm-a need you not to rile her and n'em girls up none by crying and carrying on, sweetie. And I'm-a 'specially need you not to go tearing out of Mrs. Holton's home screaming if this here *is* bad news. Can you do it?"

I know it ain't a child's place to feel this way 'bout the person that raised you, but I was disappointed in Ma something awful. She hadn't took no notice that I'd been doing a lot of growing in the pass couple of weeks.

'Twaren't but the other day I was eavesdropping and heard her tell Pa that it's a miracle I waren't born in slavery

190

'cause I'm way too fra-gile to have survived even a minute of it. Maybe I use to be a little fra-gile, but I ain't been afeared of nonsense nor run off screaming 'bout the littlest things for the longest time. And besides, it just ain't right to be calling somebody fra-gile nohow.

"Can I count on you to be growned, 'Lijah?"

"Yes, ma'am." It was gonna be hard, though. Don't nothing seem to make you want to tear up and cry more than being told not to. I was even starting to feel something loosening up and slopping 'round in my nose.

Ma kissed the top of my head again and turned me a-loose.

We started out toward Mrs. Holton's place.

Miss Duncan-the-first and Miss Duncan-the-second were tending their flower garden out front of their home.

Miss Duncan-the-first saw us and stood up and called, "Sarah? What's wrong? What happened?"

Miss Duncan-the-second stood up too. She said, "Sarah?"

Ma told 'em, "'Lijah done pick up a letter for Mrs. Holton, it come from down home."

Both the women wiped their hands on their skirts, and Miss Duncan-the-second said, "Hold on, we's coming with you. That poor, poor thing."

By the time we got to Mrs. Holton's home, what started out with me and Ma and a letter had turned into a whole parade of people. There were twelve of us: me, three babies, and eight women that were all carrying something to eat. There were pies and corn bread and chicken livers and ham and dandelion greens and grits.

There waren't a whole lot of talking going on as we walked to Mrs. Holton's.

When we got there Ma pushed me forward onto the stoop to knock. There waren't nothing but a screen door to keep horseflies out. The main door was open and I could look right into the parlour.

I knocked and Penelope and Cicely, Mrs. Holton's girls, looked up at me from where they were playing on the floor. They smiled when they saw it was me.

Mrs. Holton got up out of her chair. She was holding the same reading primer that I'd studied from five years pass.

She smiled at me and said, "Why, 'lo, Elijah. Mr. Leroy ain't working yet. My goodness, how come you's in your Sunday . . ."

She opened the door and her breathing got stuck in her throat for a minute when she saw the bunch on her stoop. She said, "Oh! Oh."

The primer slipped out from her fingers and landed on the stoop's wood floor. I handed it back to her.

She smiled at everyone and said, "Welcome. Y'all come on in."

We all pulled off our shoes and walked in.

She had her parlour set up just as nice as our'n. There was a table and a rocking chair and a bench and a big brick fireplace and maplewood floors and rugs.

She said, "I'm sorry there ain't enough chairs, but please make you'selves comforted best way y'all can."

She turned to her two children and told 'em, "Y'all go on in the garden and pick Mama some flowers. Make sure you bring me some them pretty purple and white ones."

The oldest girl said, "But, Ma, you said they ain't ready to be picked yet."

Mrs. Holton said, "I think they's ready now, Penelope."

Penelope said, "Good afternoon, y'all," then asked her mother, "Why're all these folks visiting us?"

Mrs. Holton said, "Ain't nothing to worry 'bout, darling. Now do as I say. Stay till I calls you, and don't leave the yard." She gave both of the girls a hug and a kiss.

Penelope held on to Cicely's hand and took her out through the front door.

"Can I offer y'all something?"

Ma said, "Thank you kindly, Sister Holton, but 'Lijah done pick up a letter for you in Chatham. It from down home."

Mrs. Holton told me, "Elijah, could you read it for me?" She waved the primer she was studying from. "I ain't too far 'long in my lessons."

Miss Duncan-the-first put her hand on the rocking chair and said, "Why don't you get off your feet, Sister Holton?"

"I'm fine, Miss Duncan. Really I am, but thank you kindly. Elijah?"

I started opening the letter but afore I could get my finger in it and bust the wax seal open she said, "If you don't mind, Elijah, I wants to open it."

"I don't mind atall, ma'am."

She picked the wax off the envelope and put it in the front pocket of her apron. She pulled the letter out. She looked it over then handed it back to me.

I said, "It was writ 'bout a year ago, Mrs. Holton." I looked the letter over and knowed I was gonna have to sound some of the words out. I read:

My Dearest Emeline,
    I'm hoping that this letter finds you and the children in good health. We hear many wonderful things about the Negro settlement there and are grateful that God in his infinite mercy and wisdom has seen fit to provide you and yours a refuge.

Mrs. Holton stopped me. I was afeared she was upset 'cause I stumbled on some of the words, but that waren't it atall. She looked the envelope over and said, "I believe this here's Miss Poole's handwriting. She *do* like prettying up what she say. You gunn have to tell me what some them words is, Elijah. What *refuge* mean?"

I knowed that from Sabbath school.

I said, "*Refuge* means it's somewhere that's safe."

She nodded her head.

I started back up reading:

> However I'm afraid this missive
> is not one of glad tidings. I'm afraid
> I have some tragic news I must tell
> you.

I stopped to see if Mrs. Holton needed any more explaining but she didn't. I was glad 'cause I didn't have notion the first what *mis-sive* meant.

> After a harsh forced journey
> to Applewood, John was brought
> back into servitude. Much to our
> horror, to set an example and in
> retaliation for the gold he claims

John stole, Mr. Tillman exacted a punishment so severe that due to the rigors of the march home, John's body could not endure and he went to the loving arms of our Savior on the seventh day of the fifth month in the year of our Lord eighteen hundred and fifty-nine.

He is resting peacefully in the slave burial grounds and we made certain he had a Christian service and paid fifteen dollars for a marked grave.

I am sorry to have to burden you with such news. You and the children are in our prayers. If you are so disposed to remunerate me for this expense, please forward the money to me at Applewood.

Sincerely,
Mrs. Jacob Poole

Mrs. Holton stood there. It didn't seem like none of those eight women looked di-rect in her face but I knowed they all were ready to jump in case she had a fainting spell or went fra-gile.

But Mrs. Holton didn't flinch or nothing. She said to me, "Read that part again, please, Elijah, that part 'bout John getting punished."

I cleared my throat and read, "'Mr. Tillman ex-act-ed a punishment so severe that due to the rig-ors of the march home, John's body could not endure.'"

She raised her hand. I got ready to tell her that I was middling good at reading words but lots of times I didn't know what they meant, but she shooked her head back and forth and said, "'His body could not endure.' That sure 'nough is a gentle way of putting it when one man done killed another one with a whip."

Mrs. Holton smiled at the women and said, "Thank y'all kindly for your care, but I'm-a be all right. I knowed. I knowed already.

"I been left kind of hanging since we got here but now . . . All I hopes is that he felt we got through. Spite of what Miss Poole say, that'd be the only thing what would make John rest peaceful. I hope he felt the joy and love y'all done give us this pass year."

She gave a little snuffle and I thought for sure she was fixing to cry, but she just said, "I hope he knowed how beau-tiful his girls look when they free."

Mrs. Holton sat down in the rocker and said, "He wouldn't've wanted no heavy mourning and I love him 'nough to honour that, so I'm-a be all right."

The women started in with touching Mrs. Holton and saying a lot of "sorry" and "here to help" and "call on me."

Mrs. Holton touched each of their hands and said, "Y'all forgive me, y'all been kind enough to bring all this food and here I am acting like I ain't got no manners atall. Please, let's us eat."

She stood up and went to the kitchen.

She called her children in and we all started eating.

When it came time to go, me and Ma hung back till everyone else had left. Once they'd got to talking, Ma and Mrs. Holton found out they were both from the same state down in America and the plantations they were trapped on were a couple of miles one from the 'nother. They could even call the names of some of the same people from back there. But it was all white people 'cause the people who were slaves waren't allowed to go from place to place.

We were on the front stoop and I was pulling my brogans on. Ma and Mrs. Holton hugged, and Ma said, "Sister Emeline, please, if you find you'self needing anything, come see me or send word through Eli or Leroy."

Mrs. Holton said, "Thank you, Sister Sarah. Small world, ain't it? It sure is comforting to know we's from the same place. I'm-a be all right. I's just relieved to know what happened, that's all. Ain't too much harder nor more wearying to keep up than false hopes, and I'm glad they gone. Only thing is, I caint get them words Miss Poole wrote out my head. 'His body could not endure.' It don't seem to be right. It don't seem like them should be the last words spoke 'bout John Holton."

Ma said, "Well, the body don't never endure, do it? But I hopes . . . naw, I *knows* that something inside all of us be so strong it *caint* be stopped. It fly on forever."

Mrs. Holton said, "Sister Sarah, your words been a big comfort to me, and you and all the other Buxton sisters been a big help. Thank you kindly. And thank you kindly, Elijah, for reading this letter. Me and your ma is gunn be doing that on our own 'fore too much longer."

Ma laughed and said, "You got more faith than me, Emeline. This reading and writing seem to be two them things what don't come easy once you's full growned. Ain't nothing to do but struggle on, though."

Whilst me and Ma were walking home I was 'bout to bust waiting on her to tell me how I did. You caint never be sure till you get the word from someone that's growned, but I was thinking what I just did was a pretty good sign that my days of being fra-gile were over! I hadn't cried nor let my voice get shake-ity nor even sniffled whilst I was reading the letter to Mrs. Holton.

I waren't gonna tell Ma, but I didn't think it was being

growned that got me through it. Mostly I think I didn't bawl 'cause once Ma and them women bunched up 'round Mrs. Holton with their watching, waiting eyes and hands, it felt like a whole slew of soldiers was ringing that parlour with swords drawed and waren't no sorrow so powerful it could bust through.

Once them women bunched up like that in Mrs. Holton's parlour, it seemed like they'd built a wall of Jericho 'round us, and a hundred Joshuas and a thousand children couldn't've knocked the wall down if they'd blowed trumpets and shouted till their throats bust.

Once them women bunched up in that parlour 'round me and Mrs. Holton, I couldn't've cried even if I was fragile as Emma Collins.

But I was hoping Ma would peg it on me being growned.

We were near 'bout home afore she wrapped her arm 'round my neck and pulled me in to her and said, "'Lijah Freeman, I knowed you could do it, baby! What you done was real growned, son! Wait till I tell your daddy!"

I felt so proud I was afeared I'd bust, but all that happened was that same stuff in my nose commenced to loosening up and slopping 'round all over again!

And that don't make no sense. That don't make no sense atall.

→ Chapter 14 ←

Picnic at Lake Erie!

Mr. Travis, when he's being our Sabbath school teacher, says the Lord rested on Sunday and commanded us to do the same. But, doggone-it-all, that's one lesson that ain't sticking too good with him and all the other growned folks 'cause half of every Sunday ain't spent resting, it's spent in church. And whilst Ma and Pa say church ain't work, some of the time if I had my druthers, I'd druther clean five stables and dig two miles of drainage ditch and clear three acres of woodland than sit through a whole morning and afternoon of church.

There were only two reasons that this Sunday was 'bout halfway tolerable. I ain't trying to show no disrespect, 'cause everyone in Buxton says he's either the best or the second-best white man God created, but the first reason was 'cause Reverend King was still away in England and Mr. Travis was preaching 'stead of him. Whilst I ain't disagreeing that Reverend King's a mighty good man, after all he is the one that started the Settlement, I am saying his sermons go on so long that some of the time you feel like begging, "Take me now, Jesus," 'bout halfway through 'em.

The second reason this Sunday's church was middling tolerable was 'cause right after services Ma and Pa had arranged with Mr. Segee to borrow the buckboard and one of the plow horses to carry a bunch of us children and Mrs. Holton down to Lake Erie for a picnic.

Mr. Travis gave the final "Amen," which was 'bout the only one that me and Cooter could put any enthusiasm into, and folks walked out and shooked Mr. Travis's hand at the front door, where he stood to ambush everyone.

I held back, not wanting to go through the door at the same time as Ma and Pa. Seeing us together like that seemed to be one of the main things that got Mr. Travis confused 'bout if he's your regular school teacher or your Sabbath school teacher. Afore you knowed it, he's forgot he's supposed to be resting on Sunday and starts in telling Ma and Pa 'bout how bad you're doing in Latin.

Me, Cooter, Emma Collins, and Philip Wise were the last ones out of the church.

When we got to where Mr. Travis was blocking the door, me and Cooter lied at the same time, "Very good sermon today, sir."

Mr. Travis raised his eyebrow and said, "Mr. Bixby, Mr. Freeman, *in vestra Latina maxime laborate.*"

Uh-oh. I didn't have notion the first what that meant. Seemed like he was thanking us for lying 'bout his sermon.

I said, "You're welcome, sir."

Cooter said, "You're very welcome. We really mean it."

Emma Collins coughed out a little laugh and I knowed right away we'd messed up.

We waren't even off the steps good when she said, "He told you two you need to work harder in Latin. He didn't say anything that you should answer with 'you're welcome.'"

I didn't say a word to her, I gave her my best look of pity. This waren't nothing but more of the sin of envy chawing away at Emma Collins's heart. And the sad thing was, she let it happen right in front of the church.

Pa had the buckboard and Shirl, the biggest plow horse, waiting on the road. Him and Ma and Mrs. Holton were sitting on the bench, and Penelope and Cicely and Sidney Prince were sitting in the bed. Me and Cooter and Emma greeted everyone then climbed in.

'Stead of dangling my feet off the back or the side of the buckboard, I always lean right 'gainst the middle of the bench. Not just 'cause that's where not a whole lot of bouncing goes on, but also 'cause it's a good place to be if you're interested in being right in the middle of some good eavesdropping. The land all the way from Buxton six miles south to Lake Erie belonged to the Settlement, so the ride was gonna be sort of long.

Something 'bout being in the back of the buckboard makes children forget the growned folks are a couple feet away from 'em and lots of things that shouldn't be told get said. But the same thing happens with the growned folks. They'll start in talking 'bout something and you caint believe your ears! After 'while, it comes to you that they clean forgot that there were young folks right behind 'em and things get said you ain't looking to hear. Some of the time you end up coughing or clearing flum out of your throat to let 'em know you're there, but some of the time you find out a lot of things they'd never come right out and tell you.

On this Sunday, waren't much good conversating coming from the front nor the back of the buckboard. The children decided we were gonna play abolitionists and slavers when we got to the beach and were arguing 'bout which one each of us would be. Didn't no one want to be a slaver 'cause we always ended up killing 'em. That meant we had to draw straws to see who was gonna be what. I ended up being a abolitionist and Cooter was a slave. Up front the conversating waren't interesting neither. Seemed like they waren't gonna talk 'bout nothing but crops and rain and which person got damaged by which horse.

'Twaren't long afore the clop of Shirl's hoofs and the

rocking of the buckboard and the noonday sun and Pa humming low all came together to make my head start feeling heavy and dozy. I knowed I was napping in and out 'cause one time I'd open my eyes and Emma and n'em were playing with dolls, then the next time they were all singing, then next time my eyes came up everyone was getting antsy 'cause we started to smell the lake and that meant we waren't no more'n a mile away.

Pa was still humming and Ma and Mrs. Holton were starting in on something the growned folks don't like talking 'bout much in front of us, 'bout the times they were slaves.

I'd heard Ma's story afore so I didn't have to look at her to know what she was doing as she talked. She'd keep her eyes closed and her left hand would start moving like it came alive and was acting on its own. Her fingers would commence sliding back and forth twixt her left ear and her mouth like they were tracing over a invisible welt that got whupped into her. Which was peculiar 'cause when you studied Ma's face real good you saw waren't no scar nor whelp nor mark of any kind. All you could see was Ma's smooth, dark brown skin.

"Emeline," she said, "I knows what you mean! They's got the strangest ways sometimes."

Ma was talking 'bout her own ma and pa, my grand-folks that I never met.

Ma said, "I was just a little older than 'Lijah then. Mrs. Wright surprise us all one day by telling my mama that her and Massa was gonna take me and Missy up north for the summer. Didn't give Mama no warning nor nothing. Mrs. Wright just say to Mama right out the blue that she was taking me. Fifteen minutes later me and Missy loaded up with them on the wagon heading north."

Mrs. Holton said, "They didn't say nothing aforehand 'cause they was afeared your ma woulda run with you."

This was one of the parts you didn't want to hear. It's hard to picture your ma being gave to a little white girl to play with like a pet, but that's what happened. Ma had told me that, back then, when she waren't working in the field, she was tending to this girl name of Missy.

Ma said, "Mama ain't happy 'bout it but what can she do? We s'posed to be gone for three months. I ain't never been away from Mama afore so I's scared to death, kept thinking they waren't never gunn bring me back."

Ma's hand would always quit moving at this part of the story.

"Brung me right up to a little city in Mitch-again called Flint. Massa had a brother what owned a wood mill there and some the time we all go with him down to De-troit. I 'member Mrs. Wright taking us to the river and pointing 'cross and telling Missy, 'That there Canada. That a whole 'nother country fulled up with foreigners.'"

Ma told Mrs. Holton, "I caint tell you how let down I was feeling when I looked over that water at Canada. It didn't look not one part different. Mama and all 'em other folks always saying how Canada's the land of milk and honey, but I caint see one thing different, and it ain't but a half mile off."

Mrs. Holton said, "Ooh, girl, they told us the same thing, the land of milk and honey!"

Ma went on, "Anyway, felt to me like we stayed up in Flint for two whole years, but it was only three months 'fore we start back on home. Took forever! 'Bout a hour outside Flint, Missy start in axing if we was home yet and didn't quit axing for days!

"When we in the wagon and 'bout two mile out from the plantation I starts recognizing where we at and I starts getting antsy as Missy. Mrs. Wright tell me, 'Sarah, quit acting the fool and set still.'

"I says, 'I's sorry, ma'am, I's just 'bout to bust from not seeing my mama!'

"Mrs. Wright tell me, 'Well, you'll see her first thing tomorrow. They's still plenty light and you can work in the barn, and tonight I wants you to stay with Missy. This traveling has her feeling out of sorts.'

"I knows it's back talk but I says, 'Please, ma'am, caint I see my mama for just a minute?'

"You'd-a thought I axed her for the moon. She near

backhand me out that wagon and say, 'You say one more word and I'll keep you hopping for a week.'

"Massa tell her, 'Gwen, let the child go in the field and see her ma. I'm-a give her fifteen minutes.'

"Mrs. Wright say, 'James, you's too soft on your picaninnies. They's gonna be the death of you one day. Mark my word.'"

Mrs. Holton said, "Uh, uh, uh."

Ma said, "I's so happy! After I got Missy to bed I told Mrs. Wright and she look at a clock and say, 'You got fifteen minutes. I'll cane you within a inch of your life if you's one second late.'

"Emeline, I ain't never run so hard in all my life, afore nor since. I seen Mama bent over in the field 'bout a half mile off and I feel like I's flying to get to her."

It was here that Ma's hand would commence rubbing her left cheek again.

Mrs. Holton touched Ma's shoulder.

Ma laughed and said, "Lord, if I'd-a knowed what was 'bout to happen I might not've been so anxious to see her.

"Mama hear me hollering and drop her load and run just as hard out at me. I feels like I's swimming I's looking through so many tears."

Ma's arms wrapped 'round herself.

"Ooh, did she mash me to her!

"She say, 'Chile, chile, chile! I pray every night you was gone that you come back and here you is! Look how much you growned!'

"She kiss me so much I waren't sure if my face was wet from tears or kisses. Then she ax what up north look like. I say, 'Like here 'cept there's more trees, and ain't no tabacky.' Then I throw in I seen Canada. Girl, soon's I say it I knowed by how her body lock up that I done something wrong.

"First thing I'm thinking is that Mrs. Wright done snucked up behind me and hear me say Canada. We get beat if we even say it out loud. But that waren't it.

"Next thing I know, my mama's arm uncoil like a rattling-snake and she smote me down. Hard. She hadn't never touch me afore with nothing but love, but Lord knows 'twaren't no love in that blow."

Mrs. Holton rubbed Ma's back harder.

Ma said, "I quick jumps up too scared and dumbstruck to even cry. All I done was say, 'Mama . . . why?'

"She look at me with eyes I ain't never seen on her afore. She say, 'What kinda fool I done raised? You was close enough to *see* Canada and you standing here afore me now?'

"I says to her, 'But, Mama, if I'd left I might not never see you no more!' She smote me the second time. Then she say, 'You done got took to the gates of Heaven and turned you'self back 'cause you might not never see *me* again? What make you think I wants to see you down here knowing them . . .'"

Ma looked in the back of the buckboard and spelt out, "'them d-a-m things Massa got in store for you? Ain't you got no inkling what he waiting on you to get old enough for? How daft is you that seeing me be worth more than being rid of that?'"

Ma said, "All I could say was, 'But, Mama, I waren't thinking 'bout it like that. All I could think 'bout was seeing . . .'

"Mama snatch me by my collar and hold me so close to her face that I sees fire spitting out her eyes and I smells the food she et for breakfast that morning and I feels spittle from her mouth. She say, 'Girl. If them people ever . . . *ever* take you north again and you don't try reaching Canada, I'm-a make you a promise right here. I swears on all I love that I'll wring your neck myself and won't give it no more thought than if I was wringing the neck of one n'em chickens. 'Cause if they takes you to De-troit ever again and you don't head out for Canada, you ain't got no more right to live than one n'em chickens. You ain't got no more sense than one n'em yard birds what's happy to hang 'round till it they turn to get slaughtered.

If you gets another chance and don't take it . . . or die trying . . . I swear, girl, I'll kill you myself once you get back here.' "

Ma quit moving her hand 'long her jaw and held up three fingers.

"That made three times she smack me 'cross the mouth."

Ma smiled, "I had sense 'nough to stay down after that. Folks come and pull Mama off me. I remember her screaming and crying and cursing me whilst they drag her back to work. I knowed she warcn't lying. 'Twas two years afore they brung me to De-troit again, and I knowed when we was leaving in the wagon and I kissed my mama that I waren't never gonna see her again."

Mrs. Holton kept rubbing Ma's back and said, "Sarah, I'm-a tell you some words a wise woman told me, 'Something inside so strong gunn keep you flying.' "

Ma hugged Mrs. Holton and said, "Oo-wee! I hope you cherish that woman 'cause she sure *do* sound wise!"

They laughed and Mrs. Holton said, "Girl, I do. If only you knowed how much I do. I loves her like a sister."

They stayed hugged up like that till Pa brung the wagon to a stop.

Everyone was starved out from sitting in church all day so we et afore we played abolitionists and slavers.

Folks were still bringing Mrs. Holton food to help in her mourning and she brung lots of it along. Ma had fried some chicken and baked a couple of pies too.

We spread blankets and sat in the sand to eat.

Being close to the water and hearing the lake slapping 'gainst the sand was 'bout the peacefullest thing you could think of. If I hadn't drawed the long straw and got to be a abolitionist I'd-a et and just sat there and dozed, but waren't no way I was gonna give up killing some slavers, even if they were just Penelope and Sidney pretending to be white.

Ma and Mrs. Holton gave us all big servings of good things then Ma carved up some pieces of her peach pie and dropped one on everybody's plate.

'Bout halfway through the meal I saw Pa piling a little hill of sand out of a hole next to where he was sitting on the blanket. I didn't think nothing of it till about five minutes later when he pointed at some gigantic poplar trees and said, "Is that one n'em bald-head eagles?"

Most times those eagles don't come inland far as Buxton so we all looked over at the poplars.

No one saw nothing so Pa said, "I think y'all scared him when you jumped up like that."

I looked at Pa and saw that the hole he'd been digging was gone. He'd pushed all the sand back in it. Then I saw that the piece of Ma's peach pie was gone too.

Pa could tell I put one and one together and knowed

where the pie was at. He leaned in to me and whispered, "Afore we leave, you come back over here, dig it up, then bury it real deep somewhere. It ain't right to leave it halfway buried so's some poor desperate starving wild animal might dig it up and try to di-gest it and suffer a horrible slow death."

I couldn't help laughing. But then Cooter and n'em ran off behind a bluff and he hollered back, "Help! Is there any abolitionist 'round? I'm 'bout to get dragged back to slavery by these here slavers! Help!"

I asked to be excused so's I could run after Cooter and kill me some slavers!

→ CHAPTER 15 ←

Keeping Mr. John Holton Alive

A few days later, after supper, one of Mrs. Mae's twins came banging on the door. I answered.

"Evening, Eli."

"Evening, Eb."

"Mr. Leroy told me to come here and tell you not to go di-rect to Mrs. Holton's land tonight."

This was peculiar. I was supposed to help him again.

"Did he say how come?"

Eb said, "Uh-uh, you know Mr. Leroy, he never has much of anything to say. All he said was to tell you to come by the sawmill first."

"Thank you, Eb. Tell your ma and pa I asked 'bout 'em."

When I got to the sawmill, Mr. Leroy and Mr. Polite were sitting next to a fresh-cut hunk of wood 'bout four foot long and one foot wide.

Mr. Polite said, "Here he be. Evening, Eli."

"Evening, Mr. Polite. Evening, Mr. Leroy."

Mr. Leroy said, "Evening, Elijah. I wants you to look over this here writing 'fore I starts carving it. Mrs. Holton want it to go over her door, and I ain't carving nothing for no one 'less somebody what reads tells me it make sense.

"Folks ax you to carve something, then when you do it like they want and someone reads it to 'em and it ain't nothing but jibber-jabber, they say they ain't gunn pay and I done waste all that time. So see if this here's sensical."

I could tell Mr. Leroy was mighty worked up 'bout this. That was a whole month's worth of talking for him. He handed me a piece of paper that had rough writing and lots of cross-outs on it. I read, "'These words is done so no one won't never forget the loving memory of my husband John Holton what got whip to death and killed on May the seven 1859 just 'cause he want to see what his family look like if they free. He be resting calm knowing his family done got through. The body won't never endure but something inside all of us be so strong it always be flying.'"

I said to Mr. Leroy, "Sir, some of these things *do* need to get changed. How long you gonna let me ponder on this afore I gotta tell you?"

Mr. Polite said, "Ponder? Seem to me if you was really some good at reading and writing you wouldn't need no time to ponder nothing. Just change it up 'cause it ain't ringing right to my ear."

He turned to Mr. Leroy, "I told you, Leroy, we should've got that little Collins gal. That's one bright child there. This boy ain't too far from being daft."

Mr. Leroy said, "Hold on, Henry, the boy say he need some time, I'm-a let him take his time. Mrs. Holton already suffered a lot. She don't need to be suffering no more 'cause of some jibber-jabber what's carved over her door."

I showed Ma and Pa the paper Mrs. Holton had writ and they told me it was a great honour to do this, that I had to do the best job I could.

Pa said, "You gunn have to help her take some the bite out them words, Elijah. Her pain too fresh to be locking it up so hot in writing."

Ma told me, "Poor Mr. Leroy gunn be carving for years to get all that down. But look, baby, some of them words is mine!"

I thought on it for the rest of the week. I filled pages and pages in my notebook, working on just the right words for Mrs. Holton. I thought 'bout it when I was supposed to be studying and when I was supposed to be doing chores. It even creeped up on me and made my rock fishing go real unpleasant for both me and the fish. I only chunked four outta twenty. Worst, I sent two of 'em wobbling back into the water with their brains scrambled like eggs.

After 'bout a week Mr. Leroy's patience ran out and he said, "I'm starting to agree with Henry Polite. Don't seem like changing some words 'round gunn take all this time.

Mrs. Holton been wondering where her sign's at. After your supper, come to the field and have them words ready so's I can get started. And write 'em down clear too."

It killed my appetite but I finally got something writ down just after supper. Afore I gave it to Mr. Leroy, I ran over to Mr. Travis's home so he could see if there were any big mistakes. Mr. Travis changed two words, crossed out three, put in some better punctuating, then said, "Admirable job, Mr. Freeman, admirable job."

Ma and Pa said it seemed pretty good to them, and when I told the words to Mr. Leroy he didn't do nothing but grunt, which was saying a whole lot for him.

It took him a while to carve all the letters in the wood and the day it was finished he showed it to me. It was beautiful!

He said, "She real partial to having things done fancy, don't want nothing plain, so I put some decorating on it."

In the first three corners of her sign he'd carved a tree, a bird, and some waves. In the fourth corner he put the sun and the moon. He even carved a ribbon to go 'round all the words and you'd have swored it was real. Mr. Leroy let me carry it down to Mrs. Holton's so we could put it over her door.

Soon's he drove the first nail into the wood over her door, Mrs. Holton came out to see what the commotion was.

"Good afternoon, Leroy. Good afternoon, Elijah."

Me and Mr. Leroy both said, "Afternoon, ma'am."

Mr. Leroy told her, "I's sorry, Sister Emeline, I had the boy change them words 'round some. It was too long afore."

She stepped outside, looked back up at the sign, and said, "Oh? What it say now?"

I read it to her and she smiled and said, "That's just what I wanted it to say, Elijah. Thank you kindly. And thank you kindly, Mr. Leroy, for doing such a good job. I like the way you put them things in the corners, make it look important!

"Pardon me for a minute." Mrs. Holton went back inside her home. I figured she was getting some money to pay Mr. Leroy, but when she came back she was holding on to a fancy carved box.

She reached into the front of her apron and gave me a whole nickel! She gave me money for coming up with words on a piece a paper!

I squozed it tight in my hand and said, "Thank you, ma'am!"

But even afore I could slide it down in my pocket I could hear what Ma and Pa would say.

I opened my palm and reached the nickel back to Mrs. Holton. I said, "I ain't allowed to take no one's money, ma'am."

She wrapped her hand 'round my fingers so the nickel was folded back up in my fist.

"Elijah, I insists. If you ain't gunn take it I'm-a throw it out in the yard. I'll tell your ma I made you."

That was good enough for me! Ma and Pa would think throwing money away was worst than taking it for doing someone a favour, so I didn't have nothing to worry 'bout!

Then Mrs. Holton looked at Mr. Leroy and said, "Sir. This here's for you."

She reached the wood box at him.

Mr. Leroy wrinkled his forehead for a bit then said, "Sister Emeline, I 'preciate you giving me this here box. It's some fine work. And in light of your loss I'm-a say we's even, but from now on I caint be dealing in nothing but money. Sorry if I'm seeming bold, ma'am, I ain't intending to, but I know with you having someone what was 'slaved down home, you understand."

Mrs. Holton said, "I understand. Here. Open the box."

Mr. Leroy took the box, pulled the lid off, and both him and me sucked in air like we got dunked in a barrel of cold water.

His hands commenced shaking, he busted out in a sweat and looked like his belly was aching him bad. He grabbed ahold of his left arm then whispered, "Mrs. Holton? What this?"

Mrs. Holton said, "It's twenty-two hundred dollars in

gold, Mr. Leroy. It's what I was gunn buy John Holton with. You need it more'n me now."

Mr. Leroy couldn't talk. His legs melted from under him and he ended up in a heap on Mrs. Holton's stoop. He said, "Mrs. Holton, this here'll be my wife and *both* my children. I . . . I . . . I caint turn this down. . . ."

"I ain't 'specting you would."

She walked over to where he fell and he wrapped his arms 'round her legs like a drowning man holding on to a tree in a flood.

He kept on mumbling, "I caint turn it down, I caint turn it down. . . ."

It was something terrible to see. In two shakes of a lamb's tail, all the grownedness I'd been showing lately flewed off like ducks off of a pond and I was a fra-gile boy all over again. Seeing someone strong and tough as Mr. Leroy crying made me feel like everything was turned topsy-turvy.

Next thing you knowed, all three of us were bawling on Mrs. Holton's stoop. She pulled me in to her and we were a doggone pathetic sight.

Mr. Leroy said, "Sister Emeline, I done already save eleven hundred and ninety-two dollars and eighty-five cent. I ain't gunn need all this, but I swear I'm-a pay you back, I swear it. And you ain't never gunn have to worry 'bout no work being done on your land for the rest of your life."

Mr. Leroy didn't even wipe the tears away. He was crying but started smiling at the same time. "You oughta see my oldest, 'Zekial! He was a big strapping boy when I last seen him four years ago and now he be fifteen and must be big as a oak! Me and him both gunn be at your beck and call, ma'am, I swear it! We gunn pay back every cent! Thank you, thank you. . . ."

Mrs. Holton said, "Mr. Leroy, I ain't got no doubt you gunn pay me back, but hearing that Liberty Bell toll when your wife and babies walk into Buxton gunn be near payment enough itself."

She sniffed into the 'kerchief she was holding and said, "Elijah, read what them words is to me one more time."

I'd toiled on 'em so long I didn't even have to look at the sign above Mrs. Holton's door. I swallowed down some of the looseness in my nose and said what was on the sign:

FOR THE LOVE OF MY HUSBAND,
JOHN HOLTON,
WHO PASSED ON MAY 7TH, 1859,
BUT STILL LIVES. THE BODY IS NOT
MADE TO ENDURE.
THERE'S SOMETHING INSIDE SO STRONG
IT FLIES FOREVER.

She said, "That's it, Elijah. Son, you done told the truth."

I think all three of us figured the other two waren't gonna quit bawling till we busted up one from the 'nother. Mrs. Holton was the first to untangle herself from the crying party when her two children saw what was going on and commenced bawling too. She kissed me and Mr. Leroy on our heads then closed her door kind of gentle.

I was next to leave. It was getting late and I didn't want no trouble from Ma, so I left Mr. Leroy sitting on one of the steps with his face pressed down on that box.

I ran all the way home to tell Ma and Pa the good news!

CHAPTER 16

The Preacher Comes Through

The next morning there was a knock on our front door. I heard Pa invite Mr. Leroy in so I went to give him my regards.

"Morning, Pa. Morning, Mr. Leroy."

Both of them said, "Morning, Elijah."

Mr. Leroy was holding his hat in his hand and looking like he'd got dragged through four rat holes. He said to Pa, "Spencer, I got some business I need to talk with you."

Pa said, "'Lijah, 'scuse you'self."

Mr. Leroy said, "No, Spencer, me and 'Lijah's working partners. The boy handles hisself like he's growned so I hope you don't mind if he stay."

If I lived to be fifty I was gonna remember this, the first time I got called growned! I waren't expecting this to happen for six or seven months yet!

Pa said, "Suit you'self, Leroy." He sat in the rocker and pointed at the soft chair for me.

Mr. Leroy said, "I don't know if Elijah told y'all what happened?"

Pa didn't let him know one way or the 'nother. He rocked the chair gentle and said, "What's that, Leroy?"

I sure was proud of Pa right then. It waren't until Mr. Leroy asked him that question that my mind told me in a flash that maybe I shouldn't've told Ma and Pa what happened. Maybe Mr. Leroy would've been 'shamed if I was telling folks he took Mrs. Holton's gold. But Pa didn't let on that I'd run my mouth.

Mr. Leroy said, "Wouldn't 've been no worry to me if he did tell, Spencer. Y'all raised him proper and I know the boy like to talk, but he ain't no gossip. I know there's things what children has to tell their folks."

This being growned was a lot harder than it looked. I couldn't make heads nor tails out of how Pa knowed not to say nothing 'bout me telling and how Mr. Leroy knowed that that was what I was worrying 'bout!

Mr. Leroy said, "Mrs. Holton done lent me 'nough money to buy my wife and children, Spencer."

Pa said, "Leroy, that sure is powerful good news."

Then Mr. Leroy went and ruined all this growned-up talk for me, he said, "Yes, Spencer, I don't know how I can ever . . . how I'm gunn ever . . ." and he commenced bawling again. He covered his face with his hat and sobbed. And I'll be blanged if that didn't set me off.

Pa looked at me and tipped his head toward my bedroom. I left the room and stayed outta sight, but I was still close enough for listening. After all, Mr. Leroy did say I handle myself like I was growned, and I know growned folks don't like nothing better than doing a little eavesdropping.

Pa didn't say a word. I heard the rocking chair squeaking on the floor at the same rhythm it was afore Mr. Leroy commenced crying. Pa just waited till Mr. Leroy got back in his right mind.

After 'while, Mr. Leroy said, "I 'pologize for that, Spencer. I ain't got no sleep all night, seems my mind running five different ways at once. Now that I know my family coming, seems like my mind trying to plague me with every horrible thing what might happen."

Pa said, "No need for no apologies, Leroy. These is trying times for you."

Mr. Leroy's voice was shaking whilst he talked, like he was in the buckboard on a bad road. He said, "I done work day and night for four years. Four years. I didn't reckon on having 'nough money for 'nother two years yet, Spencer. I was gunn buy 'Zekial out first, then him and me working together could buy out my wife and daughter, but Mrs. Holton's money change all that. I ain't ready for this. I don't know who I can get to arrange getting my family out. You still got any dealings with them Underground Railroad folks?"

Pa said, "Leroy, we can get this done. I'm-a talk to some

225

people in Chatham and see what we got to do. Don't you worry, we'll get this done."

Just then I heard the Preacher's voice coming through the screen door. "Spencer? I saw your door was open. Y'all up already?"

Pa jumped out of his chair quick-like and went to the door.

He said, "Morning, Zeph."

Pa walked out onto the stoop and pulled the door shut behind him. I couldn't hear what all they were saying.

After 'while, Mr. Leroy called out, "Spencer, if you don't mind, could you call him on in?"

Pa and the Preacher came into the parlour.

"Why, morning, Leroy. I missed hearing your axe this morning, thought you must have been taking a break today."

Mr. Leroy said, "No, Zephariah, it's a mighty beautiful day. I got the money to buy my family."

The Preacher called out, "Praise Jesus! This *is* a beautiful day! I can see now why you're looking so out of sorts."

Mr. Leroy said, "We was discussing how's the best way to get my family out."

The Preacher said, "What did you decide?"

Pa said, "I know some folks in Chatham what can handle this."

The Preacher said, "Not the Abrams boys?"

Pa said, "Why, yes. They's the ones."

"You must not have heard, Brother Spencer. Their pa took ill over in New York and they moved back there about six months ago."

The Preacher gave a long sigh then said, "I guess the best thing to do is wait on the next people from the Railroad that come through. It's been a while, but I don't imagine it's going to be much longer. Three, four months at the most."

Mr. Leroy must've been thinking just like me, three or four months might as well have been three or four years! I heard the chair he was sitting in scrape on the floor as he jumped out of it.

Mr. Leroy said, "I caint wait that long! There's gotta be a quicker way!"

Pa said, "I don't know, Leroy, this is something you been waiting on a long while. We best give it a little more time so we can do it right."

"But three, four months? Uh-uh! No! That's way too long! I ain't told no one this, and I 'preciate y'all not saying nothing, but I ain't been feeling myself this pass year. Seems I'm ailing all the time and caint shake it. Why, Spencer, I don't know if I got three, four months."

The Preacher laughed and said, "Brother Leroy, you're

just working yourself too hard. You're strong as a mule. No one who was sick could swing an axe the way you do."

Mr. Leroy said, "Zephariah, I caint wait. Maybe if you'd come with me I could go over to America, to Detroit, and talk to some people there. I know they got white folks what help with this."

Pa said, "Leroy, I don't think . . ."

The Preacher said, "Why, you know what? Now that you mention Michigan, I recall there's this little logging village less than an hour outside of Detroit. It's where the white man lives that helped Mrs. Lewis buy her husband down in South Carolina. I know him personally. John Jarvey, he's a mighty good white man."

Mr. Leroy said, "I remember that! 'Bout four years ago! He still there?"

"Leroy, I was there two months ago, had supper at his place. You caught me by surprise, else I would have remembered him right off. He's still making arrangements to buy folks too. Does it himself. Pretends he's buying slaves for his own plantation then spirits them to Michigan!"

Mr. Leroy said, "That's one the things what I been most afeared of. I knowed if Massa Dillon found out it was me what was buying my family, he'd double up the price or wouldn't sell 'em atall. Zephariah, you's a answered prayer!"

The Preacher said, "Naw, Leroy, this is something that's meant to be. The Lord's putting all the pieces together for you here. He's rewarding your good works. He's seeing you get what you deserve."

Pa hadn't said nothing. But soon as I heard the Preacher say the word *deserve* I knowed Pa was gonna be mighty set against this.

According to Pa, *deserve* is another one of those rattling-snake words, words that always get followed by a nasty bite.

Mr. Leroy said, "Zephariah, you think you could get in touch with this here man and make the 'rangements?"

The Preacher said, "Leroy, you know I'm hurt. You think you have to ask me to do this? You think I haven't been considering this very second how I can rearrange some of my business so that I can take care of this matter right away?"

Mr. Leroy said, "No 'fense intended, Zeph. I ain't had no sleep in a while and I'm worried something terrible."

The Preacher said, "I understand. But you do know Mr. Jarvey is going to have expenses, right?"

"How much this here man gunn want, Zeph? How much you gunn need you'self to do it?"

The Preacher said, "Personally I don't want anything. I'd pay to have your family come walking into the Settlement whilst the Liberty Bell rings. And Mr. Jarvey is a sure-enough good white man, he never charges anyone more than what it costs him. I can't say right off, but I'm thinking I should go carrying a hundred dollars or so for his expenses plus whatever it is you need to buy your family."

I knowed just what the Preacher looked like when he all the sudden shouted out, "Praise God, I haven't heard words as beautiful as *buy your family* in years, Brother Leroy!" I knowed he'd raised his arms above his head and was waving 'em at the roof.

Pa still hadn't said nothing, but it was like I could hear him frowning as the talk went more and more.

Mr. Leroy said, "How soon afore we can get this started?"

The Preacher said, "I'm leaving right now to postpone the business I had in Chatham. If you have everything together, I can get going by this very afternoon, early evening at the latest."

Mr. Leroy said, "I got some extra set aside, Zeph. I ain't axing you to do this for nothing."

The screen door opened and the Preacher called back in, "Leroy, I have no intention of profiting from anyone's misery, especially not someone as respected as you. I'm going to see if I can make arrangements with Mr. Segee to borrow a horse. The sooner we get this done, the sooner that Liberty Bell will be tolling!"

I walked back into the parlour and Pa didn't tell me to leave. He started right in on Mr. Leroy.

"Leroy, this here's moving too fast! You got to be careful. That's a lot of money you talking 'bout to buy your family, and money can make folks do some crazy things."

Mr. Leroy said, "Moving too fast? Spencer, I been waiting four years for this, four years! Ain't nothing fast 'bout none of this. Zeph is right, things just don't fall in place like this for no reason atall. There's something behind all this, something what's trying to bring righteousness into it."

Pa said, "I advise caution, Leroy. I ain't trying to bad-mouth no one, but how much we really know 'bout Zephariah? Other than him calling hisself a preacher, I ain't seen nothing really holy 'bout the man. You 'bout to give him five, six years' worth of money. That's a powerful temptation to anyone."

Mr. Leroy said, "Sometimes you just got to have faith, Spencer. Sometimes you got to believe."

Pa said, "I'm talking about what's right in front of our eyes, what we know, not no beliefs. We know Zeph don't live in the Settlement, we know he don't work regular, we know he ain't 'round for long spells of time. He's toting that hundred-dollar pistol what come from God-know-where, we know he's smart as a whip, and we know he's

231

young, real young. There's just too much what we need to ask afore you give him all that money and all that responsibility."

Mr. Leroy said, "I hear you, Spencer, but like I said, sometimes you just got to believe."

Pa said, "This ain't so much 'bout believing, Leroy. This more 'bout you hankering for your family so much that you ain't looking at things clear. I ain't one to beg, but I'm begging you to think on this and not do nothing this fast. Zeph seems to be rushing this *way* too much."

Mr. Leroy said, "I done told you, Spencer, I ain't got no more time."

He looked at me and said, "Elijah, you know Zephariah. Can he be trusted?"

Pa said real quick afore I had a chance to answer, "Leroy, it ain't the boy's place to make no judgment like that. He ain't but eleven years old. He caint look in no one's heart."

Mr. Leroy stood up and said, "Spencer, I done made up my mind. I know you doing what you think is right and I do 'preciate your concern, but I ain't got no other choice."

Pa stood up too, acting like he was gonna block Mr. Leroy's way out of the house.

They looked hard at one the 'nother. My breathing stopped.

Pa finally said, "All right, then. But just let me do one thing, one thing what will help set my mind at ease."

Mr. Leroy said, "Long's it don't delay nothing, I's listening."

Pa said, "All I'm axing is that you don't send Zephariah alone with all that money. Let's get someone else to ride 'longside him, someone we all trust."

Mr. Leroy thought for a second then said, "I don't see no harm in that. Who?"

Pa said, "You nor me caint go. We ain't got no papers and Michigan still crawling with paddy-rollers. But Theodore Highgate's got his manumission papers and his hand ain't all the way healed yet so he ain't doing no heavy working no way. Let's ax him."

Mr. Leroy said, "He a good choice."

Pa opened the screen door and stepped outside to put his shoes on. He said, "You wait here, Leroy. I'm-a be right back. Promise me you ain't gunn do nothing till I get back."

"Hurry back, Spencer. I'm gunn wait."

Pa ran off toward the Highgates' home.

Mr. Leroy sat back down and said to me, "Elijah, maybe your pa's right. Maybe I shouldn't be trusting Zeph like this."

He grabbed both my arms and looked at me hard and

233

said, "You done spent more time with him than near 'bout anyone else. You think he'd thief my money?"

I had to ponder over this. By asking me this growned-folks question, Mr. Leroy was giving me a lot of respect and responsibility so I didn't want to rush into answering him. I didn't want to say nothing wrong so I thought on it hard.

I remembered all the things that the Preacher'd done that didn't seem right. I remembered him jacklegging my fish, I remembered him telling confusing tales to the new-free folks, I remembered him thinking 'bout making me travel with that conjurer, Sir Charles. All those bad things came right to mind. But then I remembered all the good things he'd done too. Like freeing the real MaWee and searching in the woods when those paddy-rollers came and letting everyone in Buxton know I'd been gave gifts from the Lord. So I had to own up that he *did* have a good heart.

What on earth could be worst than stealing money that's supposed to buy someone's kin out of slavery? Sure, I'd seen the Preacher do some bad things, but I didn't think no one could ever do nothing that low-down and rotten.

The Preacher's heart waren't that bad, couldn't no one that knowed how hard Mr. Leroy worked ever do nothing like that to him. Couldn't no one but a demon be that cold-hearted, and even if the Preacher had a whole boatload of things that'd make you wonder, couldn't no one say he waren't a man.

Mr. Leroy gave me a shake and said, "Son? You think that man would thief my money?"

I told him, "No, sir. I don't think the Preacher would never do that. Never."

Mr. Leroy didn't say nothing more. He turned me a-loose and watched out the window.

'Twaren't long afore Pa came busting in. He said, "Theodore say he be honoured to help carry your money to Michigan."

Mr. Leroy and Pa and me shooked hands all 'round.

I heard a horse riding hard and ran out on the stoop.

The Preacher was on Champion and pulled him up out front of our home.

He said, "Brother Leroy still here, Elijah?"

"Yes, sir."

Pa and Mr. Leroy came out on the stoop.

The Preacher said, "Brother Leroy, get the money together and I'll be back as soon as I can. Now that I got this horse it won't take me near as long."

Pa said, "Hold on a minute, Zeph. Theodore Highgate's gunn go to Michigan with you."

I saw a flash in the Preacher's eyes, but he said, "Why, that'd be fine. It's going to slow things down a bit, but that would be just fine."

Mr. Leroy said, "I done thought 'bout it, Zeph, and it be best if both of y'all watches over all that money. Y'all can protect each other's back."

The Preacher jumped off of Champion and said, "Is that all that's worrying you, Leroy? Because if you're nervous about me and that money, I don't care if all of Buxton comes along. I don't want you to have a worry atall about this. I want you to be rested and comforted in your soul about me going."

The Preacher unbuckled his fancy holster. He pulled it off and reached it and his mystery pistol toward Mr. Leroy.

He said, "Here. Now, it doesn't cost near what you're paying for your family, and it's nowhere close to being as dear, but you know how I feel about this pistol. You'll be the first person to touch it since I got it. You know I'm not leaving this behind."

Mr. Leroy said, "It ain't necessary, Zeph. I trust you."

The preacher pushed it into Mr. Leroy's chest and said, "I trust you too. I trust you to hold on to this until I come back with the good word that everything's set to go." The Preacher smiled. "I'm also trusting you not to drop my pistol into any water either."

Mr. Leroy said, "Zeph, I ain't saying I don't 'preciate you doing this, but I'd feel better if you was armed whilst you carried all that money."

The Preacher pulled open his waistcoat and showed Mr. Leroy the old pistol that he'd let me shoot off once and said, "Oh, don't you worry, Brother Leroy. I'd not go into that den of vipers unprepared."

Mr. Leroy said, "In that case, Zeph, hurry on back. I'm-a make sure your pistol don't get near no water."

The Preacher said to Pa, "Tell Brother Theodore I'll be back a bit before noon. Tell him to ask Mr. Segee for a strong horse. We're going to ride hard."

The Preacher jumped back up on Champion and tore down the road toward Chatham.

Pa watched him and said, "I wish it waren't so, but I just ain't feeling good 'bout this."

CHAPTER 17

Bad News from a
Little Village in America

Time don't never go so slow as when you're waiting on someone to bring you news. Word spread 'bout Mr. Leroy being able to buy his family, and whilst him and me worked clearing Mrs. Holton's field, all sorts of folks came up to us and gave him their regards and good wishes.

Mr. Leroy didn't work no slower nor no faster whilst we waited to hear from the Preacher and Mr. Highgate. He just kept plugging away at the trees like he always did, making the same music, stopping every time someone came up only long enough to see if they were gonna tell him something. Once he saw they waren't, he was respectful but went right back at swinging that axe.

After four days crawled by, talk started up 'bout sending someone to that village in Michigan to see if there was a problem. Didn't no one own up to being worried, but everybody was.

On the fifth day after the Preacher and Mr. Highgate left, me and Old Flapjack were rock fishing at our secret lake. I'd just chunked a good-size perch and was pulling

him in when Old Flap gave one n'em snorts meaning someone was near.

I quit concentrating on the perch and raised my head. I
heard Cooter calling my name from far off.

"Cooter! I'm down here!"

He ran up on me and waited a second for his breathing
to catch up to him then said, "They bringing . . . Mr.
Highgate in . . . from Windsor . . . on a wagon!"

"Bringing?"

"Uh-huh. Some folk we . . . don't know . . . from
Windsor got him loaded on a wagon."

"How come he ain't riding Jingle Boy?"

"I don't know, Eli. They say there's a horse tied up
behind the wagon."

"Where's he at now?"

"They said he's 'bout half a hour outside Buxton. But
that was afore I left to come find you."

"What'd they say 'bout Mr. Leroy's family?"

"Didn't no one say nothing. A rider just came by and
brung the news that Mr. Highgate got hurt bad."

I said, "What 'bout . . ."

Cooter read my mind. He said, "They said the Preacher
ain't with him."

My heart sunked! That could only mean someone had
robbed 'em and killed the Preacher or snatched him into
slavery! I knowed I should go find Mr. Leroy and let him

know we got word. But after I thought on it for a second, it came to me that I didn't really have nothing to tell him. Ma's always saying, "Believe some to none of what you hear and only half of what you see." So I didn't think I should run to tell Mr. Leroy some bad news that I waren't sure had really happened.

I told Cooter, "Come on, if we run down the road maybe we can catch the wagon afore they get to Buxton."

Cooter said, "You go 'head on, Eli. I been hightailing all over these woods looking for you. I ain't got no more strength for running."

"All right, you ride Old Flapjack back and I'm-a try to head off that wagon. Gather up my fishing things and you can have two of those bass on the stringer. Take the rest to my ma."

Soon's I broke out of the woods onto the road I saw fresh wagon-wheel marks. They must've already passed. I ran back into the trees to try and cut them off farther on down. Right after I turned the first bend I could hear a wagon ahead, so I ran through the woods to where they were gonna have to pass.

It waren't but a minute later that I saw two horses pulling a big wagon with Jingle Boy tied up behind.

I waved at 'em.

The driver pulled the horses up and said, "You heading to Buxton, son?"

"Yes, sir, but I'm looking for . . ."

A hand gripped on to the stakes of the wagon bed. A man's head peeked over the side and he said, "Elijah? That you?"

I knowed it had to be Mr. Highgate but at first I didn't recognize him.

He said, "It's me, boy."

My heart dropped down into my stomach. It *was* Mr. Highgate and he didn't look nothing like the way he looked when he left five days ago.

I felt my knees get all loose and floppity, like I was gonna fall into a heap right next to the wagon.

The driver reached down and pulled me up on the seat next to him.

I looked back at Mr. Highgate.

His left eye was open but the right one was swole shut. There was a line running clean 'cross his forehead that was so straight it looked like someone had took a measuring stick then cut along it with a knife. The cut had gone bad and was bandaged up but it still was leaking something from the sides.

Mr. Highgate was kind of choking as he talked. He said, "He done shot me. He done shot me."

He waren't saying it all riled up and worried or scared and mad like you'd expect someone that got shot would say it, he was saying it like it was a surprised little prayer.

Like he was thinking if he said it over and over he might get ahold on to what happened.

"Elijah, he done shot me. He tried to take my head off."

The driver said, "He ain't been in his right mind the whole time. Keep on mumbling 'bout someone name of Zephariah."

I climbed into the wagon's bed and put Mr. Highgate's head in my lap.

We waren't but a mile outside Buxton when a bunch of growned folks came running at us. Pa was out front.

"Pa!"

Pa jumped into the wagon, looked at Mr. Highgate, and called to Mr. Segee, "Clarence, ride on to Chatham and get the doctor. He been shot."

Mr. Segee ran toward Buxton.

Pa said, "Theodore, what happened?"

Mr. Highgate said, "Spencer, I done let Leroy down. I ain't done nothing to stop him, I tried. I swear I did, but he shot me!"

Pa said, "Talk slow, Theo. Tell me what happened."

Mr. Highgate said, "Didn't nothing go right. We's cursed soon as we left Canada. Soon as we get on the ferry to Michigan, Zephariah start in acting peculiar. First thing he done is take that old pistol he showed y'all out of his waistcoat and ax me if I wanted to hold on to it. You know I ain't real partial to no kinda pistol, Spencer, so I tells him, 'No, thanks, I got my shotgun. That's plenty 'nough for me.'

"He say, 'Suit yourself.' And I'll be blamed if he don't toss that old pistol right in the Detroit River!

"I ax him how come he done that, and he say he don't need that one, he got him something better. Then he go in his saddlebag and pull out the 'xact same gun and holster like the one he give to Leroy for safekeeping, the 'xact same one! I knowed right then all them stories 'bout him killing them white twins waren't gossip atall, it was gospel!"

Pa had a look on his face like someone told him he was 'bout to get shot at sunrise. All he said was, "Awww!"

Mr. Highgate said, "Then once we get them horses unloaded off the ferry, he start in on acting like he don't know me. He won't say nothing to me. He carry on like he don't hear none of the questions I's axing him. We just plod on up the road to this little logging village.

"I ain't feeling no danger, you know how strange he be some the time. I just figure he ain't letting nothing pull him off getting up there to talk to that there white man. I's hoping 'gainst hope everything's still fine.

"Once we gets to that village he tell me it's too late to go see this white man, that we gunn have to hold on till tomorrow. I still ain't sensing nothing wrong. We pull up in this alley and I spread me a blanket and tries to get some rest.

"I has the hardest time getting to sleep, so I's just laying there with my eyes shut. Couple hours later I seen Zeph is real quiet walking off toting the bag with all Leroy's money and gold in it. I calls after him and he tell me he know where some gambling's going on and he figure if Leroy's money could buy three people what was slaves, then he could gamble him up two times that sum and free six of 'em!

"I gives him a look like I ain't 'bout to consider no nonsense such as that. Then he ax me if freeing six waren't better'n freeing three."

Mr. Highgate said, "Spencer, a chill run up my back! I told him, 'Uh-uh, Zeph, ain't no one gunn gamble none that money.'

"He laugh and say, 'Don't worry, ain't no gamble the way I play cards.'

"I tells him, 'As long as I's here you ain't playing nothing,' and I reach for my shotgun and aims it at his knee.

"He look at me cold as a viper, like he don't believe I's serious. I tells him, 'You gunn leave all that money and gold right here, else ain't both of us coming out this here alley the same way we come in.'

"He laugh again and say, 'You ain't got no idea how hard it is to kill a man.' He say, 'You ain't got the heart to shoot no one.' And he pull that pistol out the holster and hold it down at his side."

Mr. Highgate went on. "What could I do? I draws a bead right on his knee so's he can see I ain't fooling. All he do is stare me in my eye and start to raise that pistol. I caint think 'bout nothing but all them years Leroy done worked and how if Zeph left with that gold we waren't never gunn see him no more."

Pa said, "Lord, today . . ."

Mr. Highgate said, "He was right. I ain't never even point no gun at no man in my life, Spencer."

Pa said, "Ain't no one gunn fault you for not shooting him, Theo."

Mr. Highgate said, "It ain't like that, I tried! I steadies the shotgun, pulls that trigger, and . . ."

Me and Pa quit breathing.

Mr. Highgate said, ". . . and don't nothing happen, just a loud click. I ain't never heard no sound so terrible in my whole life. I *knowed* I had that shotgun loaded, and just as quick I knowed someway he done unload it. I must've dozed off and didn't know it.

"He get a smile on his face what look like death hisself, and raise that pistol till it aiming dead twixt my eyes. I 'member thinking I done let Leroy down. I 'member thinking waren't no good atall in the world if this was gunn happen, if this rapscallion was gunn get away with this crime. I 'member thinking 'bout my wife, then I 'member getting lift off my feets and I don't recall nothing else till a couple days pass.

"Once I come to, some free folks up in the logging town was tending to me. A man and his wife, mighty fine folk. Took good care of me and didn't want nothing in return."

Mr. Highgate fumbled in the top pocket of his jacket. He pulled out a piece of paper and said, "I axed 'em to write they name down so's I could send 'em some of my syrup as a kind of thank-you. They even borrowed a wagon to carry me to Detroit, then set it up with this here man to bring me to Buxton."

He handed me the paper. It had writ 'cross it in rough letters, *Benjamin Alston. 509 Wilbur Place.*

Mr. Highgate's mind seemed to leave him. I tried handing him the paper back but he pushed my hand away and said, "He shot me. He really done shot me."

Pa said, "Hold on to it, Elijah."

I folded the paper back up and put it in my pocket.

Pa said, "Theodore, try to remember. You didn't hear nothing more on Zephariah?"

Mr. Highgate said, "Mr. Alston say word was that Zeph be drinking and carousing and gambling. They say he winning big and cleaning all them white folks out they money. But I ain't in no condition to look him up, Spencer. I figure it best I get back here and let Leroy and the rest of y'all know."

Mr. Highgate started talking in that surprised little voice again. He said, "He done try to blow my head off, Spencer. He done try to kill me to steal Leroy's money!"

I knowed better. I knowed if the Preacher had aimed to blow Mr. Highgate's head off, he'd have blowed it clean off. I knowed the Preacher waren't looking to kill him.

Pa said, "Don't the woe never end? How much is we 'spected to bear? How much?"

Mr. Highgate said, "You gunn have to bring Leroy to me so's I can tell him what happen."

Pa said, "Naw, Theodore, you done everything you could. I'm-a tell him."

He looked at me and said, "Come on, son, we's gunn have to go down to Mrs. Holton's and let Leroy know 'bout this calamity."

Me and Pa jumped out of the wagon and started walking toward Mrs. Holton's land. I ain't never seen Pa's head hang so low. I knowed better than to say nothing.

Then out of the blue something came to me. This whole mess waren't no one's fault but my own! If I hadn't've told Mr. Leroy that the Preacher waren't gonna steal his money, none of this would've happened! If I'd've listened to what Pa told me and hadn't stuck my nose in growned-folks business, it wouldn't've happened atall!

You'd think I'd've come clean and told Pa, but the way he was looking, I think it would've killed him to know his own big-mouth flesh and blood was the cause of all this grieving.

We both walked and hunged our heads low as the belly on a fat snake and didn't talk 'bout nothing.

We saw Mr. Leroy from 'bout a half mile off. There waren't much you could really see, 'cepting for the sun flashing off the axe when he swung it.

When we were close enough to see the sweat flying and hear all the music, Pa called out, "Leroy!"

Mr. Leroy took one more swing and left the axe biting in the tree.

He looked at us and didn't no words need be exchanged. He squozed his eyes shut for a second, let out a long breath, sat down, and said, "What? What now?"

Pa walked right up on him and said, "Zeph done run off with the money, Leroy. He shot Theodore then left him for dead."

Mr. Leroy said, "Theodore's dead?"

Pa said, "No, he been shot, but it don't look too bad. The money's gone, Leroy. Zeph's gambling it away up in Michigan."

Mr. Leroy didn't say nothing.

Then the most terrific thing happened. Mr. Leroy showed his teeth like a madman and snatched that axe outta the oak and raised it over his head. I knowed he'd figured out who started all this and was gonna split me clean in two!

This time, my legs didn't get soft and loose-ity, they got strong. Afore he could bring that axe down, me and Mr. Leroy both screamed and I lit out for the woods. I looked back and Mr. Leroy flunged that axe toward one of the oaks on Mrs. Holton's land. It hit about thirty feet up and stuck there. Then he cut off into the woods in the other direction.

I figured he was gonna circle 'round to catch me so I ran deeper into the woods fast as I could.

I was running so hard it seemed like the trees started stepping aside, like they knowed if I hit 'em they'd get knocked clean over. I was running like the wind. I didn't feel nor hear nothing 'cepting my heart, it seemed like it jumped right out of my chest and came to rest twixt my ears.

Close as the branches on the trees were slapping by me I knowed they had to be giving me some pretty good whuppings, but I didn't feel nothing. All I was worrying 'bout was getting away afore Mr. Leroy could bring me down with his axe. All I was thinking 'bout was running faster than anybody'd ever run afore. I must have run for a hour.

I was going fast all right, but it weren't fast enough.

All the sudden there was a hand 'round my collar, and I was getting snatched right off my feet from behind and pulled down.

I hit the ground so hard and sudden that my mouth came open and I swallowed a bunch of dirt and old dead leafs.

I hoped Mr. Leroy didn't tarry when he cut me in two. I hoped I didn't get the chance to do too much screaming and begging.

I put my hands over my eyes and waited to get killed.

→ Chapter 18 ←

Kidnapped!

I don't know how long I stayed curled up in a ball on the ground afore I started hearing Mr. Leroy over top of me. He was gasping loud whilst he waited for his breathing to catch ahold of him so's he could do a proper job of chopping me up. I thought 'bout getting up and running again, but my legs were so tired and shake-ity that they waren't gonna do nothing but lay there hoping it waren't them he'd hit first.

Mr. Leroy got ahold of his breathing and said, "Boy . . . has you . . . lost your . . . natural mind?"

The peculiar thing was that even though he was having a powerful hard time talking, he didn't sound atall like hisself. He sounded a whole lot like Pa.

'Stead of cleaving me like firewood he said, "Now get up!"

It *was* Pa!

Pa kept fighting to breathe regular and said, "All I need, you taking leave of your senses at a time like this! When

251

you gunn stop this running nonsense and stand up to what's in front of you?"

I said, "But, Pa, he was gonna kill me!"

He said, "What? Why on earth would Leroy want to kill *you*?"

"He knowed it was 'cause of me all this happened. It's all my fault! I told him the Preacher waren't no thief."

Pa said, "Hush that foolishness! This ain't none of your fault, this ain't no one's fault. Leroy wanted his family so bad that he waren't thinking clear. You couldn't've said nothing to change him one way or the 'nother. Let this here be a lesson to you. You caint let your wantings blind you to what's the truth. You always got to look at things the way they is, not the way you wish 'em to be."

I knowed what Pa was doing. Since him and Ma still think I'm so doggone fra-gile they're always looking out for me, always trying to make it so I don't feel bad 'bout something I did that's total foolish. But after 'while you're old enough and you got to own up to what you did, right or wrong, and couldn't no one tell me that all this horribleness didn't start with me.

Pa said, "Come on, we gotta get back to the Settlement. I'm-a call a meeting so's we can do something 'bout catching that yellow-belly dog of a blamed thief."

I knowed better than to say anything more. Pa don't

swear much and when he does it's a sign that all talking from me is supposed to be through.

Pa said, "You near 'bout caused my heart to jump clean out my chest with all that running. You tearing off in one direction and Leroy tearing off in the other, I's too old to be chasing after folks like a hound dog. Let me sit a minute so's I can get my wind."

Once Pa's breathing catched up to him good, we headed back. I was sore disappointed in myself. Not for running off like I did, that only made good sense. Ain't nothing fra-gile 'bout running when you think you're 'bout to get axed by someone strong as Mr. Leroy. No, I was 'shamed 'cause of how far I'd got!

I reckoned I must have covered two, three miles, but once me and Pa got walking toward the road I saw I hadn't gone no more than two, three hundred feet! This was mighty puzzling, but the only thing I could figure was I must've done a lot a running 'round in circles, which would probably be why Pa caught me so easy.

Pa and the other Elders called a meeting in the church for that night. Me and Emma Collins and Sidney and Johnny had to run through the Settlement to let folks know. Most people had heard what happened and said they'd be there.

'Bout a hour afore the meeting was supposed to commence, I finished my supper and walked onto the stoop and
heard Ma say to Pa, "Then what we gunn do with 'Lijah?"

I said, "Pardon me for interrupting, Ma, but what you
mean, 'do with me'?"

Ma said, "I don't want you coming to this meeting,
Elijah. Folks likely gunn be talking a lot of bad things and
it ain't right for no child young as you to be hearing all that
nonsense. Especially since you's such a . . ."

I know it ain't right, but I butted in on Ma afore she
had a chance to get any words out 'bout me being a fra-gile
boy. I said, "But, Ma-a-a! I caint miss this! Maybe they're
gonna need my help with something."

Ma and Pa looked at one the 'nother and Pa said, "Well,
if they do, we gunn be sure to let you know 'bout it."

Ma said, "Is Mrs. Bixby gunn come to the meeting?"

Ma knowed most times Cooter's ma didn't come out of
their home. Cooter's grandma was near 'bout fifty years
old and frail and ailing and Mrs. Bixby was afeared of
leaving her for even a minute.

I said, "No, ma'am, Mrs. Bixby said her ma waren't
getting on too good and she was gonna stay with her."

Ma said, "All right, then, I want you to run on over
there and ax if it be all right for her to look after you whilst
we's at the meeting."

"But, Ma-a-a-a . . ."

Ma held up her hand to show there waren't no more to say.

Then she told me, "And you might as well ax if you can sleep there tonight and go to school with Cooter tomorrow 'cause ain't no telling when this here meeting's gunn break up, and you know how you is if you don't get your sleep."

She was making it sound like I was a baby in a crib! I said, "But, Ma-a-a-a . . ."

Pa said, "Don't be back-talking your ma, Elijah. Go get you your school clothes so you can go tomorrow morning with Cooter."

"Yes, sir."

Growned folks sure never want to give no one the respect they're suppose to get. Here I'd been working hard on not being fra-gile and Ma and Pa hadn't even took no notice of it. I went and got my clothes for school the next day and put 'em in a tote sack 'long with my school shoes and schoolbooks.

Fair's fair and it waren't the littlest bit fair that I was gonna be cut out from all the deciding what to do 'bout this mess I caused.

Whilst I was toting my clothes and such to Cooter's I started thinking on what was gonna happen at the meeting tonight. I didn't know if they were gonna put a search party together for Mr. Leroy or if they were gonna even try to get a posse up that would go to America and try to run the

Preacher down. Whatever it was they came up with, I knowed it waren't fair that I wouldn't get to know till tomorrow after I finished my chores at the barn. That waren't gonna be till after eight in the evening, and it just didn't seem right that the person that caused all this woe had to let other folks clean up behind him.

It waren't till I was just up the road from Cooter and n'em's house that another great idea started coming to me.

By the time I knocked at Cooter's the idea was set in my head.

Mrs. Bixby answered the door.

She said, "Good evening, Elijah. How you doing?"

"Good evening, Mrs. Bixby. I'm doing good, ma'am. How're you?"

"Just fine as can be." She pointed at my bag and said, "You running away from home, Elijah?"

"No, ma'am, Mrs. Bixby. Ma and Pa were wondering if it's all right if I stayed with you tonight 'cause that meeting might go on till tomorrow."

Mrs. Bixby said, "Elijah, you tell your ma anytime she need me to look after her baby, she don't even got to ax."

Doggone-it-all, didn't no one say nothing 'bout no *baby*! Seems to me ain't no one over the age of five needs to be called a baby. Seems to me even the most fra-gilest child in the world wouldn't be called a baby once he's darn near twelve year old! I was 'bout *this* close to giving

Cooter's ma some back talk, but instead I said, "Thank you, ma'am."

Then I sneaked in the lie I had to tell, "Ma wants me to walk on over to the church for 'bout a hour so I can help decide what we're gonna do 'bout this trouble. Can Cooter walk over with me?"

I figured me and Cooter would both get to eavesdrop on the growned folks' meeting.

"That's fine, Elijah, but don't be counting on Cooter to go with you. Schoolteacher Travis just come by and said the boy's acting the dunce at school again."

She opened the screen door and I saw Cooter standing in a corner with his nose mashed up 'gainst the walls.

She said, "Boy been standing in that corner so much these pass few years he done wore a spot out in the floorboards."

I said, "Yes, ma'am, and now Mr. Leroy's run off and ain't 'round to fix it neither."

Mrs. Bixby raised a eyebrow to let me know she was wondering if I was being smart-mouth. I said real fast, "I didn't mean no disrespect, ma'am."

"None taken. Here, Elijah, drink this. Your friend ain't getting nothing to eat nor drink till he learn to act right in school, and I hate seeing this glass of milk go to waste."

I drunk Cooter's milk, then Mrs. Bixby made me drink two more glasses of it till there weren't none left.

She said, "Carry your bag to Cooter's room, Elijah. And don't be trying to talk to that dunce neither. Another thing he gunn be doing till he turn thirty is keeping his mouth shut."

"Yes, ma'am."

I ran my bag back to Cooter's room and told Mrs. Bixby, "I'm gonna go back home and tell Ma you said it was fine for me to stay here tonight. Then I'm gonna go to that meeting for a while."

She said, "You be careful and hurry back. I hear Leroy done lost his mind and is wandering 'bout. Hear he done throwed one axe a hundred feet up into a tree and throwed the next one so high it poke the man in the moon in the eye."

"Yes, ma'am. I won't be long." I waren't gonna spend one minute thinking Mr. Leroy was gonna hurt no one. I knowed him better than that. That waren't nothing but some more gossip and story pretty-upping. I figured I was gonna have 'bout a hour to eavesdrop on the meeting afore I had to get back to Cooter's home.

I walked toward the church but went into the woods so I could come at it from the back and no one could see me eavesdropping. It was peculiar to see the church all lit up from candles on a Thursday night. Most times it didn't look like this 'less it was Sunday evening or 'less there was a service for someone that had gone and died.

It was also mighty peculiar 'cause there waren't none of

the regular church sounds coming out of the place. There waren't no foot-stamping nor no hand-clapping nor no tambourine-shaking to make you happy. There waren't even none of the choir's singing to make the place seem so warm and comforted and cozy that afore you knowed it, some growned person was digging their elbow in your ribs to wake you up. But I knowed why the church was so different tonight, and it waren't 'cause of the full moon neither. Tonight folks waren't interested in nothing but straightening out my mess.

There were only a few folks there already. They were keeping their voices low inside the church and only once in the while could I understand somebody shouting out "Yessir!" or "Lord almighty!" Those were interesting things to hear but what was more important was hearing what had made folks call out so.

If I was gonna eavesdrop proper I'd have to crawl right under the church's floorboards. I 'membered what Pa said 'bout people that use to be slaves and how they never let a chance at being late get by 'em, so I knowed I was gonna have to wait out here for a while till the church filled up and all the stragglers had made it in.

I was *this* close to being out of the tree line when I heard a twig snap behind me. I did what every fawn in the woods does whenever it gets come up on by surprise, I froze right where I was at.

But it was too late, afore I could turn 'round to see what was sneaking up on me, a rough hand came 'cross my face from behind and I was getting squozed 'round the middle, lifted off my feet, and toted back into the woods!

I'd seen how when a mouse gets grabbed up by a cat, it won't fight or twitch or do nothing to try to get away. I'd seen that and never could get in my head why it happened. I use to think if it was me that got snatched like that, I'd fight and kick and make that cat earn eating me up. I always use to say that I waren't gonna go down that cat's throat without a fight, without at least getting me some good bites in on his tongue as I was getting swallowed. But I could see now that I was wrong, 'cause once this haint or this killer or this kidnapper or this slaver or this demon that had grabbed me lifted me up in the air light as a piece of straw and pulled me deeper into the woods, I knowed there waren't no sense in fighting or nothing. I was feeling just what that mouse must've been feeling. I didn't want to drag things out none by tussling. I just wished this getting killed would be over quick.

→ CHAPTER 19 ←

A Ball Starts Rolling . . .

Whatever snatched me up was starting to get tired. The way it had me mashed up 'gainst it I could feel its heart flopping 'round in its chest like a fish that had got throwed up on the land. It commenced breathing hard and finally dropped me on the ground.

Soon's it let me go I forgot all that nonsense 'bout mice and cats and I tried to light out for the trees. I didn't get far 'cause a root seemed like it reached up and tripped me back to the ground.

You'd've thought with as many times as I been stumbled up and throwed to the ground I'd've learnt to keep my mouth shut once I was 'bout to hit, but that's another one of those lessons that don't seem to stick 'cause soon's I banged down, I got a mouthload of twigs and dirt and dried-up leafs.

I felt 'round to see if maybe I could get ahold of a chunking stone and go down fighting, but my fingers waren't running over nothing but more roots and twigs. I turned 'round to see what it was that had snatched me and saw a sight that terrorfied me to my soul!

'Twas Mr. Leroy!

And he looked just like someone that had died but didn't know it!

He was holding on to his left arm and breathing hard.

He said, "Elijah, I needs you."

I spit the dirt and leafs out of my mouth and told him, "I'm sorry, Mr. Leroy, I didn't know he was gonna steal your money, I swear I didn't know, sir!"

Mr. Leroy held up his hand so's I'd give him a chance to catch on to his breathing.

He said, "Boy, I know you didn't know nothing . . . ain't no one's fault but my own and that thieving fool's. But I do hope . . . you gunn help me out. Elijah, I'm lost, I ain't got no one else what I can turn to."

Mr. Leroy leaned up 'gainst a tree and kept having a hard time finding his breathing. I stood up and went over to him, and said, "Mr. Leroy, I don't care what you and Pa say, I know it's 'cause of me that all this happened, and I'll do anything you want to try to help, sir, anything. All you got to do is tell me."

What Mr. Leroy said made my blood run cold and my legs get shake-ity.

He said, "I got to go to that village in Michigan and see if any of that money's left. And if it ain't none left,

I'm-a find Zephariah and shoot him down for stealing my dreams of getting my family out. I'm-a look him in the eye and make sure he die a terrible death."

I'd heard tell 'bout people that you could look at and see death was walking right next to 'em and when I looked at Mr. Leroy and heard the hard, cold way he was saying those words, I knowed what that meant. Some of those words might be freed people prettifying things, but some of it was real! It was easy to see that death had its arm 'round Mr. Leroy, propping him up, taking its time, waiting to walk with him into Michigan to grab ahold of the Preacher.

Mr. Leroy put his hand on his side and I saw he was wearing the Preacher's fancy holster and mystery pistol. All the sudden I didn't feel so brave.

"But, sir, I caint help with that. I don't know where he's at."

Mr. Leroy said, "I needs you to come with me 'cause I caint read, 'Lijah. Plus I ain't comforted dealing with white folks like you is. I ain't got the intention of letting no man, not even no white man, pull me off from what I got to do, and I need you to help."

"But, Mr. Leroy, there're slave catchers over in Michigan. How we gonna stop someone from trying to kidnap us?"

"Boy, the way you talks, no one in the world gunn think

you ever been no slave. All they got to do is look at you, they know you born free. And if we got to use this pistol, then we got to use this pistol."

"So does that mean you're gonna *force* me to come with you, sir?"

"I'm terrible sorry, Elijah, but a ball done started rolling downhill what ain't gunn be stopped. We both going to Michigan."

"Then that means I ain't got *no* choice, sir?"

"I'm afeared not, son."

I told him, "Great! I was just making sure, Mr. Leroy. I know if Ma and Pa found out I went to Michigan on my own accord, they'd skin me alive once I got back! This way I can tell 'em, and tell 'em true, that I got kidnapped and I ain't gonna be in near as much trouble! Thank you, sir."

Mr. Leroy said, "I do hope you ain't gunn be talking no spools of nonsense whilst we's going. I really caint take that, Elijah. I think it be best if we goes along being quiet."

"Yes, sir!"

Mr. Leroy said, "I borrowed a horse from the barn. We gunn make good time."

We walked deeper into the woods. Jingle Boy's reins were tied to a tree. Mr. Leroy climbed on his back and reached down to pull me up.

I began seeing that Mr. Leroy hadn't done no planning 'bout this. It was like Pa had said, he waren't seeing things the way they were, he was still seeing things the way he wanted them to be.

I said, "Mr. Leroy, we caint just go right off to Michigan like this, sir. Cooter's ma's expecting me to go to her house tonight."

He turned 'round and said, "So? If things go good, you's gunn be back tomorrow, day after, at the most."

"Well, sir, if I don't show up tonight they're gonna think something happened to me, and I ain't meaning to be disrespectful, sir, but folks are saying you lost your mind and are out in the woods wandering 'bout chunking axes at the moon. If they put those two things together they're gonna figure you grabbed me and we're heading to Michigan. And Pa likes you a powerful lot, sir, but if he thinks you kidnapped me he's gonna come ripping out after us like his hair's afire. Then there's gonna be some big problems and we ain't gonna be able to catch ahold of the Preacher."

Mr. Leroy reined in Jingle Boy and said, "That makes sense. What you think we should do?"

"Let me go back to Cooter's home and tell Mrs. Bixby that Ma and Pa changed their mind and that I caint spend the night there. That way Ma and Pa will think I'm sleeping at Cooter's, and Cooter's ma will think I'm sleeping at home. It won't be no big problem that I miss school tomorrow. Ma and Pa will figure I'm there. Then with tomorrow being Friday, I gotta do my chores at the barn right after classes and then they'll think I went fishing, so won't no one know I'm kidnapped till after eight o'clock tomorrow evening. By that time we'll be back. Won't we? We caint be back no later than Saturday, sir. I got a big examination on Latin verbs Monday and I ain't done the proper 'mount of studying yet."

Mr. Leroy said, "I knowed it was the right thing to bring you 'long. You got a real keen mind, Elijah. I figure you can think us through near 'bout anything. I'm powerful sorry I got to drag you into this, son. You keep in mind you's saving me. But you gunn have to work hard on cutting down on some that talking you like to do."

I showed Mr. Leroy the quickest way to get to Cooter's through the woods.

Afore I jumped off Jingle Boy's back Mr. Leroy turned 'round to look me hard in the face.

"You know if you was to take off, there ain't nothing I could do. You tell me now, Elijah, you tell me so's I ain't gunn waste no more time waiting on you. Is you gunn come back? There any need for me to wait, or should I just leave now, alone?"

I raised my right hand and told him, "Mr. Leroy, sir, I swear on my mama's head that I'm coming right back."

I slid off Jingle Boy and ran out of the woods and down the road to Cooter's home.

The screen door was shut but the main door was open. I knocked.

Mrs. Bixby held the door open and said, "That sure waren't long."

I tried to look sad and said, "No, ma'am, folks waren't too much in the mood for talking."

She said, "So what they gunn do? They gunn try to run that thief down?"

Uh-oh! I said, "They made me leave afore I found out."

She laughed and said, "That's good. I's kind of surprised your folks let you go to that meeting in the first place." She looked over in the corner, where Cooter was still mashing his nose up 'gainst the walls. She said to me and him both, "But, Elijah, you's a whole lot more growned than some other folks your age."

I said, "Ma and Pa changed their mind, ma'am, I caint stay with you all tonight. I gotta go back home and go to school tomorrow and go do my chores right after class and then go fishing. I'm-a probably be out of everyone's sight till near 'bout eight tomorrow evening, maybe a little later if the fishing don't go good, and judging by the way it went the other day I might even be later than that, so no one should think I got kidnapped and come looking for me till probably a whole lot later than most times."

I tried to look sadder.

She said, "That's fine, Elijah, you can stay on some other night. Your bag's where you left it at."

I walked into Cooter's room to get my bag, but I reached inside and got a paper and a pencil to write a note. I went over to the window so's the full moonlight would let me see.

I wrote:

DEAR COOTER,
    HOW ARE YOU? FINE I HOPE. I'M
DOING GOOD ACCEPT THAT MR. LEROYS
GONE AND KIDNAP ME AND TOOK ME
FIGHTING ALL THE WAY TO MITCHAGAIN.
WE'RE LOOKING FOR THE PREACHER
AND MR. LEROYS MONEY. HE AINT
CRAZY NOR TRYING TO HIT THE MAN IN
THE MOON HE JUST WANTS HIS FAMILY
BACK. I BEGGED HIM NOT TO TAKE ME
BUT HE SAY I GOT TO GO. WE GOING TO
BE COMMING BACK TOMMOROW ROUND
SUPER TIME. TELL MY MA AND PA THEY
DO NOT GOT TO SEND NO MONEY AND
THEY DO NOT GOT TO WORRY CAUSE MR.
LEROY SWORED HE IS GOING TO TAKE
GOOD CARE OF ME.

Cooter's ma called out from the parlour, "Elijah? What you doing? It don't take that long to get no bag."

I said, "I'm sorry, Mrs. Bixby. I was writing Cooter a note to say I'll see him tomorrow since I ain't allowed to talk to him."

She said to Cooter, "See? How come you ain't more like that boy?"

I had to finish quick.

SINCIRILY, YOUR FRIEND,
ELIJAH FREEMAN

I read what I'd writ and figured I'd best put in one more part.

P.S. DON'T GIVE THIS TO MY MA AND PA
UNTILL SATURDAY MORNING ELSE MR.
LEROY WILL CUT MY THROAT AND BLEED
ME LIKE A PIG.

I had to put the throat-cutting part in 'cause every once in the while my luck ain't real good, and whilst I can most times count on Cooter to do what's wrong, he might've got afeared and tried to do what was right with this. But if he thought I was gonna get bleeded like a pig, I knowed he'd do what was wrong and wouldn't tell no one.

269

I went back into their parlour and said to Mrs. Bixby, "Ma'am, can I give this note to Cooter?"

She said, "Go 'head on, Elijah, then hurry home. Tell your ma I ax 'bout her."

"Yes, ma'am."

I went to Cooter 'bout as close as I could get and said, "Cooter, this here note's for you."

I put the note in his hand.

Long as she was in the room, Cooter was real good at doing everything his ma told him to do and he waren't 'bout to move his nose out of that corner. He looked at me from the side of his eyes and I blinked twice at him and he blinked twice back at me. I felt better 'cause that meant he knowed that note was powerful important and needed to be studied hard.

I said, "Thank you kindly, Mrs. Bixby, and good night."

"Good night, Elijah." Then she said to Cooter, "Where's your manners at? Say good night to Elijah."

Cooter kept his nose plumb in that corner and called out, "Good night, Eli."

"Good night, Cooter."

I left the Bixby home and started down the road toward my own home. Soon's I was far 'nough along that I knowed Mrs. Bixby couldn't see me, I cut into the woods and headed back to where I'd left Mr. Leroy.

He didn't smile or nothing, but I could see it was a weight off his mind to see me. He said, "I knowed you was a good man, 'Lijah."

He reached down and pulled me up onto Jingle Boy. I wrapped my arms 'round Mr. Leroy's waist and said, "Now I got to go back home and get some things I'm gonna need, Mr. Leroy. Ma and Pa must be at the meeting by now so no one won't see me."

Jingle Boy picked his way through the trees heading toward my home and I asked Mr. Leroy, "How far off is this village in Michigan, sir?"

"Ain't far atall, Eli. Less'n a hour from De-troit on this here horse."

"How're we gonna know where to look for the Preacher?"

"He ain't gunn be hard to find if he there."

That didn't make no sense, that didn't make no sense atall. If the Preacher really had stoled Mr. Leroy's money, seemed to me like he'd try to make hisself *real* hard to find.

I said, "But, Mr. Leroy, what if he's gone? He shot at Mr. Highgate five days ago. I don't think he's gonna be waiting 'round for no one to come get him."

Mr. Leroy pulled Jingle Boy to a stop. He turned 'round and looked in my face and said, "'Lijah, what you want me to say? I ain't got no other choice but to go and try to find him. I ain't got no other choice of getting my family back. You can talk all you want, we's going to Michigan."

I knowed right at that second how smart my pa was. He was 'xactly right when he said Mr. Leroy was looking at things the way he wanted them to be, not the way they really were. But I also knowed that if I waren't there to try to think things through for Mr. Leroy, there waren't no way atall he was ever gonna find the Preacher. I knowed Mr. Leroy's heart was so bust-up that I was gonna have to do the thinking for both of us.

Mr. Leroy let me off Jingle Boy a ways in the woods so's I could walk up to our house. When I got there my heart quit beating 'cause when I pulled the door to go in, Ma and Pa were pushing it to go out. They were as surprised to see me as I was to see them.

"'Lijah, what you doing here? Caint Mrs. Bixby watch you?"

"Yes, ma'am, she said she can watch me anytime you want. 'Cepting she's confused and called it looking after your baby."

Ma smiled and said, "Well, she don't know you too old to be called no baby, do she? We ain't gunn say nothing to her 'bout it, though. She don't mean no harm."

"Yes, ma'am."

Pa said, "Answer what your ma axed, Elijah. What you doing here?"

I lied, "I forgot my geometry schoolbook and had to come back."

"Well, run on in and get it, son. We's just 'bout to leave."

"Yes, sir."

Doggone-it-all! Waren't gonna be no way to get no food nor provisions for this trip with Ma and Pa waiting on me. I went back into my bedroom and picked up another tote sack and put a book in it. I got ready to leave my room then stopped 'cause I got to thinking 'bout something. Since me and Mr. Leroy were 'bout to take a dangerous trip and he had the Preacher's fancy pistol in case anything bad happened, I thought maybe I should take something along too.

I put about twenty of the best chunking stones I had into the sack then lifted the end of my mattress and pulled Mr. Taylor's sullied knife from underneath. I looked at it and let the moonlight shine off the blade. I practiced stabbing at a paddy-roller then stuck it in my bag.

Then I dug 'round in my box till I found the piece of paper that Mr. Highgate had gave to me. I looked at the name of the man who'd helped him then stuck the paper in my pocket.

I looked 'round my room to see if there was anything else that we might use on this adventure. I didn't know what it was, but something made me start feeling a little fra-gile. I didn't know if it was 'cause this might be the last time I'd ever see my room again, or if it was 'cause I knowed if I did make it back, Ma and Pa were gonna be outta their minds with being mad at what I'd done. I sniffed the looseness back down in my nose then went out on the stoop.

Ma said, "Everything all right, Elijah?"

Doggone-it-all, Ma was hearing things that waren't being said again!

"Yes, ma'am."

Pa said, "Don't you worry, son. Things has ways of working theyselves out."

"Yes, sir."

I hugged my ma and pa for maybe the last time. They told me to be good and we all walked off the stoop. They went left and I went right.

Mr. Leroy was still where I'd left him at in the woods. He pulled me back on Jingle Boy. I took the paper with the address out of my pocket and said, "Sir? This is who we're gonna look for once we get to that village in Michigan. Mr. Highgate said he's a mighty good man."

For the first time I can ever remember since I've knowed him, Mr. Leroy smiled! And I caint say which looked more unnatural, him trying to smile or Old Flapjack trying to run.

He said, "'Lijah, this here's gunn turn out all right. I feel it in my heart."

Me, Mr. Leroy, and Jingle Boy started heading southwest, getting ready to catch ahold of the stealer of dreams!

→ CHAPTER 20 ←

The Death of Mr. Leroy

I said it afore and I know there ain't many folks who're gonna agree with me 'bout this, but riding a horse ain't nowhere near as good as riding a mule. 'Specially when you're galloping hard down a bad road heading for Windsor. 'Specially when you know the man you're riding behind ain't got no intention of stopping till you're on the ferry that goes 'cross the Detroit River. 'Specially when it feels like they'd gone and stretched out the road twixt Buxton and Windsor by another couple hundred miles!

Why, I was getting bumped 'round on Jingle Boy so much that I knowed those glasses of milk Cooter's ma made me drink had gone and churned theirselves into a big lump of butter in my belly! And whilst I'm mighty fond of butter, it ain't nowhere near as good tasting if the way it gets into your belly is as milk.

All I could do was squeeze my eyes shut, mash my face into Mr. Leroy's back, hold on tight, and hope that all that butter waren't gonna try to fight its way back outta my throat. Big and hard as it had got, it wouldn't probably come back out without a whole lot of choking involved.

I wanted to holler up at Mr. Leroy that maybe he was running Jingle Boy too hard, but like he'd told me, it was like a ball had started rolling down a hill and waren't about to be stopped.

After the longest time, I could smell water and Mr. Leroy eased up some on Jingle Boy. I opened my eyes and saw we were in Windsor at the end of a road that had a big ferry sitting on the river!

Me and Mr. Leroy jumped off, and once things inside of me quit shaking, I patted Jingle Boy's chest. He was sweating something fierce and breathing hard, like it was a cold, cold winter day. He looked at me like he was wondering how come I let Mr. Leroy pound him that way. His eyes were wild as a hurt deer's.

I said, "Mr. Leroy, sir, we ran Jingle Boy way too hard! He's 'bout to die, sir! I best take him down into the river and water him and cool him off."

Mr. Leroy said, "Depends on when that ferry's leaving. You go ax them white men. Horse gunn be fine. Y'all up here baby 'em too much."

I said, "Yes, sir. But maybe you should take him down to the river, Mr. Leroy, and maybe you should take a dip too, you're sweating just as much as Jingle Boy!" I didn't tell him, but his eyes were looking just as wild as the horse's too.

The white men said the ferry waren't leaving for forty-five minutes. I told Mr. Leroy and took Jingle Boy right on into the river. He dropped his head down and drank long and hard, blowing bubbles up all 'round his mouth. I found a bucket with a hole in it and used it to scoop water up on his flanks. They shivered and shooked but I knowed he liked it.

After 'while he quit drinking and started breathing regular.

Mr. Leroy called out, "Elijah, bring that horse on up here. We gotta be first on so's we's first off."

I took Jingle Boy back up to the landing and told Mr. Leroy, "Sir, it ain't no use to run Jingle Boy this hard. If he dies or pulls up lame it's gonna take us twice as long to get up to that village and three times as long to get back to Buxton. I know this horse, sir, and he ain't up to hours of hard running like this."

Mr. Leroy looked out 'cross the river at Detroit. He said, "I suppose you right. We ain't gunn push him as much from here on."

That near 'bout took my breath away, those were words of respect! Here I waren't nothing but a child and he saw what I said was right and agreed to go 'long with my plan!

I guess it's like what Cooter's ma said, that I'm a lot more growned and smarter than most folks my age.

Once we got off the ferry in Detroit I looked back over to Canada.

I ain't disputing that I'm a whole lot smarter than most other children who're near 'bout twelve years old, but I couldn't for anything see how come a river made so much difference. How could one side of the river mean you were free and the other side mean you were a slave?

When you looked at the trees in Canada and the trees in America they seemed to be the same trees, like they could've come out of one seed. Same with the rocks and the houses and the horses and everything else that I could compare, but the growned folks could see big differences that waren't plain to me.

Mr. Leroy kept his word, and whilst the shaking was still worst than it would have been on Old Flapjack, it was tolerable better than the ride to Windsor.

The logging village was 'bout five or six times as big as the square in Buxton.

Mr. Leroy told me to get the paper out that had the man's name on it who'd nursed Mr. Highgate. First person we saw that waren't white, he made me ask, "Excuse me, sir, we're looking for Mr. Benjamin Alston. He lives at five-oh-nine Wilbur Place."

The man said, "That be old Benji. It's on down the road a bit, but you ain't gunn find him there. He most likely out back of the tavern this time of night."

"Where's the tavern, sir?"

The man pointed up the road and said, "Right yon." He told Mr. Leroy, "That's a mighty fine horse you got there, mister."

Mr. Leroy didn't answer so I said, "Thank you kindly, sir."

Mr. Leroy was looking hard up at the tavern.

He said, "What he doing out back a tavern?"

"They's gambling. Stakes ain't much, but it's 'bout all the entertaining you gunn find 'round here."

Mr. Leroy said, "You hear tell if a man from Canada what call hisself Preacher been gambling with anyone 'round here?"

The man laughed and said, "A preacher what owns up to sinning, huh? Ain't heard of no such man in these parts. Naw, that would've stuck with me."

Mr. Leroy pulled his coat aside so the man could see the Preacher's pistol and said, "He's toting a gun same as this here one. Same holster too."

The man smiled and said, "Oh, *him*! Yessir, he was gambling up here a while back. He done cleaned all these here fools out then went looking for some bigger fish to fry.

Last I hear he went on over to gamble with some n'em white men. I don't know where they playing at, but one of 'em back behind the tavern would."

This was great news! Maybe the Preacher had won enough by now to really buy six more slaves out of America! Maybe we didn't have no cause to come up here tearing after him!

Mr. Leroy said, "Thank you kindly."

He reached down to pull me onto Jingle Boy.

'Twaren't far atall to the tavern. When we got there Mr. Leroy tied Jingle Boy out front and told me, "If they's any trouble you light on out for this horse and go home. Just follow that road south."

I said, "Yes, sir."

He pulled the pistol out of the holster and put it in the pocket of his waistcoat. He never took his hand back outta the pocket.

We walked 'round back of the tavern and came up on a bunch of men squatting down and talking loud.

Once we got up on 'em I saw the Preacher waren't there. The men were tossing two little white square boxes with dots all over 'em up 'gainst a wall. There was lots of swearing and lots of coins being passed 'round and American dollar bills being waved back and forth and held squozed up in fists.

Mr. Leroy said, "Pardon me. Any y'all know a man

name of . . ." He gave me a nudge. I took the paper out of my pocket again and read, "Mr. Benjamin Alston."

One of the men said, "Who axing?"

Mr. Leroy said, "He help a friend and I needs to talk to him."

The man said, "What friend he help?"

Mr. Leroy said, "Man name of Highgate, come from Buxton. In Canada."

The man who'd asked all the questions stood up and said, "I'm Benji Alston. What can I do for you?"

Mr. Leroy said, "Thank you kindly for helping Theodore, sir."

"'Twaren't nothing. Someone bushwhack him. All I done was give him a place to rest and call a doctor. That's one lucky man. Doc say a half a inch closer, he'd have been killed for sure. How he doing?"

Mr. Leroy said, "I hear you might know where I can find the man what got a gun like this here one."

Mr. Leroy pulled his hand outta his pocket. He had the gun pointing back at hisself so no one wouldn't get the wrong idea.

A bunch of grumbling and scowls came over all the men once they saw that gun.

Mr. Alston said, "Hesh, couldn't none y'all say for sure he was cheating. Man might've been having a good roll of luck."

Someone said, "Luck, my foot!"

One of the other men said, "He got done with us and said he was looking to bet for some real money, said he wanted to go up 'gainst some white folks. They was gambling over in Culpepper's, but that was earlier this week. Shoot, I figure if that man was smart 'nough to cheat all us, he *have* to be smart 'nough to know better than to gamble with no white folks."

Mr. Alston said, "Last I heard he was over at the East Lee stable yesterday. But I ain't sure I believe it. That's where them slavers is staying."

Slavers? My blood ran cold!

Mr. Alston said, "Y'all best be careful if you plan on going over to that stable. Them paddy-rollers there ain't to be trifled with. Got them one the biggest, baddest bear-fighting dogs I ever seen up north."

He told us where the stable was and I thanked him.

I don't know what it was, if it was the talk about the slavers or the talk about the bear-fighting dog, but soon as we started walking back to Jingle Boy, Mr. Leroy commenced to looking mighty worried and afeared. And it tore my heart out.

I said, "What's wrong, Mr. Leroy? Should we go get us some help from somewhere?"

Mr. Leroy grabbed his left arm and started breathing like he'd just been chopping oaks.

He said, "Elijah, ain't . . . no . . . one gunn help me. It just be you."

Ain't nothing in the world that'll get you feeling fragile quicker than seeing a growned person you know is hard as nails looking afeared.

"But, Mr. Leroy, what's wrong? Why're you looking like that?"

He said, "We got to get to that stable, boy. We got to move quick."

He climbed up on Jingle Boy slow and in parts 'stead of jumping up the way he regular did.

He didn't put his arm down to pull me up.

He said, "Lead the horse yon, Elijah, through the back way."

I grabbed Jingle Boy's reins and led him north.

We got 'bout a half mile when I said to Mr. Leroy, "Sir, maybe we should get you some rest afore we go to that stable, maybe we need to . . ."

I looked back just as Mr. Leroy started sliding off of Jingle Boy. It seemed like he was moving so slow that he was sort of floating down toward the ground, like he was just gonna settle soft and light as a feather. But when he landed on his face, there was a horrible heavy thump and things commenced moving again like they normal do.

"Mr. Leroy!"

I ran back and kneeled down beside him.

His eyes were open but he was blinking more than he would most times.

I said, "Please, Mr. Leroy, please get back up!"

I shooked him and he said, "No. You got to go in that stable and get that money, boy. He done thiefed the money for your mother and sister, 'Zekial!"

Mr. Leroy was out of his mind!

I said, "Please, sir, I ain't Ezekial, I'm Elijah, Elijah Freeman!"

He grabbed my arm and said, "Is you gunn do it? Is you gunn get that money, boy?"

I started going all fra-gile. Things commenced loosening in my nose.

He said, "Promise me . . . promise me now!"

What could I do? I whispered, "I ain't Ezekial, I'm Elijah."

He said, "Promise me! Promise me you'll get that money and if he done lost it, promise me you's gunn gut-shoot him!"

"Please, Mr. Leroy, please get up. Please don't leave me here alone!"

He said, "Son, caint you see I'm dying? Please tell me, please tell me you's gunn get the money for your ma and sister. That ain't much. 'Zekial, how come you ain't telling me?"

His voice was getting softer and softer and that was worst than if he'd been yelling.

Finally I said, "I promise, sir, I promise I'll do it."

He smiled and whispered, "Take that pistol, boy."

I pulled the mystery pistol out of the fancy holster and put it in my tote sack.

He coughed twice and something dark and thick started leaking out of his mouth and nose.

The last things he said were, "I love you, son. Tell your ma I . . ."

His eyes stayed open but I knowed they waren't seeing nothing.

I shooked him and said, "Mr. Leroy? Oh, please, Mr. Leroy!"

I ran back to Mr. Alston to try and get some help.

I busted right in on the men and yelled, "Excuse me, sir, Mr. Leroy fell off the horse and ain't moving!"

Mr. Alston said, "What you say, boy? Calm yourself down and don't be talking that fast."

I catched my breath and said, "Mr. Leroy fell off the horse and ain't breathing!"

They ran back with me and bunched up 'round where Mr. Leroy was laying.

Mr. Alston looked at Mr. Leroy and put his hands over his eyes to close them. He said, "Son, he pass. Y'all kin?"

"No, sir."

"Y'all's both from Buxton?"

"Yes, sir."

"You got anyone up here what can look after you?"

I started to say no but knowed if I did and if Mr. Leroy really was dead, they waren't gonna let keep my promise, they waren't gonna let me hunt the Preacher down and get Mr. Leroy's money back.

I said, "Yes, sir, my aunty lives just over yon." I pointed south.

Mr. Alston said, "We gonna have to get the sheriff, boy. Tell your aunty she need to come claim him else they gonna put him in the paupers' field."

I said, "I'll have to tell my pa in Buxton. They'll come and get Mr. Leroy."

I grabbed Jingle Boy's reins and never looked back.

A promise is a promise and I waren't 'bout to let Mr. Leroy down. I was gonna find the Preacher if it took me ten years. And I was gonna start with the East Lee stable.

So Mr. Alston and the other men wouldn't get suspicious I headed south, pretending I was riding hard back to Buxton.

→ CHAPTER 21 ←

Terrorfied in America!

I circled 'round and started back north. I saw the stable from two blocks off. There was a hitching post just down from it so I tied Jingle Boy and commenced walking the rest of the way. I dug five of the chunking stones out of my tote sack and put three in my left hand and two in my right. I didn't have notion the first what a bear-fighting dog would look like so I hoped five stones would be enough in case me and it had a disagreement.

As I got right on the stable, it happened in a flash. First thing that came to mind was Pa telling me that I didn't never have to worry 'bout no barking dog, that it was barking 'cause it was just as scared as me. He said it was the quiet dog I had to be afeared of. That was the kind of dog that waren't interested in scaring no one, it was only looking to bite something big and meaty off of you.

Afore I seen anything I heard the sound of a chain rattling, then a hard grunt like something heavy was changing directions sudden-like. Other than those soft sounds this bear-fighting dog was quiet as a owl diving at a mouse.

I saw a big black blur coming at me and, at the same time as I tried to get out of the way, I throwed left-right-left hard as I could.

I heard a chain sing from getting pulled taut and the bear-fighting dog's paws hit me square in the side so strong that the last two chunking stones flewed out of my hand. I waren't nothing but a dead duck!

A spray of the dog's slobber splashed on my face and I hit the ground hard, knocking my breathing right out of me. The dog still didn't bark or nothing but his front paws pressed like fists into my ribs. All I could do was wonder if he was gonna rip me apart or squeeze the life out of me by standing on my chest.

I closed my eyes and waited to get suffocated or tored limb from limb.

But didn't nothing happen. I opened my eyes and saw the dog was out cold, his head was lolling up 'gainst my side. The head was huge, just 'bout the size of a five-month-old calf's head, and was covered with scars. He was breathing fast, like he'd just chased a rabbit, and little snorts of dust were blowing up with each breath he took. His feet were twitching like dogs do when they're having a nightmare.

Just that quick I noticed my ribs. It felt like someone had run a knife into 'em and I looked down. The nails from one of the bear-fighting dog's front paws had disappeared into the front of my shirt and my blood was starting to leak out. I rolled from underneath the dog's legs, then rolled twice more and laid in the dirt waiting for my breathing to catch back up to me.

After 'bout five or six big gulps of air I pulled my shirt up to see if any bones were poking through. There waren't nothing there but three tiny holes where his claws had gone in and only one hole was bleeding atall. I felt to make sure waren't nothing broke. Other than poking three holes in me, it seemed like the bear-fighting dog hadn't done nothing worst than knock the air out of my chest.

I stood up and put two more chunking stones in my hand then walked over toward the dog. One of my stones had caught him right twixt the eyes. I knowed it was the second left-hand one I chunked. There was a big knot swelling up there already. His tongue was hanging out from twixt long yellow and brown teeth that were 'bout the size of bear claws. There was a little puddle of mud spreading in the dust where his tongue was resting. I didn't think I'd hurt him too bad, but I waren't gonna wait 'round to find out.

I leaned against the door that led into the stable and pushed.

When you first walk into a room in a house, or into a clearing in the woods, or into the inside of a stable like this one, they have a way of telling you they know you're there. It ain't nothing particular noticeable, but the air inside of 'em changes like it's saying, "I'm watching you." Some of the time it seems like the air's smiling and saying, "I'm watching *over* you, come on in," and some of the time it seems like it's all a-frowning and saying, "I'm watching you, and you *best* be careful." But I'd got into this stable so quiet and sneakish that *nothing* knowed I'd cracked open the door, held my breath, and took a step inside.

I eased the door back shut, stood still, and waited for my eyes to get use to the dark.

All I could see was black, but going by what I was hearing, I figured there must've been five or six horses held up in here. There was the *swish-swish-swish* of tails going at flies, there was the *bumpty-bump-bump* of hoofs shifting and scraping whilst trying to get comfortable, there was the steady, easy, deep breathing of animals that had been worked hard trying to get some sleep. There was also a slow *woo-woo-woo* sound from a barn owl hid out waiting for a mouse to make a mistake.

It didn't sound like there was nothing to worry 'bout . . . right off.

I let air come out of my mouth easy and breathed back in through my nose.

I knowed just like that that there was something terrible wrong inside this stable.

It waren't the horses, they smelt the same as Buxton horses. That waren't peculiar.

It waren't the smell of the straw on the floor neither, but I could tell that whoever's chore it was to keep it clean waren't changing it regular enough.

I could even smell that there was a goat or two somewhere in here . . . all those things were easy to tell and usual. But there was something else mixed up with the all-the-time stable smells, something that just waren't sitting right.

It waren't like a rat had curled up in a hole somewhere and died then commenced to swelling up and rotting, but it waren't far from that. Or like a mule had et something bad and was ailing and leaking sickness, but it was kind of akin to that.

It waren't one n'em sickroom smells neither, one n'em rooms they tell you you ain't got no choice but to go into and say good-bye to someone that looks like they should've died a year afore, but it waren't exactly the back side of that kind of stinking.

I didn't have much time to study on what the strange smell was 'cause my eyes started getting use to the dark and were picking out things, and when it comes to choosing to pay attention to your nose or your ears or your eyes, you gotta listen to your eyes every time.

Then my heart stopped beating, my blood ran cold,

and time stood still! Someone was standing over at the other end of the stable!

I acted like a fawn all over again. I quit breathing and frozed all my muscles dead where they were at. Maybe whoever it was hadn't seen me.

My eyes were slow getting more use to the dark and, doggone-it-all, I started suspecting I knowed who I was seeing. At the other end of the stable was the Right Reverend Deacon Doctor Zephariah Connerly the Third, the stealer of dreams!

But, just like the smell in the stable, something waren't right about him.

He was watching me from the other end of the stable and I was pretty darn sure it was the Preacher, but as he real slow started getting more and more lit up and less and less gray and shadowish, I began doubting what I first saw.

He was being *too* still.

The Preacher always had something moving on him, either his hands or his legs or, most of all, his mouth. It just waren't sitting right seeing him standing there with his arms raised up on both sides of him and his head ducked down like he was studying something in the dirt. Or maybe that waren't it atall. Maybe he was doing the same thing I was doing, freezing every muscle so's I might not see *him*.

We both stood still, frozed that way for the longest time waiting to see which one was gonna move first. But finally my legs took to twitching and feeling that they were 'bout to bust out afire. The Preacher was better at this standing-still business than me. He didn't move a finger. He kept his arms up there patient as a rock, quiet as a scarecrow.

But something just waren't right.

I started stealing closer to him one slow step at a time.

Then I heard a humming sound so near to my left-hand side that my blanged legs and breathing frozen up all over again. Whatever it was that was making that sound was so close that even my eyeballs locked where they were at. I kept 'em straight ahead on the scarecrow-that-might-be-the-Preacher. Then, slow as maple sap on a cold day, I started sliding my eyes off to the left, off to the direction that the humming sound was coming from.

The only thing I could make out was that someone had leaned some dark bundles or sacks up 'gainst the left hand side of the stable. There were five of 'em all sitting the same space apart one from the 'nother.

The noise commenced again, sounding like someone fishing 'round trying to figure which song they were 'bout to hum.

I knowed I best quit holding my breath, else I was gonna be forced to breathe in so hard it'd make a racket. I eased air back into me like a bellows being pulled open slow and easy.

I moved my eyeballs just the tiniest bit more and saw exactly what it was that was making that music humming sound.

It was one of the bundles!

I ain't never gonna know if it was 'cause of the slow way air was sliding back into me or if it was 'cause my eyes finally could make out what they were seeing, but my head got light and afore I could do anything my senses took off, squawking and flapping away like a flock of pheasants in a field.

Next thing the stable floor felt like it was rising and dropping like a fresh-dried bedsheet being snapped and shooked afore it got folded.

The way things were jumping 'round and with my wits flewed away, it didn't make no sense to try to keep standing. I knowed I'd best get ahold of something till the floor steadied itself, else I'd pitch into the dirt.

But it was too late. I looked at the humming bundle again and saw that it had arms!

Four live, moving arms!

Two of 'em were tiny and mostly still and two of 'em were big and moving!

I couldn't believe I'd come all the way to the United States of America to see my first haint!

I didn't have no chance to get ahold on to nothing, my legs gave out and I crumpled toward the ground. I'd gone and got myself right in the middle of being fra-gile again.

When your senses leave you sudden-like and you start falling, you don't have the time nor the notion to put your hands up so's not to hit your head. Everything goes limp and flops like okree. And since your head's the thickest part of you and most times leads the way down, it's always first to bust the ground. But this time, I did remember to keep my mouth shut.

Part of the floor must've had planks laid down in it, 'cause when my head hit, there was a loud sound like a axe chopping a thick oak. That one good hit to my skull made me see stars and it was *terrible* loud 'cause each and every one of those bundles that was on that wall came to life and unfolded itself with a powerful horrible sound!

The commotion they made when they moved was enough to wake the dead! Not from being loud, but from being terrorific. It waren't no human sound atall, but something 'bout it did bring people to mind. It was groans and rough breathing mixed up with the same noise that the chain on the dog outside had made. Which got me thinking I was soon 'bout to get ripped to shreds by the brothers and sisters of the dog that I'd chunked.

Only difference was now the sound was timesed by five and was added to a bunch of whimpers and the hard sucking in of air.

What I was seeing waren't five sacks atall, nor five dogs looking to settle scores for me chunking their brother, nor five evil spirits come to life. None of that. What I was seeing was worst than all those things totaled up together.

What was on the wall of the stable couldn't've been nothing but five squatted-down demons that had been captured and chained by someone who was sending 'em back to Satan so they couldn't snatch no one else's soul!

I looked over to where the Preacher was, hoping he'd do something to help but got my attention drawed back quick to the chained demons. The four-armed one that was humming made a shushing sound at the rest of 'em and started talking! Talking in English too!

It whispered out to me, "Hoo-hoo! Is you real or is you a haint?"

I lifted my head from the floor and without thinking what I was talking to said, "Pardon me, ma'am?"

She was the only one 'mongst the bunch that looked like a woman, and I ain't sure if it was the right thing to do to call a haint "ma'am," but the word came out anyway.

As she got clearer- and clearer-looking, I wondered if she was a haint atall. She was starting to look just 'bout like a regular woman, but a regular woman that was afeared and had four arms.

But the way her eyes locked on me, I was pretty sure this *was* a regular woman. I also saw she didn't have no clothes on 'cepting a rag hanging 'cross one of her shoulders.

Seeing a growned-up person naked like that was so

shocking that I snatched my eyes off her and looked down at the dirt in front of her feet. There were thick bands of iron hugged 'round her ankles connecting up to some locks and chains that were keeping her where she was at. I was just as embarrassed to see these chains as I was to see that she didn't have no clothes on. I looked at the others so's not to shame her.

The rest of 'em were men and they waren't wearing nothing atall, not even a rag. Their ankles were covered with the same kind of thick iron shackles as the woman's. Their eyes were all on me and they were looking just as scared and confused and surprised 'bout seeing me as I was 'bout seeing them.

The four-armed woman hissed again, "Is you a real boy?"

I waren't sure how to answer her. If she *was* a haint and thought that I was one too, she might not do nothing to me. 'Sides, who else but a haint's gonna have four arms? But if she *waren't* a haint and I told her I *was* one, maybe she'd put some kind a haint-killing conjure on me and I'd be dead anyway.

'Stead of looking at her, I put my eyes up in the rafters of the stable, which was easy to do since, whilst my mind was trying to figure out how to answer her question, I was still spread out on the floor being fra gile. The waiting owl stared back down at me.

I figured I'd best answer her with the truth. I said, "Yes, ma'am, I'm a real boy."

She whispered, "If you's a haint, get on outta here. If you's a real boy, cut that foolishness and pick you'self outta that dirt!"

I tried to get back on my feet. I got up but kept my head down. A choky, coughing sound came from the woman and I couldn't help but look. The sound was too tiny for a growned woman to be making. I saw a little black head and two little black arms coming out of the rag that was stretched out 'cross her front. It was truly a load off my mind when I could tell that, even with it dark as it was in the stable, she didn't have four arms atall! She was a woman holding on to a baby!

Then I understood! These waren't no chained demons! These were five runaway slaves and a baby that had been caught! I knowed what they were but my head kept spinning anyway.

She said, "Boy!"

"Yes, ma'am?"

She said, "If you's real, go by them horses in that stall behind you and fetch that bucket of water, but keep heshed! One n'em paddy-rollers be over yon lickered up."

I looked to where she was pointing and saw another bundle on the right-hand side of the stable. 'Cepting for the shotgun leaned up 'gainst him, you'd've never knowed it was a white man.

There was a leather bucket hanging from a nail so I went and brung it and the drinking gourd that was next to it over to where the woman with the baby was squatted down.

She reached out and touched my hand like she was making sure I was real, then said, "Thank you, boy!" She dipped the gourd in the water and propped the baby up so's it could get a drink.

The baby hadn't showed no signs of being alive past a cough or two but once it saw the water it sprunged up and commenced kicking its legs straight out and clawing at the gourd and sucking and slurping and lapping at the water like it hadn't had nothing to drink in two years.

The sound of the baby going at the water stirred the men up something fierce. Two of 'em reached their hands out at me and strained up 'gainst their chains so's to get close to the bucket as they could.

The woman mashed her finger 'gainst her lips and said, "Hesh them chains! You wants to wake that white man and get this here boy killed? They's plenty water here, just you wait!"

She waved her hand 'round a lot whilst she was talking to the men, like they couldn't hear her good.

She eased the gourd away from the baby and said,

"There now, darling. Go slow. Ain't no point making you'self sick."

But the child waren't having none of her cautions. It snatched back at the gourd and bit on the side of it, breathing in water, splashing its mouth 'round like a sparrow in a puddle.

The baby commenced coughing again and the woman took the gourd away. She dipped it back in the bucket and took a long pull herself. Two more times she did this, draining the gourd dry then taking a breath so deep and so hard that it brung to mind someone who'd dived under a lake then come back up right afore their lungs were 'bout to bust.

She said, "Thank you, thank you kindly. Now give them men some."

I stepped over to the man closest to her and set the bucket in front of him. He looked at it then looked up at me. He raised his hands and I saw that his arms were tied up with heavy chains that were dangling off of his wrists.

I didn't know what to say or do.

Ma and Pa and all the growned folks in the Settlement had told us plenty of stories 'bout folks in chains afore, and a couple of people in Buxton even have thick, shiny scars on their ankles and wrists from wearing 'em, but seeing the chains real waren't the kind of thing you could imagine. It waren't the kind of picture that words could paint.

Maybe the growned folks were trying not to scare us when they told stories 'bout folks being chained up, 'cause judging by the way these people looked, I knowed we waren't getting the whole story. I felt my legs getting unsolid and rickety all over again.

The woman said, "Boy! It's just *my* hands what's free so's I can tend my chile. Them men's arms is chained and they caint reach they mouth. You's gunn have to help 'em."

I dipped the gourd into the water and raised it to the man's lips so he could drink. His eyes were blood red and swole up and crusted so's you'd've thought he'd had a good, long, hard cry. But there was something in his eyes that told you that this waren't the kind of man that was likely to be bawling, no matter what happened to him.

Things had run out of his nose and were making the hair on his lip look gray, but up close he seemed too young to be showing age that way. He was too strong-looking. He was one n'em men that's got every muscle poking right out of him, sort of like if he waren't careful they'd come ripping right through his skin.

His lips were cracked with long, bloody splits dividing 'em every little bit. His hair was caked up on one side with blood or mud like he got chunked there by a rock and never took the time to wash it out.

He had one of his legs stretched out front of him, and there was a big rip outta the skin by his knee. It had got sewed up, but not real good. It must have been from that bear-fighting dog.

He ducked his head at me once then drank just as hard as the woman and the child.

She said, "He the chile's pa. Him and them other three's all full-blood Africans. He don't talk a whole lot of English, but he ain't lost his manners so much that he ain't gunn say, 'Thank you kindly,' has you, Kamau?"

The man ducked his head again.

I said, "You're welcome, sir," and once he had his fill I went down the line watering the other men.

The last one waren't a man atall. He was a boy that looked like he was a little younger than me. His eyes were red and swole up and crusted too, but there waren't no doubt what caused this on *him*. It was crying. Even dark as it was, I could still see the gray tracks the tears that had run down his cheeks left. His nose was crusted up and leaking even more than the man's. It was terrible to see.

When he looked up at me all I could think to do was pull my hand up in my sleeve then reach my cuff over to wipe his nose and mouth off. He saw me raise my hand and flinched back like he was expecting me to bust him in the face, but he saw what I was trying to do and leaned in. Soon's I wiped his nose I gave him some of the water.

Once he had his fill he bent down and pulled my arm so's my hand was at his lips. He pressed his mouth there. It ripped at my insides something harsh. He was acting like giving him a drink of water waren't no different than giving him a twenty-dollar gold piece. He wouldn't turn my hand a-loose. He started mumbling some African talk against it then commenced to crying in quiet jerking noises that made his teeth rub up against my skin and made the chains on his arms and legs rattle.

I pulled my hand away and all the sudden I knowed what the odd smell in the stable was. It was fear. It was the smell of five growned folks and one baby that were afeared of everything.

And that smell and the sight of these chained folks and the sounds they made every time they moved started making me sick to my stomach. I know it don't seem right, but all I wanted to do was get away from this boy, to get away from these people afore I throwed up. I left the bucket at the boy's feet and stumbled three steps backward.

The woman whispered, "No, chile, you's got to put it back jus' like it was. You's got to leave it like ain't no one been in here."

When I got the bucket and gourd back she said, "Come close and keep your voice down. What you doing here? You work in this stable?"

They'd scared me so bad I'd plumb forgot about the Preacher!

I remembered what I'd swore to Mr. Leroy and told

her, "No, ma'am, I'm searching for the man that stoled my friend's money."

I looked to the other end of the stable and the Preacher was still standing there, pretending he waren't hearing none of this. I drawed Mr. Leroy's pistol out of my tote sack so's the Preacher could see this waren't no bluff and said a little louder, "He's gonna give me Mr. Leroy's money back else I'm gut-shooting him down like a mad yeller dog."

Having a gun in your hand when you knowed you were gonna use it to shoot a human person made it feel a whole lot different. When I'd used the Preacher's old rusty gun to shoot stumps and stones, it didn't feel nowhere near's heavy as this one. The mystery pistol was shaking and sliding back and forth in my hand same as a weather vane in a January storm.

The four Africans drawed back once they saw that gun and the way it was jumping 'round in my hand. You could tell they knowed what a pistol like this one could do to somebody.

The woman said, "Now I seen everything. A boy holding a man's gun fixing to shoot someone! But if you's set on killing that man, you's too late, chile. Looky there. He breathed his last just 'fore sunset.

"Had quite the mouth on him, that one did. I knowed they waren't taking him nowhere. I knowed when they brung him in here and bust his teeth out and split his tongue in two. They ain't never gunn treat no one what they's looking to sell like that. What they done with him waren't nothing but play, nothing but sport.

"But you tell your friend if that man stoled something from him he done paid a terrible price for it. You tell him that man stayed alive way pass what you'd-a thought someone could, and he never begged, and he cursed them paddy-rollers with every blow they put on him, cursed 'em right to the end."

So the Right Reverend Deacon Doctor Zephariah Connerly the Third was dead. I was 'shamed 'cause, wrong as it might seem, the first thing that came flooding into my heart was reliefness 'cause that meant I waren't gonna have to keep my word and kill him.

I could see now it was ropes that were keeping the Preacher's arms spread out to the sides. He was strunged up twixt two beams. Another rope was wrapped 'round and 'round his neck and was pinching his throat narrow and tight. I knowed I waren't never gonna be able to look at Emma's old doll, Birdy, again without calling up thoughts 'bout the Preacher.

The next thing that came into my heart made it sink right down into my brogans. There waren't no clothes on the Preacher 'cepting for a bloody rag 'round his knees. Mr. Leroy's money must be all gone!

The woman said, "Put that thang down 'fore you hurts someone!"

I put the Preacher's gun back in my tote sack.

She said, "Who you belongs to?"

She could see I was having a powerful hard time taking my eyes off the Preacher, so she pulled at my arm. When I still couldn't quit looking at him she turned my face so's I was looking dead at her.

"Who you belongs to?"

The only thing I could think to say was, "No one, ma'am. I'm my ma and pa's boy."

She said, "You sure do talk peculiar. Where you born? You from this here town?"

I said, "No, ma'am, I was born free in the Buxton Settlement, in Canada West."

"Canada!"

"Yes, ma'am."

She said, "How far's us from Canada?"

"It took me and Mr. Leroy near 'bouts a hour to ride it, but we waren't tarrying atall. We were probably riding the horse too hard."

She said, "A *hour*?"

"Yes, ma'am."

"Naw, say that ain't the truth. Say that a lie, boy!"

"No, ma'am, that's the swear-'fore-God truth."

For the first time since I met her she smiled. She held

the baby away from her and said, "Honey, I guess we just snakebit. We run all that time and falls one little hour short. One hour, chile, we was that close. I 'spect we so close we might even be breathing that free Canada air."

I started to tell her that mostly the wind blows the other way, from America over into Canada, but I figured that waren't what she was talking 'bout.

I said, "Where's that man taking you, ma'am?"

She said, "I 'spect me and Kamau and the baby's heading back to my missus in Kentucky. I caint say where they taking them other three. They don't talk no English atall and Kamau say they don't talk the same African he do."

I remembered all the stories we'd heard in classes about abolitionists and how they'd risk their lives for people who were just like these folks. I remembered how those stories got you so excited and mad and worked up that you wanted to charge down into America and free *all* the slaves. I remember how those stories near 'bout made you cry when the growned folks would tell you how they felt when they finally got to Buxton and they pressed their left hands onto the Liberty Bell and they finally knowed how it felt not to be owned by nobody.

I thought 'bout all the times me and Cooter and Emma and our friends played abolitionists and slavers, the way we had to pull straws to see who would get to be the abolitionists 'cause didn't no one want to pretend to be somebody bad as a slave owner. I remembered how we'd act like we were sneaking up on a plantation to kill the lot of slave masters and make a run for Canada with some happy, smiling, free slaves. I remembered how easy it all was.

But now I could see our playing didn't have nothing to do with the truth. I could see how it was a whole lot harder when things were real and you had to worry 'bout shotguns and chains and coughing little babies and crying folks without no clothes. Folks that were the same as me and Ma and Pa, 'cepting they were near dead. 'Cepting they gave off a sad, peculiar smell. 'Cepting they were chained in a way that I ain't never seen even the wildest, worstest animal chained.

I knowed right then that if I got out of this stable in Michigan alive I waren't never gonna play abolitionists again. Not just 'cause all the fun had been took out of it, but mostly 'cause I knowed I waren't brave enough to even *pretend* to be one of 'em. I knowed it would be kinda like pretending you were a angel. It was the kind of thing that would make you 'shamed the next time you ran into a real angel or a real abolitionist. It was the kind of thing that shouldn't be involved in no sort of game.

I looked at the woman and swored to myself, shotguns and chains or not, I was gonna figure a way to get her and these Africans out of here!

CHAPTER 22

Busting Free!

I asked the woman, "How many of 'em is it that's stealing you, ma'am?"

She said, "They's that one pass out yon and one what they calls Prayder and his two boys. And a ornery dog."

I calculated real quick, swallowed hard so's there wouldn't be no backing down, and said, "Ma'am, I can creep up on that man that's asleep and try to get the keys to those locks away without rousing him, and if he does wake up and I got to use this gun then I got to use this gun. Then I'll let you all loose and we'll have a shotgun too and when those other slave hunters come running we all could . . ."

Ideas were jumping at me hard and fast and it seemed like the more harder and more faster they came the more they were bumping into one the 'nother and the more confusing and worthless they were sounding, even to me.

But I couldn't quit talking. Quitting talking was the same as quitting everything so I said, "And when we get to Buxton, the folks'll welcome you and help you set up a farm. Even some of the white folks'll help. And we're always looking out for people who're trying to get free, and when you get there me and Cooter are gonna ring the Liberty Bell 'round a hundred times. That comes out to twenty times for each one of you. And don't no paddy-rollers come there else they get tarred and feathered and run out of town on a rail, or they disappear and ain't never heard from no more. And even the white folks that don't want us there get mighty riled when Americans come into Canada and try to tell 'em what to do, and once we get there, Emma Collins ain't gonna have to trick you out of the woods 'cause I'm-a bring you all the way there myself and I . . ."

I looked over at the four other people who were back to leaning their heads twixt their knees and breathing in a way that told me they waren't gonna run nowhere. They didn't look like a bunch of tired, beat-down people no more. They were back to looking like five bundles throwed up 'gainst a stable wall.

It was too much. Mr. Leroy dying, the Preacher getting killed, the smells, the way the chains rattled, and the naked folks looking so scared and whupped and tired, it was just too much. The stupid and confusing ideas quit coming and got their place took by a stinging in my eyes and a loosening in my nose and a choking in my throat.

It waren't nothing but some powerful fra-gile-ness, and when it comes, there ain't nothing you can do to stop it. It's like a ball got rolling down a hill. So all I could do was cry.

Same as the chained-up runaway boy that was younger than me, I quit talking, covered my eyes, and cried.

The woman switched her baby to her left hand and covered my mouth with her right one. She'd done it gentle but her hand was rough as old barn wood 'cross my face.

She said, "Now, chile, you got to settle down. You gunn wake that white man, then what gunn happen to you? We caint be having no talk 'bout you sneaking up on no one in they sleep killing 'em.

"You shoots that thang off and every white man and boy in the country gunn be in here in no time. 'Sides, I sees you's a proper-raised chile. You caint be having no murders resting on your soul."

I sucked some of the looseness out of my nose and said, "But, ma'am, how'm I gonna get you out of here? I know you're tired but I got a horse outside that's the second-fastest in all of Canada and if we're careful we can ride him hard and maybe we could even borrow some of those horses there and wouldn't no one have to walk and . . ."

She laughed. "My word! You sure is one bad little mister! First off you gunn shoot a white man what's sleeping, then you gunn help bust some slaves out they chains, then you gunn steal some horses! Why, chile, with all the mischief you got planned, white folks gunn have to hang you once then cut you down and string you up 'nother two or three times!"

She rubbed her rough hand 'cross my hair. "Boy, there ain't gunn be no horse stealin' and there ain't gunn be no more running. Caint you see we all run out? 'Sides, that drunk man over yon ain't got no keys. Massa Prayder and his boys keep 'em, and keep 'em all separate too."

I remembered Mr. Taylor's sullied knife!

I told her, "I have this!" I reached in my tote sack and pulled out the knife. I said, "It wouldn't make no noise if I cut that drunk one's throat and then took his shotgun and then we could . . ."

She gave me a snatch and said, "Hesh! Look at you, how you gunn cut some man's th'oat? Tender as you is, I reckon you ain't never even cut the th'oat of no hog, has you?"

"No, ma'am, but I ain't never felt this way afore."

"Well, you ain't gunn start no th'oat-cutting now. How old is you?"

"I'm-a be turning twelve in 'bout ten months, ma'am."

"Twelve year old and free! And look at them proper clothes and shoes you wearing! And listen to the ed-u-cated way you talking. It sure don't sound natural coming out of you but you sound as ed-u-cated as the missus' chil'ren theyselves. I knowed soon's I seen you, you ain't never been no slave. With that and you 'pearing outta thin air like you done is why I waren't sure if you was a haint or not."

"But how're we gonna get you free?"

"You caint, chile."

"But I got this knife! Maybe I can gouge those chains out of the wood they're mounted in."

I looked where the chains were joined up to the wall. It waren't wood atall. The chains came right outta rock.

She gave me another snatch and said, "Boy, stop! Them paddy-rollers ain't leaving nothing to chance. This ain't no 'musement to them. This how they live. This what they do. If they don't know nothing else, they knows how to hold slaves and they knows how to keep us held."

I said, "Maybe if I pull the chains I can . . ." I snatched at where the chains were put into the rock. ". . . I can tug 'em free. Sometimes if you want something bad enough, your dreams get answered, sometimes if you're scared enough, you get so strong you can do near anything. . . ."

I pulled even harder on the chains and told her, "Everybody in Buxton knows 'bout how Mr. and Mrs. Alexander were clearing stones out of a field by theirselves and had loaded 'em all up in a wagon and he had to crawl underneath the wagon for something and the wheel busted off and his leg was pinned and there waren't no help 'round and 'stead of having a fit, Mrs. Alexander got so afeared and mad that she picked up the whole end of the wagon herself so's he could crawl out! A whole wagon full of stones! And she ain't nowhere near strong as me!"

I snatched again, but it was like the chains were laughing at me.

The woman reached down and held on to her ankle where the iron band was. She said, "Honey, you gunn bust my leg 'fore you bust that rock. Don't you think if getting afeared and wishing something to happen would make it true, that these here chains would've turned to dust long ago? You think you wants to pull us free of these chains more than me and them Africans does? You think you got more strength and wanting in you than us?

"*Than me?*

"Chile, you need to quit your agitating 'fore you ends up shackled too. Some things just ain't meant to be changed."

She was right, and soon's I knowed it, my legs quit working again and I fell in a heap at her feet. She pulled me up and cradled my head in her arm.

She wiped my eyes and said, "Lord! If you ain't the swooningest thang I ever seen!"

She held my chin in her hand. "Listen here. Don't you be fretting for us. You stop this crying, you just riling that African boy up, honey. You don't wanna make things no worser for him, do you?"

I hadn't thought of that. I was just being selfish.

She said, "You caint know it, but you's the shiniest thing what we's seen in a long, long, *long* time. Seeing you's the next best thing to seeing Canada. Seeing you shows me the whole thang ain't no dream."

Her baby coughed again and she kissed it on the forehead then kissed me on mine.

She pushed me so's she could look me right in my eye and said, "Now. Listen good. You gotta get on outta here, but 'fore you go, that there pistol you has, it real? It ain't no chile's toy?"

"No, ma'am. That's a real hundred-dollar gun."

"Do it work?"

"Yes, ma'am."

"Do it got bullets?"

"Yes, ma'am."

"It hard to shoot?"

"No, ma'am, I saw the Preacher shooting it and it has got a kick, but if you're ready for it, it ain't much. But you do gotta be strong."

"*You* ever shoot it 'fore?"

"No, ma'am. But I shot the Preacher's other gun, and it was just 'bout the same."

She smiled. "Well, honey, I s'pose if a little passing-out, freeborn thang like you can shoot a pistol, ole Chloe can shoot it too."

I looked at Mrs. Chloe's arms. They were like thick, twisted, black rope.

She grabbed my chin with her hand again so I was

looking her right in the eye and she said, "Lemme hold that gun."

I pulled the mystery pistol outta my tote sack and put it in her hand.

She said, "It sure is lighter than it look. Now show me how it work."

I showed her the same way the Preacher had showed me.

She said, "That all?"

"Yes, ma'am."

"How long after you shoot it one time 'fore it set to shoot again?"

"It's a revolver, ma'am. Soon's you pull the trigger it'll fire again, but you gotta make sure you aim it real careful and hold your breath afore you fire the next time."

"And if it shoot a man one time he gunn die?"

"You hit him in the head or the chest, ma'am, he's gonna die. And if he don't die right off, he soon will. And if he don't die soon he's gonna spend the rest of his life wishing he had."

"And how many times this gunn shoot 'fore it through?"

"That's a six-shooter, ma'am."

She said, "That be just perfect."

My mind did the totaling and, counting the baby, there were six of *them*!

Afore I could ask her what she wanted to do, she grabbed my chin again and said, "Now, chile, you think you gunn be shooting something with this here pistol 'fore you back in Canada?"

"No, ma'am, but . . ."

She said, "But nothing. Maybe it be best if I keep this gun."

It waren't a question.

I looked at the way it was resting easy in her hand and knowed I couldn't have took it back if I wanted to. I said, "Yes, ma'am, maybe that's the best."

I wished I could do something more. I didn't see how they were gonna bust outta here with just the gun if they couldn't get off of the wall. And she was right, once that gun commenced shooting, all the folks in this town would come running. And how far were they gonna get with no clothes if they could bust out? And what if she waren't gonna use the gun to shoot those slavers? What if she really was gonna use the gun to shoot . . . ?

I couldn't even think 'bout that.

She set the pistol behind her and nodded over to where the Preacher was hanging and said, "'Fore you go, you tell me what that man over yon done stole that make it worth y'all leaving Canada and coming down into this?"

I tried to look over at the Preacher but she pulled my face back to her. I told her everything that happened with Mr. Leroy and the Preacher and Mrs. Holton's gold.

She listened careful then said, "So now that your thief

done died, is you heading di-rect back to Canada or is they some other white men's th'oats 'round here that you need to cut?"

"No, ma'am, I'm going right back. I got a examination in Latin so I gotta be in school on Monday."

She looked hard at me and said, "School?"

She said it again, *"School?"*

"Yes, ma'am."

She took the longest time to say anything else. She closed her eyes and squozed her baby.

After 'while she smiled and said, "Here. Come hold my chile whilst I get this here shackle 'justed. I thinks all your tussling done bust one n'em scabs open."

I said, "I'm sorry, ma'am, I was only trying to . . ."

She said, "Hesh, boy. My word! You sure do like the sound a y'own mouth, don't you? Just be still and hold on to my chile."

I took the baby from her. It was a little girl.

She said, "I see you know how to hold a baby."

"Yes, ma'am, some of the time I watch over the children in the nursery."

The woman reached down with both hands and wiggled the iron 'round her ankle then looked at me. She seemed surprised and said, "Now that's truly 'mazing! I ain't never seen such a thang in all my days! Why, looky how that chile just let you hold on to her! Look how easy she be resting in your arm! Looky there!"

The baby looked up at me. The woman acted like she wouldn't've been no more surprised if she'd just seen Moses hisself part the Red Sea.

She said, "I ain't never . . . ! Why, I believe that gal do love you, boy! I done spoilt her something terrible and she don't let no one hold her without she holler her life away! I do swear that baby love you! Why, I think she must believe you her brother. I ain't never seen such a thing my whole life. That chile do feel you some kinda kin 'cause she ain't never let no one but me and Kamau hold her so. She do, boy, looky there she really love you!"

Tears were coming outta the woman's eyes but she was still smiling.

I looked down at the girl. She was a stringy sickly thing.

I didn't think she loved me atall. I thought the only reason she waren't raising Cain was 'cause even though she was being toted and waren't doing no walking with heavy chains on, she still looked just as beat and wore down and tired and whupped as her ma and pa and n'em other three Africans. But I couldn't figure out why this woman kept saying that this girl loved me.

She said, "You sees it, don't you, boy? You sees what I'm saying?"

319

Then I did! I started seeing some of what was going on! This was some of that talk that growned folks do where they're saying one thing out loud but you're supposed to be hearing lots of other things at the same time! This woman was treating me like I was growned! She was acting like I could understand what she was meaning on the back side of her words!

I tried hard as I could to see why she was pretending that me and the little girl were kin, but nothing would come, doggone-it-all! This was just like one n'em surprise examinations Mr. Travis bushwhacks us with in school. No matter how much you know on the subject, if he just starts asking all sorts of unexpected questions, your mind and brain seize up like a pump in the winter. Even if I *did* know what this woman was saying, it waren't gonna come to me now. It waren't gonna come 'cause of the surprise.

I felt something terrible, but she was wasting her time. I still couldn't speak or understand this growned-folks language. I couldn't think of *nothing* past how to get these folks freed, and it looked like there waren't nothing I could do.

She tried again. "Do you see how much she love you, boy?"

I told her, "No, ma'am, I don't see nothing like that."

I reached the woman's baby back to her. She looked at me hard. Her hands were shaking when she took the girl from me.

She cut out all the talking 'bout love and held her baby tight.

I was whupped. All I could do was look down and shove my hands in my pockets.

Then, like I was getting a message, my fingers curled 'round the piece of paper in my pocket!

I pulled it out and saw the name of the man who'd helped Mr. Highgate and who was looking after Mr. Leroy's earthy remainders, Mr. Benjamin Alston! Mr. Highgate told Pa he was a mighty good man. I knowed what to do!

I whispered, "Ma'am. It's come to me! I can get someone to help us! I'm-a be right back!"

She said, "Boy, don't come back in here once you done left. You need to get back to Canada quick as you can."

"But, ma'am, I ain't gonna be alone. I know some men who'll help free you! They use to be slaves theirselves. Once they hear 'bout you they'll get you outta here in no time atall!"

"Listen to me, boy, once you leave don't you come back. Ain't no one gunn help us. You just risking y'own life for nothing. Get on back to Canada. I don't mean maybe."

I picked up my tote sack and went to the door of the stable. I looked back at the woman, raised my right hand, and said, "Ma'am, I swear on my ma's head that I'm gonna come back with help. Don't you fret, we're *all* gonna be in Buxton afore the sun comes up!"

CHAPTER 23

Riding Hard Back to Buxton

When I opened the stable door I already had four chunking stones in my hand just in case the bear-fighting dog had woke up. He looked like he was feeling a little better. His tongue had gone back in his mouth and he was making a tiny whining sound, but he was still laying on his side with his eyes shut. I stepped over him and ran to Jingle Boy. We headed back to the tavern fast as we could. I kept hoping the men hadn't left. As I got closer my spirits started lifting. I could hear they were still back there gambling!

When I busted 'round the corner I saw Mr. Alston squatting 'gainst a wagon wheel watching the other men tossing the white spotty boxes. Ain't nothing like a hard galloping horse that'll get folks' attention. All the men jumped up like they'd got caught doing something wrong.

I jumped off Jingle Boy and yelled, "Mr. Alston! Mr. Alston! They got people they're taking back to slavery! They're 'bout to march 'em out tomorrow! They got a woman and her baby and some Africans and a boy who ain't no older'n me! But we gotta hurry! And they killed the Preacher and got him hanging in the stable!"

Mr. Alston grabbed ahold of me. "Slow down, boy! What you saying?"

It took a second for my breathing to catch up to me, then I said, "There's four paddy-rollers that's kidnapped six people and are taking 'em down south! We can get 'em out! There's only one watching over 'em di-rect and he's passed out from drinking! There's even a baby! We can get 'em out!"

He said, "We can do *what*?"

The other men looked hard at me and Mr. Alston.

"We can get 'em out, sir. They're feeling pretty low but once we get 'em going toward Buxton I know they'll lively up some!"

One of the gambling men laughed and said, "Man, pass me them dice. That boy crazy."

Mr. Alston turned me a-loose and said, "Son, you needs to get to Canada and tell your people 'bout that man what die. How come you ain't left yet?"

"Yes, sir, I will, but they're taking these runaways out first thing in the morning! We gotta free 'em now! I swored to Mrs. Chloe we'd get her out!"

Then I remembered how afeared the men were when

they told me 'bout the bear-fighting dog. I said, "Oh! You don't need to worry. I already knocked the dog cold. It's all right!"

Mr. Alston said, "Boy, I ain't playing. You needs to get on your horse and get your people. Ain't no one freeing no one. This ain't Canada, this America. They ain't nowhere near the same. I do truly feel for them poor souls what's been caught, but they gots laws here. If we was to get tangled up in this mess they be selling *us* down the river. Ain't no one 'round gunn help. It was the sheriff what let them slave hunters lay over in that stable."

One of the men said, "Didn't no one bust me free when I was in 'Bama. Why'm I gunn risk my neck for some folks I don't know what's stupid enough to get caught?"

I didn't know what to say.

I turned to the men and said, "But we're all . . ."

The one with the dice cuffed me upside my head.

"You heard the man, get on outta here. Don't no one want to be hearing none of the mess you talking. We ain't 'bout to brook your nonsense. 'Sides, I'm on a roll, you messing with my game!"

I said, "But they're near dead, they caint barely . . ."

The man punched me in the chest, knocking me down and sending the breath right out of me.

Mr. Alston grabbed ahold of him and said, "Ain't no need for that!"

The man yelled at me, "Boy! You best get away from me 'fore I kills you! We done told you, ain't nothing can be done! You best get you'self back to Canada. We don't need none y'all freeborn Buxton fools coming up here making no trouble for us! I ain't 'bout to go back and be no slave."

I got up and started running back to Jingle Boy.

I was so dumbstruck I couldn't even cry.

Jingle Boy snuffled at me when I got to him. I crawled up on his back. I headed him out toward the road and felt something leaping 'round in my belly. Next thing I knowed I was leaning over and throwing up my supper from Ma and the milk from Cooter's ma. I throwed up over and over till waren't nothing coming out of me but bitter water that I ain't got no recollection of drinking. Once that was gone, I throwed up air whilst my guts twisted and jumped.

I knowed this didn't have nothing to do with the bear-fighting dog hitting me in the side nor the man punching me in the chest. I knowed this waren't nothing but my conscience talking to me 'cause I was gonna have to break my promise to Mrs. Chloe. There waren't no sense in going back to the stable to try and free her and them Africans. The best thing I could do was ride Jingle Boy hard back to Buxton and see what Ma and Pa would say we should do.

But my conscience knowed that by the time I got down

325

there and they put a posse together and came all the way back up here those slavers would've took Mrs. Chloe away and there wouldn't be no way to figure out where.

I had to choose twixt going back and telling her no one could help or getting to Buxton quick as I could 'cause maybe, *maybe*, something could get done. But my conscience was chewing at me and choking on my guts 'cause it knowed that was a waste of time. The gambling man was right. Couldn't nothing nor no one help now.

The tears finally came. I was gonna listen to Mrs. Chloe. She told me not to come back. I dug my heels into Jingle Boy's sides and pointed him south, down the road to Buxton.

→ Chapter 24 ←

The Revenge of
Mr. Frederick Douglass!

I was pushing Jingle Boy harder than I should've, but it was for a good reason. Not just 'cause I wanted Ma and Pa's help on this confusion, but also 'cause with Jingle Boy running so hard, I was hoping that the only thing I'd want to think 'bout was hanging on tight so I wouldn't get tossed. But it waren't working, all his bumping and jarring couldn't make me quit thinking.

I thought 'bout how my conscience and Ma's cookie jar snake were pretty much alike. Seemed that no matter how hard and fast I tried to run away from either one of 'em, I ended up carrying it right along without even knowing I'd done it. 'Bout the only difference twixt the two was that it 'peared the snake had been a whole lot easier to toss down and be rid of than my conscience was gonna be.

Me and Jingle Boy waren't even a mile out of the little logging village when I pulled up the reins and stopped him.

It waren't nothing 'gainst the horse but, doggone-it-all, I wished I was riding Old Flapjack instead.

If this was Old Flap we'd've been going so slow that I wouldn't've had no choice but to try and figure out what to do. All the bouncing Jingle Boy was doing whilst he galloped made it so's I waren't able to get ahold of a thought and work it all the way through. And even though there was some comforting in that, I knowed I had to stop him afore I made a real bad choice.

The thought that was mostly plaguing me was Mrs. Chloe talking that growned-up language then looking so disappointed in me when she saw I waren't understanding it.

Growned folks have whole slews of ways of crushing your spirits if you're young. And if I got one weakness to what they do, it ain't when they holler at me or switch me or chase after me to try and 'buke me. If they really want to squash all the happiness out of me, it seems all they gotta do is tell me they're disappointed in something that I did.

It's even worst when they don't come right out and say they're disappointed but instead look at me and wrinkle their brow then turn away whilst shaking their head a little. They seem to get so doggoned sad. For some reason, that hurts more than any switching or beating they can lay on you.

If I was gonna think this through, I knowed I was gonna have to quit worrying 'bout the disappointment and put all my thoughts on the growned-up language Mrs.

Chloe used on me. I know it had something to do with her lying 'bout her baby loving me so much, something that both of us knowed waren't true, but I still couldn't cipher what it meant. How's a baby gonna love someone they ain't never seen afore? And how's a baby's ma gonna lie like that? That don't make no sense, that don't make no sense atall.

But why *did* she want to pretend that me and that girl was some sort of kin to each other, that there was something strong twixt me and . . . ?

I'm gonna sound like I'm being boastful and pridesome, but what I'm 'bout to say is the truth, and if it's the truth it ain't boasting:

Why, my brain is so powerful amazing that some of the time it leaves me dumbstruck!

Here all these things had been happening and trying to pull my mind away from what was right in front of me, then in two shakes of a lamb's tail my brain told me what Mrs. Chloe was really saying! It even told me *why* she said it!

And that ain't nothing but more proving of what I been saying all along, riding a mule's a whole lot better than riding a horse. Why, if I hadn't pulled Jingle Boy up, I'd be halfway to Buxton by now without getting a chance to have a proper thought, and it might be too late!

I dug my heels into Jingle Boy again and headed him

hard north, back toward the little logging village, back to the stable.

The bear-fighting dog had got back up on his feet. His tail was twixt his legs and he was staggering 'round and whining and looking like he waren't seeing too good. If I'd've been fra-gile as Emma Collins I'd've felt sorry for him, but I recalled the bite on Mr. Kamau's leg and the three new holes I had in my side and I didn't feel no sorrow atall.

I throwed left hard as I could and caught him in the same spot as afore. He didn't make a sound, he dropped like a sack of rocks.

I stepped over the dog and eased the stable door back open. This time when I went in, a hinge squeaked and the stable could tell I was there.

I looked at the bundles to the left and my heart stopped, my blood ran cold, and time stood still!

Even though my eyes waren't all the way use to the darkness, I could still see the hole in the barrel of the mystery pistol that Mrs. Chloe was aiming right twixt my eyes! And whilst it had been waving and jumping in my hand, it was steady as iron in hers.

I whispered, "Mrs. Chloe, it's me!"

She took the gun off of me.

She said, "I *told* you not to come back!"

She looked back at the door, and afore I could answer, she said, "Now, where them men you was talking 'bout?"

"They couldn't help. They were too scared."

She set the gun behind her and picked her baby up.

The disappointment was still in her eyes when she looked at me. I noticed a long time ago when it comes to disappointment, once a growned person feels it for you, you ain't nothing but a dead duck, 'cause caint nothing be done to change their mind.

I took another deep breath so there waren't gonna be no backing off from talking growned, which when you look at it seems to be a powerful lot like lying.

I said, "Mrs. Chloe, pardon me swearing, but it's the blangedest thing! I was riding Jingle Boy back to Buxton and something was bothering me and I couldn't figure out what it was, then it came to me just like that!" I snapped my fingers.

She just watched me hard.

"When I first saw your daughter I was so stupid-fied and shocked that my mind played a low-down, rotten trick on me, but once I got on that horse, I knowed what was plaguing me, I knowed what was wrong! It came to me that that there girl's the spittin' image of my baby sister that died of the fever two years pass!"

Mrs. Chloe kept watching me.

I lied, "Yes, ma'am, my little sister that pass two years ago looked exactly like your baby."

She said, "Chile, I'm sorry to hear that. I know your'n and your ma's hearts must be busted."

I said, "Thank you, ma'am. You're right, Ma's heart's busted so bad she won't stop mourning and she's tossed out all her clothes that have any kind of colour in 'em and she won't wear nothing but black 'cause the doctor told her the Lord waren't gonna bless her with no more children."

Mrs. Chloe didn't say nothing. She looked at me and shooked her head up and down one time.

I said, "And now Ma's always saying what she wouldn't give for just one more look at my baby sister."

She said, "Your poor ma. Your poor, poor ma."

I took this as encouragement to lie some more, to keep trying to talk this secret language.

I said, "She's always moping and even terrorfying folks by wandering 'round in the woods at night and saying she'd give anything for one more look, that my sister went too fast, that Ma didn't have the chance to tell her no proper good-bye."

Mrs. Chloe said, "That's a tragedy. I see through you what a good woman your ma is. She sure done raise a fine boy in you, a fine, fine boy. What kind of world we living in when a good woman like your ma have to shoulder that kind of load and caint have no more babies?"

Once you start lying, it ain't hard to keep going. It's like a ball starts rolling down a hill. But I knowed I had to prettify the story even more. I said, "Yes, ma'am, she goes on and on talking 'bout how she would die happy if she could get just one more look at my sister.

"Then she'll say, if God was truly just and kind, like she knows he is, maybe not only would she get a chance to see my sister one more time, but maybe there'd be some way she could raise another child."

I watched Mrs. Chloe's eyes hard, the same way I watch Mr. Travis's. If you're reciting something to him and you're doing good, you can tell by his eyes, you know you just gotta keep going on. Mrs. Chloe's eyes were doing the same thing.

I said, "Ma's always saying she don't care if she birth it or not, all she's longing for is another little girl to look after and raise. Why, ma'am, the way she's dragging 'round and carrying on is 'bout to drive me and Pa mad."

Mrs. Chloe said, "I hopes you and your pa is kind with your ma, boy. Ain't nothing in the world worse than birthing a little one then losing it. Nothing. I done lost three myself, two what was sold away and one what die asleep. This gal here my last."

I was through. I was so 'shamed of myself for lying that I couldn't talk no more of this growned-folks language.

I was 'bout *this* close to slipping into another one n'em

fra-gile spells when Mrs. Chloe studied me and said, "So what you think we should do, son?"

"Ma'am?"

"What can me and you do that'll give your poor ma some comforting?"

I knowed what she was really asking, but I didn't know how to answer her.

All I could say was, "I was wondering, ma'am, if maybe you'd let me borrow your baby and carry her to Buxton so I could show Ma how much she favours my sister?"

Mrs. Chloe's eyes looked just like Mr. Travis's did if you got all the way through conjugating your Latin verbs without no mistakes.

I said, "Confused as Ma is, maybe she'll think this is my sister and she's getting one more look."

Mrs. Chloe drawed in a long hard breath. For the second time she sounded like she'd been underwater and had come back up just afore her lungs were 'bout to bust.

I raised my right hand and said, "I swear on my ma's head I'll look after her real good, ma'am. You saw how good I held her. I swear she'll be safe, and once I swear, I ain't got no choice but to keep my word. I swored I was gonna come back, didn't I? I swear she'll be safe if you let me borrow her."

I thought I'd messed up on this growned-up talking, I thought I'd said the wrong thing 'cause Mrs. Chloe made a sound like she'd just got gut-punched. But she whispered, "Chile, chile, chile. That's just the thing that we can do . . . that's just it."

She kissed the baby's eyes and told her, "You see, sweetheart? I promised. I promised you you waren't going back to Kentucky. I promised you I waren't gunn allow you to go back, only I never thought it'd be like this! You know I never would've done nothing to hurt you 'less it would spare you a whole life of hurt, don't you? Never, baby.

"Something told me to wait, and I ain't never had no fear nor softness in me, so it was something else. And lookit here. Lookit what my waiting done brung. Lookit this here boy. He *did* come back. *He come back!* And I ain't never been so proud of no young man in all my days."

She looked up at me.

She said, "You's all I got left."

I couldn't tell if she meant me or her baby.

She kissed her daughter's eyes again and said, "'Stead of this being your last night it turned to your first."

She told me, "Don't you cry, boy. Don't you dare. I ain't never loved nothing in my life more'n I loves you right at this minute. Ain't nothing for you to be crying 'bout. Only reason any of us need be crying is if, come tomorrow, you waren't nothing but a dream, nothing but my mind conjuring something to stop me from doing what I was gunn have to do. But you is real, ain't you?"

I wanted to say, "Yes, ma'am," but all I could do was shake my head up and down and keep sucking the looseness back up into my nose.

She said, "I knowed it. Don't seem like a haint or a dream would be fainting and crying much as you do. 'Sides, I done me lots of dreaming and I ain't never yet had one near beautiful as you is. Never."

She said, "'Fore you go you take her on over to her pa and let him hold on to her one last time."

She reached me the baby. Her hands were back to shaking.

I carried the child over to the big African and reached her out to him. His hands could only come up so high, but it was high enough that he could cradle her bottom and put her face on his.

She grabbed at his hair and he mashed his rough, cracked lips into her cheek. He kept his face there, closed his eyes, and took four or five deep breaths like he was trying to get the smell of her deep into him. He held her as far away as the chains would go then said something to her in African.

His voice was deep like thunder. He reached her back to me and said, "Boy. Go! Go, now! *Uh-san-tay. Uh-san-tay sah-nah.* Thank you much kindly."

I was wrong afore when I said it seemed couldn't nothing make this man cry.

I took the girl from him and turned to the woman to see if she wanted to hold her baby again. She was back to leaning 'gainst the wall like a bundle and her hands were covering her eyes. But she was smiling.

There waren't nothing more to be said.

I put the girl in my right arm and got a chunking stone ready in my left hand for the dog outside. I peeked back out of the stable door and saw the dog was still stretched out on the end of the chain, the mud was drying up 'round his tongue, and he waren't moving a lick. It looked like his nightmare was over.

Afore I stepped through the door, Mrs. Chloe said, "Boy. What you called?"

I said, "Elijah, ma'am."

Then, so if she did bust out and got to Canada, she wouldn't make the mistake of asking for the other Elijah, the white one up in Chatham, I told her, "I'm Elijah, Elijah of Buxton, ma'am."

She said, "Well, son, you done proved what you said afore. You proved that if you wants something horrible bad enough, sometimes dreams has a way of finding you. You done lift something heavier than any wagon of stones off my heart, Elijah of Buxton. Thank you."

"You're welcome, ma'am."

I looked back into the stable. Everything was dark and foggy again.

I said, "Ma'am? What's your baby's name?"

The African man said, "Too-mah-ee-nee!"

The woman said, "He call her Too-mah-ee-nee, but I calls her Hope. You make sure you thank yo' ma. You make sure yo' ma tell Hope when she done growned . . ." Miss Chloe stopped and covered her mouth with her hand for a second. She pulled it away and said, "You make sure your ma tell Hope her pa full-blood African. And he say he use to be a king. And I believe him."

"Yes, ma'am, I will. And I'll tell her her pa's name's Kamau and her ma's name's Chloe and she's got two names, Hope and Too-mah . . ."

Mr. Kamau said, "Too-mah-ee-nee, she our Too-mah-ee-nee."

I said, "Too-mah-ee-nee."

Mrs. Chloe said, "How you gunn 'member all them new names, 'Lijah?"

I told her, "I ain't good at mathematics, ma'am, but I'm real good at rememberizing things. Plus I got me a pencil and some paper in my tote sack and I'm gonna write 'em down."

She said, "Stop! You writes? And reads?"

"Yes, ma'am."

"You *is* truly, truly a miracle. But you gotta quit pressing our luck. Y'all gotta get on outta here."

As I stepped back out of the stable, Mr. Kamau said, "Chloe, let *me* have gun."

She said, "Man, hesh. Where you gunn hide it if I gives it to you? I'm-a keep it cover up in this here rag till Prayder and them worthless boys comes in the morn with our clothes.

"Way I sees it, Old Scratch gunn owe me big 'cause bright and early tomorrow morn I sure am 'bout to send him back four of his cursed souls and one of his good-for-nothing dogs.

"'Sides, Mr. Kamau . . ." She laughed kind of soft. ". . . if you's the mighty African king you's always claiming you is, and you wants this here pistol so bad, why don't you come on over here and take it from me?"

There was a wait then the stable was fulled up with another soft laugh, this one deep and rumbling.

He said, "I love you, Chloe."

She said, "Aww, hesh, Kamau, I love you too."

Their soft laughs, that boy's bawling, and those chains rattling and scraping are sounds I'm gonna be hearing for the rest of my life. Even if I live to be fifty.

I wrapped the baby's arms 'round my neck and ran to where I'd tied Jingle Boy. I took two of my chunking stones out of my tote sack and put 'em in my pocket. I throwed the other ones and Mr. Taylor's sullied knife on the ground. I gentle set Hope Too-mah-ee-nee in the empty tote sack and tied her 'round my back, same as the women in the fields. And we started for Buxton.

Twixt Jingle Boy already being run too hard and me being careful whilst holding on to Hope Too-mah-ee-nee, we went easy and didn't get to the ferry in Detroit till near daybreak. She'd been a good baby and hadn't cried or nothing all the way there. Mostly she pulled at the hair on the back of my head.

Whilst we waited for the ferry to carry us to Windsor, I started wondering what would happen to Hope once we got to Buxton. But I knowed pretty quick. I knowed Mrs. Brown was probably gonna be able to buy some cloth with some colour in it from MacMahon's Dry Goods.

When the sun started peeking over the trees on Belle Isle I knowed I had to welcome Hope to Canada the right way, the same way growned folks do.

I pointed over to Canada and said to her, "Looky there! Look at that sky! Ain't that the most beautifullest sky you ever seen?"

'Stead of looking where I was pointing she looked at the end of my finger.

I put Hope Too-mah-ee-nee on my shoulder, pointed over at Windsor, and said, "Looky there, look at that land! Look at those trees! Have you ever seen anything that precious? It's the land of the free!"

She kept watching my finger

"Now look at yourself, have you ever seen someone that looked so gorgeous?

"Today you're truly free, and you choosed the most beautifullest, most perfectest day for doing it!"

I raised her over my head and said, "All I'm wondering is, what kept you?"

She smiled at me, reached her hands down at my face, then spit up water all over me.

Even though most times getting throwed up on ain't the kind of thing you're gonna laugh 'bout, I did anyway.

I wiped my face off, pulled on Jingle Boy's reins, and led him up the ramp to the ferry.

It got me thinking 'bout Mr. Frederick Douglass, and it might sound like I'm being prideful again, but I knowed that once I got this little girl back to Buxton safe, I was pretty doggone sure waren't no one gonna remember what happened twixt him and me ever again. I knowed it was like he'd finally got his revenge and would quit plaguing me!

Once we set foot in Canada I put Hope Too-mah-ee-nee back in the tote sack. I decided I waren't gonna take no chances by running Jingle Boy too hard. I made him go mule speed 'stead of horse speed. It took a lot longer that way, so we didn't get to the west part of Buxton till sometime 'round noon.

And Hope slept the whole way.

❖ **AUTHOR'S NOTE** ❖

What an interesting, beautiful, hope-filled place the Elgin Settlement and Buxton Mission of Raleigh was and is. Founded in 1849 by a white Presbyterian minister named Reverend William King, the Settlement was first shared by Reverend King, fifteen slaves whom he had inherited through his wife, and six escaped slaves who awaited them. Reverend King felt there was nowhere in the United States that these African-American slaves could truly know liberty, so he purchased a three-mile by six-mile plot of land in southern Ontario on which he and the freed slaves could live. The population of Buxton at its height ranged from an estimated 1,500 to 2,000 escaped and freed people. Though there were a few other settlements of refugees from slavery in Canada at that time, Buxton proved to be the one that thrived. Even into the twenty-first century, several hundred descendants of the original settlers still live in the area, farming the land their ancestors hewed from the once thick Canadian forest.

The relative success of Buxton can be attributed to two things: First is the will, determination, courage, and sheer appreciation of freedom that steeled the spines of the newly freed, largely African-American residents. In the face of great opposition by some Canadians, they fought and worked hard to maintain the promise of the North Star. They took themselves from the horrors of southern American slavery into the land of the free, Canada. Every day they awoke was filled with hardship, every day they awoke was filled with the joy of freedom. In *Legacy to Buxton*, a detailed history of the Settlement, author A. C. Robbins cites a Paul Laurence Dunbar poem to describe these brave people, and I can't think of a more fitting tribute:

> *Not they who soar, but they who plod*
> *Their rugged way, unhelped, to God*
> *Are heroes; . . .*
> *Not they who soar.*

The second reason the Buxton Settlement thrived is the set of strict rules that were instituted by Reverend King. People who chose to live within the Settlement's boundaries were required to purchase, with the assistance of very low interest loans, a minimum of fifty acres of land which they had to clear and drain. Their homes had to be a certain size with a minimum of four rooms and were set thirty-three feet from the road. The front of each home was to be planted with a flower garden and the back was to have a vegetable garden or truck patch.

Economically, Buxton was fiercely and deliberately self-sufficient and eventually had its own sawmill, potash mill, brickyard, post office, hotel, and school. There was even a six-mile-long tram that carried lumber from Buxton down to Lake Erie, where it was loaded on ships to be sold throughout North America. Buxton's school developed such a sterling reputation that many white families in the area withdrew their children from the local government schools and sent them to the Academy at Buxton instead. Many Native Canadian children also were educated at the school.

While I have fictionalized some aspects of *Elijah of Buxton*, much of the story is based on fact. Although there is no record of a terrible accident, Frederick Douglass actually did visit Buxton, as did abolitionist John Brown, though not at the same time. One of Buxton's earliest inhabitants, a young girl, made the journey to freedom in the same way Elijah's ma did, by escaping from her mistress on her second trip to Detroit. The Liberty Bell was indeed rung whenever a newly freed person reached the Settlement. This five-hundred-pound brass bell was cast in Pittsburgh in 1850, and was paid for by the pennies, nickels, and dollars saved by former slaves as a tribute to the people of Buxton.

Unfortunately, during the 1920s the church that houses the Liberty Bell was sold, and today the bell remains in a completely enclosed tower, not seen by anyone. The Canadian government recently donated a generous $20,000 for a replica of the bell to be made and placed on the grounds of the Buxton National Historic Site and Museum, but the casting had to be done through estimates. It is my hope that the Liberty

Bell will someday again let freedom ring over all of Buxton. To learn more about the bell, visit my Web site, www.nobodybutcurtis.com.

I strongly recommend taking a trip to North Buxton. It's almost impossible not to be deeply moved while looking out on fields that were cleared by people who risked their lives for the dream of freedom. It's almost impossible not to feel a sense of joy that is a tiny fraction of the joy former slaves must have felt when they first saw the school at Buxton. A place where their children would be learning everything from simple addition and subtraction to calculus, everything from English to Greek. It is almost impossible not to look to the Buxton sky, be it rainy or sunshiny, and think, "Ain't that the most beautifullest sky you ever seen?"

Go to the Buxton National Historic Site and Museum and get a feel for what life in Buxton was like a century and a half ago. The museum's publication *Something to Hope For* is a fascinating overview of Buxton's history. An actual original cabin and the original schoolhouse on which I based places in *Elijah of Buxton* still exist on the grounds of the museum, along with the original cemetery. A huge celebration is held in Buxton every Labour Day when more than 3,000 descendants of former slaves from all over the United States and Canada come to celebrate and honor their ancestors.

Buxton is an inspiration, and its importance in both American and Canadian history deserves to be much more recognized. I feel so honored to have been able to set my novel in such a beautiful place.

Christopher Paul Curtis
Windsor, Ontario
March 2007

AFTER WORDS™

CHRISTOPHER PAUL CURTIS'S
Elijah of Buxton

CONTENTS

After Words™ guide by Anamika Bhatnagar

About the Author

Christopher Paul Curtis was born and raised in Flint, Michigan. The second of five children, Christopher always loved reading, but as a child he didn't find many books that, as he says, "were about me." After graduating from high school, he took a summer job hanging car doors on the assembly line at Fisher Body Flint Plant No. 1, figuring he'd make some good money before starting college at the University of Michigan-Flint in the fall. It turned out that the money was *too* good to walk away from, and Christopher's summer job ended up lasting thirteen years! While the experience left him with a lifelong aversion to getting in and out of large automobiles, it also gave him a chance to do something that would eventually change his life — to write. He and his work partner came up with a plan: Instead of taking alternate turns putting the doors on Buicks as they rolled down the assembly line, each of them would hang *all* the doors for thirty minutes straight, giving the other a half-hour break. Christopher took the opportunity to write in his journal. Though he hated working in the factory, writing allowed him to forget where he was, for thirty minutes at a time.

While working at Fisher Body, Christopher continued taking classes at night. He was supposed to be studying political science, but he found himself drawn toward writing fiction. A few years after leaving his job at the plant, Christopher took a year off to write a book. He spent his days at the children's room of the Windsor Public Library in

Windsor, Ontario, writing this new story out by hand. In many ways, Christopher's writing became a family affair, with his son, Steven, typing up his drafts on the computer, and his daughter, Cydney, and his niece, Ilara, adding musical and editorial comments. Steven was the very first person to read about ten-year-old Kenny Watson's family road trip to Alabama — the story that became *The Watsons Go to Birmingham — 1963*, Christopher's first book.

Christopher submitted *The Watsons* to the Delacorte Press First Young Adult Novel Contest. The story didn't win the prize, but Delacorte decided to publish it anyway. *The Watsons Go to Birmingham — 1963* went on to receive a Newbery Honor and a Coretta Scott King Honor, and its success finally allowed Christopher to consider writing as a full-time career. Christopher's second novel, *Bud, Not Buddy*, was inspired in part by his grandfathers, Earl "Lefty" Lewis, a pitcher in the Negro Baseball Leagues, and Herman E. Curtis, bandleader of the Dusky Devastators of the Depression. In 2000, it was awarded the Newbery Medal and the Coretta Scott King Author Award, among many other honors and accolades. Christopher's other novels include the Golden Kite Award-winning *Bucking the Sarge*, *Mr. Chickee's Funny Money*, *Mr. Chickee's Messy Mission*, and this book.

When he is not writing, Christopher enjoys playing basketball and collecting old record albums. To learn more about him, visit him online at www.nobodybutcurtis.com.

Q&A with Christopher Paul Curtis

Q: *How did* Elijah of Buxton *come about?*

A: *Elijah of Buxton* came to me very easily — in a way that was far different from any other book I have written. From the word "go," Elijah and I became close friends. When I'd go to the library to write, it was as if he were anxiously waiting for me, waiting to tell about his life, his worries, and his adventures. I knew I wanted to write something about slavery, but I can't think of a more difficult subject to write about. When I write, I like to put myself in the place of a character and try to imagine what that person's life would be like. But I'm just not able to imagine what it would be like to be a slave, to be completely dehumanized — and even worse, to have to teach your children that they too have to give up their humanity.

Q: *What made you decide to set Elijah's story in the Buxton Settlement?*

A: Actually, the first chapter I wrote ended up being one of the last chapters of the book, and at the time, I didn't know it was going to be set in Buxton. Once I found out more about the characters I'd created and about the community in Buxton, which I'd visited, the idea of setting the story there just grabbed a hold of me. Buxton is about forty miles from Detroit, in Canada, and about two hundred descendents of the original settlers still live in the area. It was a terminus of the Underground Railroad, so many former slaves settled there after escaping from the U.S. By setting Elijah's story there, and by making him the first child born free, I was able to look at slavery without being actually in it.

Q: *Was it difficult to write this book?*
A: You might think it would have been, but Elijah just spoke to me and it took me about six months to finish. That's a *very* short time for me.

Q: *What is your writing schedule like?*
A: I still get up at five in the morning every day — I always worked an early shift at the factory, and I can't seem to break the habit of waking up before everyone else does. Early mornings are my editorial time. From five until about eight, I take whatever I wrote the day before and try to beat it into a story. From nine until noon, I go to the Windsor Public Library and write. That's my creative time, where I just let the story go. A lot of what I write won't end up in a book, but it gives me a little background on what I'm writing about. I can tell that I'm getting the story right when the editorial part becomes much shorter than the creative part.

Q: *Do you plan to write another book about Buxton?*
A: Buxton has such a rich and fascinating history that there are surely hundreds more stories to tell. I hope to tell a few more of them myself.

A Brief History of the Elgin Settlement at Buxton

The Elgin Settlement, commonly known as the Buxton Settlement, was founded in 1849 in what is now North Buxton, Ontario, Canada. It was established by a Presbyterian minister named William King, who was a slave owner himself through his late wife, the daughter of a Louisiana plantation owner. Reverend King did not believe in the ownership of one human being by another, and he became a staunch abolitionist who supported ending the practice of slavery in the United States. While working as a pastor in Chatham, Ontario, Reverend King came to a decision: He would no longer own slaves, and he would do something to help the fugitive slaves who had fled the U.S. to find freedom in Canada. He approached the leadership of the Presbyterian Church of Canada and requested their permission to build a church and a school for the fugitive slaves. The Church agreed, and they also helped him create an association to establish a settlement where the former slaves could live and prosper. The association, and eventually the Settlement, were named for James Bruce, the Earl of Elgin, the Governor General of Canada West.

In 1848, Reverend King moved the fifteen slaves he owned from Louisiana to Ohio, a free state where his family had a farm. There, he told the slaves that they were free to do as they chose: They could strike out on their own, as free men and women, or they could join Reverend King in Canada, where he and the Elgin Association had purchased land which the former slaves could buy and settle upon. All fifteen chose to remain with Reverend King, and when they arrived in Buxton in 1849, they found several other refugees from America waiting there. These former slaves had heard of Buxton, and they too wanted opportunities for their families and their children. Together, these men, women, and children became the first residents of the Elgin Settlement at Buxton.

Although there were other settlements for former slaves in the area near Chatham, Buxton was destined to become the most successful — in part because of the strict conditions for ownership that Reverend King and the Elgin Association established. The 4,300 acres of the Settlement were to be divided into fifty-acre lots, which were to be sold exclusively to former slaves and free blacks. The land would be sold at a reasonable price, with a down payment of $12.50 to be paid within a year, with the remaining balance to be paid off over time. By creating these rules, Reverend King made sure that the new residents of Buxton would have the chance to build their own community without having to worry about white settlers, some of whom did not want the former slaves living there, trying to buy up the land.

There were other rules to ensure that the community was a pleasant place to live, unlike the shacks many of its residents had lived in when they were slaves. For instance, each fifty-acre plot had to be drained and cleared, and houses built on them had to be placed thirty-three feet from the road. Each house was also required to have a picket fence, a flower garden, and at least four rooms. All the children would be required to attend school, as well as help out with chores.

The adults would also be given an opportunity to attend school, and they would work together to drain the land, cut down timber to clear it, and build the Settlement's homes and church with the lumber they harvested. Because Reverend King was a religious man, he also established a rule forbidding the sale of whiskey and other liquor in the Settlement.

Of course, it would take time for the Settlement land to be cleared, so Reverend King bought a huge farm nearby that had enough room to house Buxton's first settlers until their own homes could be built. The work was hard, but together, the settlers made progress. On Sundays, Reverend King held church services in his house while waiting for the Settlement church to be completed. By April 1850, the settlers had built their own cabins and had erected a building that could be used as a church and a school. All the residents of the Settlement and nearby towns were invited to attend both. On the first day of school, ten black children and two white children showed up, and over time other white residents of the area began to send their children as well. Classes for adults were held at the school at night, and many white residents who lived nearby also attended. The Buxton school soon became the finest in the area, and it got so crowded that a second school had to be built. The subjects taught included Latin, Greek, and other high-school level courses, as well as domestic skills. Later that year, a group of former slaves and free people in Pittsburgh joined together to provide a gift to the school: a five-hundred-pound bell that would ring each morning to call the students to class. The Liberty Bell was also rung at six in the morning and nine at night to remind the residents of Buxton that slavery continued to exist in the U.S., and it is said the bell sounded every time another fugitive escaped to freedom by entering the Settlement.

Buxton continued to grow in size after the passage of the Fugitive Slave Law of 1850 in the U.S. That law allowed slave owners to capture escaped slaves who had made it to freedom in the northern U.S. The only truly safe place for former slaves to go was Canada, and many of them settled in Buxton. In its earliest years, Buxton relied mostly on agriculture to sustain itself, and crops included corn, wheat, potatoes, beans, and peas. The residents also raised livestock, such as cows, oxen, horses, sheep, and pigs. But with the arrival of new residents, Buxton quickly grew into a successful commercial center. A brickyard and grist mill were established, and a tramway was built to float logs down to Lake Erie where they could be shipped out. The ash from burnt timber was used to make fertilizer, and lumber was converted into barrel staves. Soon, Buxton's many businesses included a general store, a blacksmith's shop, a shoe factory, a hotel, and a bank. As Buxton continued to prosper and grow, many residents became active in local government. After living in the Settlement for three years, Buxton's residents became naturalized citizens of Canada West, a British territory, and the men of Buxton became eligible to vote.

As the abolitionist movement continued to grow in the United States, the political turmoil eventually led to the American Civil War. The conflict slowed the rate of migration into Buxton, and Buxton's residents anxiously awaited the outcome. While the men of Buxton were eager to help fight for the cause of abolishing slavery in the U.S., they were not allowed to serve in the all-white Union army at first. Eventually, the Union army created all-black regiments, and seventy or so men from Buxton enlisted. After the war ended and slavery was formally abolished, hundreds of Buxton's residents returned to the United States to search for their families. Many of them returned to their former hometowns, using their education and the skills they learned in building Buxton to better the lives of the newly freed slaves in the American South.

Sources:

Civil War by John Stanchak, Dorling Kindersley Publishing, Inc.

Something to Hope For by Joyce Shadd Middleton, Bryan Prince, and Karen Shadd Evelyn, Buxton National Historic Site and Museum

Buxton through the Years: A Timeline

1812 — Reverend William King, the founder of the Elgin Settlement at Buxton, is born in Ireland. His family later moves to the United States to escape the Irish potato famine, and he eventually marries the daughter of a Louisiana plantation owner. Although he is against slavery, King becomes a slave owner himself through his wife.

1843 — King decides he cannot continue living in the United States as a slave owner, and he moves to Scotland to study to be a Presbyterian minister. While there, he also becomes an active abolitionist.

1846 — After completing his studies, Reverend King is assigned to become a missionary in Chatham, a town near Lake Erie in Canada, a country where slavery is outlawed.

1848 — Reverend King and his fifteen slaves travel to the free state of Ohio. King grants them freedom and tells them they are welcome to join him in Canada, where he plans to create a settlement that will allow former slaves the opportunity to own land and support themselves.

1849 — The Elgin Settlement is founded on a property of 4,300 acres of land in Buxton, Ontario.

1850 — Buxton's first school opens, with twelve children attending on the first day. The "coloured inhabitants of

Pittsburgh" present the citizens of Buxton with the Liberty Bell. That same year, in the United States, the Fugitive Slave Law is passed, forcing officials in the free states of the North to capture and return runaway slaves to their owners in the South.

1851 — A brickyard is opened, and it produces 300,000 bricks in its first year of operation. Buxton Savings Bank is established, and the Settlement continues to grow and prosper.

1858 — Abolitionist John Brown visits Buxton, and in 1859 launches a raid on the town of Harpers Ferry, Virginia, helping incite tensions between abolitionists and slave owners.

1860 — Abraham Lincoln is elected president of the United States. In December, South Carolina becomes the first state to secede from the Union.

1861 — Other states secede and form the Confederate States of America. In April, the Confederate army attacks U.S. troops at Fort Sumter in South Carolina, starting the American Civil War. When the Union army creates all-black regiments a year later, approximately seventy men from Buxton enlist and join the war.

1865 — The Confederate general Robert E. Lee surrenders on April 9. On April 14, President Lincoln is assassinated in Washington, D.C. Later that year, the Thirteenth

Amendment to the U.S. Constitution is ratified, permanently abolishing slavery in the U.S.

1873 — The Elgin Association, which oversaw the Settlement, is officially dissolved as many Buxton families have returned to the U.S. since the end of the war.

1887 — Reverend King leaves the Settlement. He dies in Chatham in 1895.

1999 — The Buxton Settlement is designated one of Canada's National Historic Sites.

Sources:

Civil War by John Stanchak, Dorling Kindersley Publishing, Inc.

Something to Hope For by Joyce Shadd Middleton, Bryan Prince, and Karen Shadd Evelyn, Buxton National Historic Site and Museum